PRAISE FOR THE WRITING OF MARGERY SHARP

"A highly gifted woman . . . a wonderful entertainer."
—*The New Yorker*

"One of the most gifted writers of comedy in the civilized world today." —*Chicago Daily News*

"[Sharp's] dialogue is brilliant, uncannily true. Her taste is excellent; she is an excellent storyteller." —Elizabeth Bowen

Britannia Mews
"As an artistic achievement . . . first-class, as entertainment . . . tops."
—*The Boston Globe*

The Eye of Love
"A double-plotted . . . masterpiece." —John Bayley,
Guardian Books of the Year

Martha, Eric, and George
"Amusing, enjoyable, Miss Sharp is a born storyteller."
—*The Times* (London)

The Gypsy in the Parlour
"Unforgettable . . . There is humor, mystery, good narrative."
—*Library Journal*

The Nutmeg Tree
"A sheer delight." —*New York Herald Tribune*

Something Light
"Margery Sharp has done it again! Witty, clever, delightful, entertaining." —*The Denver Post*

Something Light

Something
Light

a novel

MARGERY SHARP

OPEN ROAD

INTEGRATED MEDIA

NEW YORK

Copyright © 1960 by Margery Sharp

Cover design by Mimi Bark

ISBN: 978-1-5040-5087-6

This edition published in 2018 by Open Road Integrated Media, Inc.
180 Maiden Lane
New York, NY 10038
www.openroadmedia.com

To
Geoffrey Castle

Something Light

PART ONE

Chapter One

——— ❋ ———

I

Louisa Mary Datchett was very fond of men.

Not all women are, not even those to whom matrimony is the only tolerable state; for these often like men as husbands, as other women like them as lovers, and others again as small boys. Louisa liked men. If a bus driver halted for her at a pedestrian crossing, her upward glance was disinterestedly affectionate— there he sat, hot and conscientious, minding his own masculine business, no awareness of her save as a possible hazard to his time schedule—and there stood Louisa, liking him; and if on the island of her refuge she observed an old gentleman in a garish tie, striped red and yellow like a ripening pimento, her sympathetic imagination at once ranged over the whole field of English cricket—Dr. Grace, Ha'penny Down, "O my Spurling and my Hornby long ago"—as she mentally wished him on to a happy day at Lord's.

These examples, however, are merely illustrative. Most men were reciprocally aware of Louisa. If she paid for her rangy height by cheeks thin as a whistling boy's, if her fox-colored hair was turning like an autumn leaf—here a streak of cinnamon, there a dash of pepper—she had nonetheless only to stand still in any public place, at a bus stop or outside a telephone booth, and as to Red Riding Hood up came a wolf.

—Yet did she respond, and Louisa usually responded, how many a wolf turned nursling! To be listened to (wife not understanding wolf), to be found employment (wolf out of work), to have musical instrument (wolf potential member of dance band) got out of hock! It was extraordinary how swiftly they appreciated her special temperament.

Older acquaintances took it for granted. In June '56, Louisa gave evidence as to character three times in one week. This was a record, but only in its own field; no one, least of all Louisa, ever counted the times she got suits back from the cleaners, washed socks, or carried prescriptions to the chemist . . .

Bachelors in lodgings going down with influenza employed their last spark of consciousness to telephone Louisa. Sometimes their landladies telephoned her. Publishers of books commissioned but overdue telephoned Louisa. She was constantly being either sent for, like a fire engine, or dispatched, like a lifeboat, to the scene of some masculine disaster; and fond of men as she was, by the time she was thirty she felt extremely jaded.

II

"You know what?" said Louisa to the milkman. "I feel jaded."

"No one would tell it to look at you," said the milkman handsomely. (Louisa was wearing a rather rowdy housecoat, zebras on a pink ground, and the overnight skin food gave her face a healthy shine.)

"I'll tell you something else," said Louisa. "I dare say I'm what suffragettes chained themselves to railings for."

"My Auntie was a suffragette," offered the milkman.

"I dare say I'm even Bernard Shaw's Intelligent Woman, I'm the independent self-supporting *femme sole*, up the Married Women's Property Act and I hope Ibsen's proud of me."

"He'd be a fool if he wasn't," said the milkman.

"And I spend as much time running about for men as if I was a Victorian nanny."

"Why not take a spot of cream?" suggested the milkman.

"Thanks, I will," said Louisa. "And you might leave a yoghurt for Number Ten."

The milkman glanced at the neighboring door—not more than a yard away, in the converted house where dwelt Louisa—and cocked a deprecating eyebrow.

"To go down with yours as per usual?"

"Well, of course," said Louisa.

"Which is okay with me 'n the dairy," said the milkman, "but you'll regret it at the month's end."

III

Louisa knew damn well she'd regret it. Yoghurt for Number Ten (an indigent and vegetarian flautist) was becoming a noticeable item on her monthly budget, moreover his very gratitude was a nuisance, since besides teaching the flute he fabricated costume jewelry out of beechnuts. Louisa had a whole drawerful; it attracted mites.

Standing cream jar in hand, as the milkman clattered on—

"It's not the suffragettes who'd be proud of me," thought Louisa bitterly, "it's the Salvation Army. I may be the modern woman, the *femme sole* with all her rights, and I'm very fond of men, but it's time I looked out for myself. In fact, it's time I looked out for a rich husband, just as though I'd been born in a Victorian novel . . ."

IV

A rhythmic tapping on the party wall called her back inside her room. Number Ten had formed the pleasant custom of thus conveying his morning greetings—usually with the opening phrase of a Beethoven sonata. Louisa, who wasn't musical, knew this only because she'd been told, and herself customarily banged back no more than "Rule, Britannia." She did so now—POM, pom-pom-pom!—set down cream jar on sink, and returned to her meditations.

For once, rarely, contemplating an abstract conception: the position of the independent woman in modern society. Better their lot by far, Louisa was sure of it, than that of the timid Victorian wife trembling at a husband's frown. (On the other hand, not all Victorian wives were timid; Mrs. Proudie, for instance, browbeating her bishop, couldn't have been wholly fictional?)—Better their lot, again, than that of the Victorian spinster with no other economic resource than to become a bullied governess. (But some governesses achieved the feat of becoming bullies themselves.) Louisa had a higher opinion of women than might be expected; for those committed to any vocation, a genuine, wistful regard. If it was they who'd inherited the world the suffragettes fought for, that was fine with Louisa. But considering the average run of independent self-supporting modern women—

Here Louisa broke off to consider the case she knew best: her own. The way she, individually, supported herself was as a photographer of dogs. (Originally, of men and dogs; but the men became more of a hobby, also dogs didn't need retouching.) A nation of dog-lovers hadn't let her starve; but she noticed Number Ten's yoghurt on her milk bill. She was certainly independent, she hoped intelligent; and possessed only five pairs of stockings, two laddered.

—Considering the average run of independent self-supporting modern women, Louisa honestly believed they'd all be better off with rich husbands.

"And I'm one of the average," thought Louisa.

This obviously, given her special temperament, wasn't strictly accurate, but Louisa was in no mood to split hairs; the general proposition stood.

Her eye traveled to the row of photographs adorning her mantelshelf. As though in summary of her career, they showed about two dozen men, all broke to the wide, and in pride of place My Lucky of York, champion greyhound '56 to '58, the best provider Louisa'd ever struck. Besides photographing him, she backed him regularly at short but safe odds.

Or used to; My Lucky had been retired after the last season.

"I need my breakfast," thought Louisa.

V

She always had breakfast. With a really good dinner in prospect Louisa frequently skipped lunch, as after a really good lunch she could carry over, on cups of tea, till next morning; but she never went without breakfast. She instinctively agreed with the essayist Hazlitt that only upon the strength of that first and aboriginal meal could one muster courage to face the day. She now turned on a tap, filled a kettle, lit a gas ring, laid the table and reached down the coffee tin, all without moving her feet. Such are the advantages, to the long-armed, of a kitchenette-dinette.

Louisa's domain offered several other advantages: it was actually a divan-bedroom-bathroom-kitchenette-dinette. Except in very coldest weather, fumes from the penultimate area warmed all dependencies. There was a flap that let down over the bath, very convenient for ironing or making pastry on, and plenty of room, in the bottom of the hanging cupboard, for such essential stores as shoe polish and sardines. Some tenants found it a nuisance to be perpetually carrying down paper bags of tea leaves, potato peelings and other organic matter besides, to be deposited in one of the communal dustbins by the area steps; but such was the *genre de la maison*, and by a civilized convention they never recognized each other when so engaged, particularly if on the way out in evening dress. Louisa didn't mind in the least, and it was only because she'd temporarily run out of paper bags that her sink basket now over-flowed—and smelt a bit.

The table itself was gay with brightly striped oilcloth, china of several patterns, and paper napkins advertising cider. It was also, comparatively speaking, laden: marmalade and margarine elbowed a whole untouched loaf (the sustaining rye variety, with poppy seeds on top), and there was even a half slice of toast left over from the day before, which Louisa intended to tidy up first. The cream was merely an extra.

Louisa looked at it uneasily.

"What am I *doing* with cream, anyway?" thought Louisa. "I can't afford it, it was sheer greed . . ."

By a fortunate coincidence, however, she had promised to look in that afternoon on a producer of off-beat plays recovering from bronchitis. She took just one spoonful, neat, and set the jar on the window ledge outside to keep cool for Hugo.

The kettle boiling, she made her coffee and sat down.—How good the bread and marmalade—marmalade masking the flavor of margarine—how good the taste of coffee, enriched by an aftermath of cream!

"You know what?" Louisa addressed the absent milkman. "I'm actually on velvet."

She chewed with conscious deliberation, making each mouthful last as long as possible; was careful not to lose any of the poppy seeds. There was no hurry; she had no professional engagement that morning—or indeed that day. A nation of dog-lovers obviously wouldn't let her starve, but the whole week was in fact a bit of a blank, in the dog line. . . .

"I'll take it easy," Louisa consoled herself. "I'll have a good easy . . ."

On the thin party wall Number Ten rapped again.

"Miss Datchett?"

"Outside the door," called Louisa impatiently.

"Thank you, I have found it," called back Number Ten. "Thank you very much.—Just to say, Miss Datchett, I have the box quite ready!"

With sinking heart Louisa recalled one of her rasher promises: she was going to try and peddle some of his horrible beechnuts for him round the artier and craftier boutiques.

She recalled also Hugo down with bronchitis, and a Hungarian sculptor for whom she was finding a studio. Dogs might be lacking, but never men, to keep her occupied . . .

"I feel jaded," thought Louisa.

At that moment the milkman yodeled again. (On top of everything else, she had a histrionic milkman.) She opened grudgingly, while her coffee cooled.

"Hope on, hope ever," said the milkman. "There was a letter for you below; I've brought it up."

Chapter Two

I

Louisa didn't often get letters. (She got telegrams, or picture post cards.) She examined the envelope with what she afterwards believed to be prophetic interest.

It was large and expensive, and the writing was unfamiliar, for F. Pennon had never written to her before.—Indeed, Louisa didn't even know, till she read the letter inside, that his initial was F.

Upon large expensive paper, headed Gladstone Mansions, W.I.—

My dear Louisa (wrote F. Pennon)
I hope you may remember me from Cannes last spring— the lonely old bachelor you were so kind to? I remember you very well indeed, and would very much like to see you again. Will you come and have tea with me as soon as possible? I remember your saying you enjoyed a good tea, and scones and honey shall await you here daily. I telephoned you several times during the last week, but you were always out—though not, I sincerely trust, out of Town.

May I say, à bientôt?
F. Pennon

Prophetic interest or no, Louisa had at first some difficulty in placing F. Pennon at all. That week at Cannes had been hectic: it was the single burst of luxury her career had ever brought her, when an Italian film star whose poodles she'd photographed in London summoned her out to the film festival to photograph them again with additional publicity. In gratitude for the gesture Louisa cooperated wholeheartedly—even to the extent of faking a Rescue by Poodles in Rough Sea—but she'd also enjoyed herself.—*How* she'd enjoyed herself! Among so many breath-takingly beautiful women, each *soignée* to the last eyebrow, Louisa's harum-scarum looks seemed to bring many a cameraman relief. (The likenesses of Bobby and René and Kurt still hailed her from the mantelshelf, affectionately dedicated in three languages.) With Bobby and René and Kurt, Louisa, whenever off poodle-duty, had for a week made such carefree fiesta, the details were naturally blurred . . . Thus when after a little thought F. Pennon's image finally emerged (like a weak negative in the hypo bath), it was merely as that of the man Bobby hit with a roll.

And who'd been so nice about it—the image became more precise—they asked him over to their table—at the Poule d'Or, at the Moulin Vert?—and who'd afterwards rather strung along with them, picking up the bills.

Which he invariably paid by check . . .

Louisa found herself remembering this quite clearly—and indeed it was a circumstance to excite general admiration: absolutely anyone in Cannes took F. Pennon's checks. And not only took them, but if necessary cashed them . . .

Than which there is no more infallible sign, as René pointed out, of truly formidable riches.

At this stage in her recollections Louisa carried the letter back to her kitchenette, and there dissected it like a biologist dissecting a frog.

II

My dear Louisa . . .

He knew *her* Christian name. But then men always did.

I hope you may remember me . . .

Louisa had. With an additional effort, however, she now recalled something of F. Pennon's appearance: he resembled a Sealyham. Whether it was because of this that she also recalled him as elderly—all Sealyhams looking elderly from puppyhood—or whether it was the other way round, she wasn't quite sure. "Let it pass!" thought Louisa, reading on.

. . . would very much like to see you again.

He'd liked seeing her at Cannes. A certain shy attentiveness had been unmistakable; it was upon Louisa, they all agreed, his benevolence was chiefly directed—the others just cashed in. She herself, having such a good time, merely scooped him up into her all-embracing bonhomie without learning so much as his initial. (His address was indeed peculiarly stiff: like a Sealyham's. "Come on over, this is Uncle Bobby apologizing!" shouted Bobby. "The name is Pennon," said Mr. Pennon; and Mr. Pennon he'd remained to them throughout the week.) But attentive he'd certainly been, in a cagy way, and Louisa seemed to remember him more than once providing her with aspirins.

Her eye traveled on.

I remember your saying you enjoyed a good tea . . .

What meal didn't Louisa enjoy? It was a pity she hadn't said a good dinner, or even a good lunch; even so, F. Pennon plainly recalled her slightest word.—At this point Louisa opened the window, reached in the cream, and poured a good dollop into her coffee.

I telephoned you several times . . .

Yes, but why only *during the last few weeks?* A year had elapsed, since Cannes; it was now May again. Perhaps he'd been abroad again, thought Louisa; perhaps he'd been abroad the whole time? He was certainly staying on at Cannes, and she had a vague recollection of his mentioning South Africa.—In any case, *several times*—let alone *as soon as possible*—he was eager enough now!

May I say, à bientôt?

"The more *bientôt* the better!" thought Louisa warmly.

Then she read the whole letter through again, and came to a swift decision.

Her first impulse was to telephone herself; on second thoughts she sent a telegram. She felt that a preliminary, disembodied conversation would somehow take the dew off their meeting—and wasn't the day hers to name? WITH YOU FOUR-THIRTY LOUISA, dictated Louisa confidently. She very nearly made it a Greetings Telegram, only none of the forms suggested by the operator seemed quite to meet the case.

As has been said, she had no professional engagements; and could easily take round Hugo's cream in the morning instead of the afternoon.

III

"You seem to have had a whack at it already," said Hugo ungratefully.

He was sitting up in bed, his thin little neck protruding from a dirty turtle-neck sweater, under a counterpane littered with play-scripts. These however were so maculate already, with tea, cocoa and gin, that an additional drop of cream wouldn't make much difference.

"I had good news," apologized Louisa. "I took it, quite honestly, for you—at least my subconscious did—then I had good news, and a spot somehow got into my coffee. Eat it up, it'll build you."

Hugo fished a teaspoon from under his pillow, dipped and licked.—The lenient gulletful improved his manners.

"What sort of good news?"

"I'm going to get married," said Louisa.

It is remarkable how swiftly, once seeded, the idea of matrimony burgeons in a woman's mind. Some women indeed think of practically nothing else until they stand gazing like startled fawns through a cloud of white tulle veiling; Louisa was so far from being one of these, if she passed a society wedding, two hundred housewives outside identifying themselves with the bride, Louisa identified herself with the photographers. When she opened F. Pennon's letter, only half an hour had elapsed since her conversation with the milkman, and her subsequent meditations on the lot of the independent modern woman, and her final conclusion as to the desirability of rich husbands all round; when she finished reading, her decision was as swift as if she'd been trained in a first-class finishing school. She was going to marry F. Pennon.

She was even slightly annoyed that Hugo should now regard her with evident astonishment.

"And why not?" inquired Louisa coldly. "I'm not a hag yet!"

"My dear! No reason in the world," exclaimed Hugo, genuinely shocked. "You're *very* attractive. I mean, that's why I was surprised— you have such a good time knowing such dozens of men."

Louisa looked at the stack of dirty plates on the floor beside his bed. In a few minutes, she supposed she'd be having a good time washing them. Quite possibly Number Ten imagined she'd have a good time peddling his beechnuts. "And whose fault is it?" thought Louisa honestly. "It's not men's, it's mine. I've asked for it, I've made a hobby of it, I've been the original Good Sort . . ." She was damned if she'd wash Hugo's dishes, but neither would she do him injustice.— As he suddenly coughed like a sick sheep, she hadn't the heart even to disillusion him.

"Of course you're right," agreed Louisa. "I've had a marvelous time. Particularly with you, Hugo dear. I still think I'll get married."

"I suppose it *is* the modern thing to do," coughed Hugo, recovering aplomb. "I'm so old-fashioned, I just live in sin."

Louisa cast an understanding but expert eye over the traditional attic. There wasn't room, between peeling wall and unwashed window, to swing a cat; but love (or sin), Louisa was aware, in the circles in which Hugo moved rather throve on squalor. Not a stocking, however, hung to dry . . .

"I know you'd *like* to—" began Louisa sympathetically.

"My dear good girl," snapped Hugo, now annoyed in turn, "I assure you I slept with Pammy actually last night."

"Then when you've still got bronchitis it was very silly," said Louisa. She paused, and looked round again. Not a stocking, not a flower!—and not a thermometer. "What *I* mean is," explained Louisa, "if you were really *living* in sin with Pammy, she'd be here now, looking after you in sin."

"Actually she's got a rehearsal," said Hugo sulkily.

"Which is precisely the point," said Louisa.—She paused again, suddenly and surprisedly aware of what she really had in mind; which was, briefly, that she herself wouldn't be giving up work (as she fully intended to do, upon marrying F. Pennon) solely because F. Pennon could support her, but also because she recognized certain reciprocal claims. If F. Pennon had bronchitis, she, Louisa, wouldn't be out photographing poodles! Nor was the idea unwelcome; in fact she desired such claims—on her time, on her affection; *but from a husband.*

Louisa looked at Hugo thoughtfully. She was very fond of him. He was a brave little twirp. Not one of his off-beat plays had ever succeeded, he currently stage-managed at an Outer London rep.; and though it was there, in the drafty wings, he caught his bronchitis, so dedicated was he that he crawled from his bed and back into the drafts each night. Louisa was not only fond of Hugo, she admired him. His dogged, masculine single-mindedness, in the face of so much discouragement, struck her as little short of heroic. All the same she felt, suddenly, extremely tired of him.

"It's time I had some proper claims made on me," thought Louisa, "before I turn into the original Mother Figure . . ."

She stood up.

"Darling, you aren't *going?*" protested Hugo incredulously.

"I've got to look in at the shop," said Louisa.

"But you haven't told me about your Intended. I'm all agog, honestly I am! Who is he?"

"Someone I've known for quite a while," said Louisa.

"Has he any money?"

"Quite a lot," said Louisa, rather sharply. "But that's not only why I'm marrying him."

By now, strangely enough, it was true.—Who more mercenary than Louisa, that very breakfast-time, as she contemplated her lot as an independent modern woman? Who more mercenary than Louisa as she dissected F. Pennon's letter and sent off her wire? During the intervening hours, she had grown fond of him. In a sense this was only to be expected, she was fond of most men; the fact remained that though his money was an essential factor, she now thought of F. Pennon with genuine affection, and thoroughly resented, on his behalf, Hugo's tone.

"What a lucky girl you are!" congratulated Hugo, all unconscious. "I suppose he isn't by any chance interested in the theater?"

"Not that I know of," said Louisa—at the door.

"Because if he *should* be," called Hugo, "you might just drop a word—at some tender moment, you know—about my Aristophanes in modern dress . . ."

IV

"And when's it to be?" inquired Mr. Ross interestedly.

"Well, I'm not quite sure yet," said Louisa. "But I can't see why we should wait."

"Just give the word in good time," said Mr. Ross, "and me and the boys'll have a whip-round. Congratulations again—though I must say the place won't seem the same without you."

It wasn't much of a place, Louisa's shop. Fortunately as a photographer of dogs she had no need of any chichi studio, her subjects posed either *en plein air* or in their own homes; in fact she hadn't a studio at all, but merely rented darkroom space off Mr. Ross at a highly un-chi-chi address in Soho. (Mr. Ross's subjects, though anthropoids, were also photographed *en plein air*: on the pavement outside Burlington House.) The accommodation suited Louisa very well, however, and she and Rossy had shared many a companionable cup of tea, as they were doing now, by the gas ring on the back landing.

"Not that we'd expect," added Mr. Ross delicately, "to be *asked* ..."

"Good heavens, why not?" exclaimed Louisa. "You don't think I'm going to drop all my old friends?"

"If you're wise you will," said Mr. Ross.

Louisa looked at him as she'd looked at Hugo: he stood up better to her scrutiny. He wasn't so very much the elder, his sharp-cut suit and pointed shoes were as much of a group-uniform as Hugo's dirty sweater and duffle coat; his oily black locks, styled to kill, inspired no confidence in the conventionally-minded. But his eyes were the sagacious eyes of the Jew; and he was genuinely concerned for her.

"When embarking on a new life," said Mr. Ross earnestly, "make a clean break. You're marrying a well-to-do man, you're going to have a nice home: so okay, don't clutter it up with old pals. I'm speaking against my own interest, your society's been a real pleasure; but I've seen again and again how it doesn't do. My own sister," said Mr. Ross unexpectedly, "married into a chain store. But do *I* drop in on 'em, Saturdays? Not me. It wouldn't answer."

"Why not?" asked Louisa uneasily.

"Hampstead and Whitechapel. The grape 'n the grain. In your case, let's say, Knightsbridge 'n—"

"Paddington," supplied Louisa.

"That where you live? I didn't know," said Mr. Ross. "I don't know, either, that you mayn't have some very classy friends—"

Louisa shook her head.

"Then take my advice, give 'em the go-by. Make a clean break.— And don't fret about me missing the champagne," added Mr. Ross humorously, "just pour me another cup of char."

V

Before so momentous an appointment Louisa naturally returned home to embellish her appearance; and met Number Ten on the stairs. He looked even seedier than usual—as though the mites were beginning to get at him too; also his vegetarian breath smelt unpleasantly of garlic. Without a pang, Louisa mentally gave Number Ten the go-by.

Without a pang, she felt, she could give Hugo the go-by. She could give them all the go-by, gladly—the whole shiftless bunch of men she was used to being fond of . . .

"Rossy's dead right," thought Louisa. "It's time I made a clean break."

Chapter Three

I

There could still be no stronger proof of her special temperament (which Louisa was now determined to repress, but Rome isn't built in a day) than the fact that she could enter Gladstone Mansions not only without dismay, but with positive exhilaration. Most women got the willies.

The first impression produced by the interior was of being underground. Seen from without, twelve massive stories reared almost tower-like; once past the great oak and ground-glass doors the catacomb illusion was complete. A cautious use of electricity left in shadow the high, coved, cavernous ceiling; on the walls, a paper originally representing marble now looked like wet granite. At intervals upon it naked skulls, like the trophies of cavemen, thrust up branching antlers or simple horns. Stray visitors from the provinces, peering uncertain through the heavy doors, felt that a Natural History Museum ought to be brighter. Only the specialist eye of a British club-man—and Louisa's—at once recognized the entirely appropriate threshold to the most expensive flats in London, single gentlemen only.

When one rang for the lift, nothing happened.—This was all right with Louisa, who had arrived a trifle early; in any case, she would no more have minded waiting than a scholar minds waiting in a library, or a botanist in a herbarium, or a kindergarten mistress in a show of infant handicraft. She had all the heads to look at. The legend beneath an *Oryx indiensis*, "Shot by Major Cart-wright-Jones, Himalayas 1885," filled her with vicarious pleasure. (Though fond of animals, she was fonder still of majors, and besides had never seen an oryx on the hoof like a major in his boots.) A Colonel Hamlyn had bagged a wildebeeste, the Hon. C. P. Coe a moose; Louisa mentally tramped veldts with the one, slogged through tundra with the other—she was having, so to speak, a last orgy—and marveled as always at men's gratuitous heroism . . .

F. Pennon didn't appear to have shot anything. Even so, Louisa could well imagine some future nostalgia on his part, and easily promised herself to respect it.

An ancient clock coughed the half-hour. She rang again, and now in the lift shaft something happened. Iron vitals rumbled; machinery shuddered, ropes strained, wheels ground; it was like the birth of the Industrial Age. Rudimentary yet effectual, a great iron cage descended, groaned to a halt, and gaped. Casting a last affectionate thought towards Colonel Hamlyn, Major Jones and Mr.Coe—whom no one else had thought of, let alone with affection, since about 1910—Louisa stepped hardily in.

"F. Pennon, third," said Louisa. "What a splendid lot of heads!"

"The relatives don't claim 'em," replied the lift man morosely.

His aged features, unused to expressing anything but apathy, readjusted themselves to express a dislike of small talk. Louisa admitted her error, recognized, and applauded, a complete absorption in the remarkable task of making six hundredweight of iron go up and down, and held her tongue.

Up they labored. An eye attuned to the cavern below instinctively sought, between the probably hand-forged bars, for some daubing of elk or mastodon on the lift shaft's naked brick. But it was bare as a pot-hole.—To be ejected, at the Third, into civilization, nonetheless came as a shock, even though one was still, unmistakably, in Gladstone

Mansions as well. The long narrow corridor still gave the impression of being underground, if only as in a mine; upon the walls, instead of horns and skulls, hung steel engravings—but each commemorating some disaster to British arms. (*The Charge of the Light Brigade*, the *Loss of the Royal George*, the *Retreat from Corunna*.) Louisa passed appreciatively between them, identified the door she sought, and used the *Death of Nelson* as a mirror to repowder her nose.

II

"F. Pennon?" inquired Louisa.

"Miss Datchett?" inquired the old manservant.

He might have been the lift man's twin brother; but Louisa was now too intent on her own affairs even to ask if they were related.— Behind him stretched a typical Gladstone Mansions sitting room— furnished apparently with sarcophagi, carpeted apparently with churchyard moss, the whole gloomy vista closed by curtains not absolutely black, but nonetheless suggestive of a first-class French funeral. The only points of brightness were the silver tea set ready on the tea table and the eager gleam in F. Pennon's eye as he hurried towards her out of the circumambient gloom.

Louisa scrutinized him with natural interest. Her memory had been generally accurate: like a Sealyham he was broad through the chest and rather short-legged, but though not tall he was at least as tall as she was (and she could always wear flat heels), and his graying hair had exactly the springy roughness of a Sealyham's coat. (Louisa could easily imagine herself dropping a kiss on it at the breakfast table.) In age she judged him about nine—or rather sixty—and though she could have wished him younger, he looked fit as a fiddle.

"My dear Louisa," exclaimed F. Pennon, "how good of you to be so prompt!"

He had her hand even before the manservant stepped back, clasping it enthusiastically between his own.—Where now was his reserve, his peculiar stiffness of address? All swept away, thought Louisa happily, in the joy of seeing her again!

"It's a pleasure," said Louisa sincerely.

Indeed it was, to see him not only so spry and so delighted, but also, quite obviously, nervous. (He was far more nervous than Louisa; but then she already knew his fate.) He fussed. He fussed over finding her the most comfortable chair, and over the disposition of the tea things. (There were the scones, there was the honey, also a plummy cake shaped like an Edwardian toque.) He asked her to pour out. The weight of the teapot almost sprained her wrist, but how gladly she bore the slight twinge! "Family plate," thought Louisa—for not even Gladstone Mansions would supply solid silver. The sugar bowl alone could have been pawned for thirty bob. (How different a cup of char with Mr. Ross!) Merely to handle the solid silver sugar tongs, good for at least half a guinea, Louisa took three lumps.

"This is just," sighed Louisa, "what I like."

"You used to take lemon," said F. Pennon anxiously.

There was lemon too, sliced wafer-thin in a silver shell. Not to disappoint him, Louisa added lemon. F. Pennon himself spooned honey onto her plate, beside the hot scone. Then he sat back and watched her eat with an expression of rapture.

"How well I remember," he exclaimed, "that week at Cannes!"

"Oh, so do I!" said Louisa.

"We did, didn't we, get on rather well?—D'you think you could call me Freddy?"

"Easily," said Louisa—she was only too glad to find it wasn't F. for Ferdinand.

"You attracted me at once," continued Freddy, in happy reminiscence. "I don't mind telling you I was a bit annoyed—being hit with that roll—then I saw *you* at the table, and that's why I came over. What a thundering piece of luck it was!"

"For me too," said Louisa.

"You really mean that?—I don't live here regularly, you know," said F. Pennon, "I've a house as well, outside Bournemouth."

The transition was abrupt—how nervous he was, poor F for Freddy!—but Louisa grasped the implication at once. Wives being obviously tabu, in Gladstone Mansions, he wanted her to know about the house.—Not in Knightsbridge; outside Bournemouth. Mr. Ross however had scarcely erred.

"I can't imagine anything nicer," said Louisa encouragingly.

"I hope you'll think so when you see it. That is, if you do see it. I want you to see it.—But I'm going too fast," said F. Pennon anxiously. "I'm rushing things. Have a slice of cake."

Though she hadn't finished her scone, Louisa accepted it willingly. His nervousness was beginning to be infectious, and eating always steadied her.

"Not that I don't like it here too," added Freddy, with a touch of wistfulness. "I do. I like it uncommonly."

At the thought of all he was giving up for her, Louisa's heart quite melted—particularly as Gladstone Mansions was just the sort of place she liked herself. How different, the huge, solid room, from a divan-bedroom-bathroom-kitchenette-dinette! Even its gloom was tranquillizing—like a thoroughly wet day when there is no question of going out. If Freddy's eye was wistful, so was Louisa's; but no one was ever less of a dog-in-the-manger.

"Why not keep it on?" she suggested kindly. "Then you could pop up to town on your own."

"You really think I might?" exclaimed F. Pennon, brightening at once. "It wouldn't cause . . . misunderstandings?—My dear Louisa," cried F. Pennon enthusiastically, "how right I've been about you! I knew I was right, even on so very brief an acquaintance as ours was at Cannes! You're the only woman, I tell you frankly, I've been able to think of—"

Louisa swallowed fast. She didn't mean to receive his proposal in form with her mouth full.

"—to turn to," finished F. Pennon, "in a jam."

For one moment—and alas, for one only—incredulity numbed Louisa's brain. The moment passed. After but the briefest pause, during which she resisted an impulse to dash the scone to the ground and grind it into the carpet—

"Here we go again!" thought Louisa resignedly.

III

Resignedly she composed herself to listen. She also put another scone on her plate, beside the slice of cake, to make sure of supplies. Though where were now her rosy hopes, if she ate enough tea she could do without supper, and so be at least a meal up.

"Fire ahead," said Louisa.

It was encouragement of a sort. At any rate it was encouragement enough for F. Pennon. He drew a deep, already assuaged breath.

"I don't suppose even you can realize," he began earnestly, "how a man feels—a man of my age—when the woman he's worshiped for twenty years is at last free to marry him."

Louisa sat perfectly still. The words were a final blow, and in the circumstances a shattering one. Yet what fidelity they exhibited! Twenty years! How different, such true devotion, thought Louisa, from the untidy amours of her familiar circle! Chagrined as she was, she felt her heart melt.

"Perhaps not," she said kindly. "Tell me."

"He feels terrified," said F. Pennon.

IV

Another moment passed. As though upon some emotional switch-back, Louisa had scarcely time to alter her expression—in fact she was still looking reverent—before it was necessary to speak.

"I thought you said you'd *worshiped*—?" began Louisa.

"Yes. But from afar," said F. Pennon.

"How far afar?"

"Argentina. For the last *eighteen* years, she's lived in the Argentine. She married a man in business there—a splendid chap," said F. Pennon warmly. "Now he's dead."

"You mean you haven't *seen* her for eighteen years?" marveled Louisa.

"That's right. His business rather went downhill, d'you see, and they couldn't afford to come home. But of course I've written to her. We wrote to each other," said F. Pennon, warming up a little, "every month . . ."

"You mean love letters?"

"I suppose you might call 'em so. I know Enid told me they added meaning to her whole existence.—So they did to mine," said F. Pennon. "I'd no other attachments, never wanted any; but once each month I'd turn aside from—well, money-grubbing—and just give myself up to sweeter things. I used to keep a special evening, settle down at that desk with perhaps a spot of brandy—"

"And a dictionary of quotations?" suggested Louisa.

"Just to refresh my memory," said F. Pennon simply. "Enid liked me to put in poetry. She's particularly fond of Tennyson. One way and another, taking all my letters together, I dare say you'd find the whole of *Maud*. And then of course there'd be a letter each month from *her*, and I kept a special evening for them too. It was ideal . . ."

Louisa could see that it had been. Now that she wasn't going to marry him herself, now that she regarded him dispassionately, she could see it was the very thing for him: a sentimental attachment—a *long-distance* attachment—neatly compartmented from, not interfering with, the solid comforts of Gladstone Mansions. It was a particularly galling reflection that she herself, at Cannes, had no doubt been merely an Enid-surrogate—F. Pennon on holiday, with time for sweeter things on his hands . . .

"Did she teach you to carry aspirins?" asked Louisa abruptly.

"Enid? As a matter of fact, yes. How did you guess?"

"Never mind," said Louisa, beginning to eat again. "Go on. Where do I come in?"

But Freddy was still gazing nostalgically towards the writing desk.

"I'd just bought a new seal, an agate," he mourned. "It had *Semper Fidelis* on it.—Now the poor chap's dead!"

"And I suppose Enid expects you in Buenos Aires?" prompted Louisa, not quite patiently. "I still don't see where *I*—"

With an effort he jerked himself back to the present.

"Actually her boat docks the day after tomorrow," said F. Pennon. "She's *come* . . ."

Though still eating fast, Louisa met his desperate eye with renewed sympathy. Who wouldn't, thought Louisa, in such a situation, be terrified? To worship afar for eighteen years, and then to have one's idol all at once within reach! And not only within reach but positively, so to speak—and soon now, indeed, without metaphor—in one's lap! For Louisa had no doubt in the world, she read it in F. Pennon's every agitated glance, that in those monthly letters he had absolutely committed himself. Enid had come home to marry him.

"Congratulations," said Louisa, "and cheer up. When does she get to London?"

"She isn't coming to London," said F. Pennon. "She's going straight to my house at Bournemouth.—What else can she do? She hasn't a penny, poor gel—and I can hardly pay her hotel bills! So she's going to Bournemouth. That's where we're going to meet. And that's where I want *you* to come too," said F. Pennon rapidly, "dear Louisa, just to help me over the hump."

V

Louisa swallowed the last crumbs of plum cake and rose. At least she had had a good tea.

"Dear Freddy," said Louisa, "not on your life."

Just as Hugo when she left him on his sickbed, Freddy stared incredulously.

"But, Louisa—"

"I quite see why you've been telephoning me," said Louisa, more kindly, "I even see that it wasn't a bad idea. You've still, so far as I can judge, got to marry her—"

"Of course I'm going to marry her!" cried F. Pennon, with belated fervor. "Dammit, I *want* to marry her! Only I can't, I tell you I positively can't, be all alone with her for the first few days. There's got to be a—well, a buffer. Come to Bournemouth just for a week—"

"You could hardly introduce me as a buffer," said Louisa coldly.

"Of course not. I shouldn't think of it. You'll be a friend I have staying with me. Probably she'll take it for a delicate piece of chaperoning. I dare say she'll *expect* chaperoning—"

"Duennas, in Argentina, are probably still all the go," agreed Louisa. "Haven't you any female relatives?"

"No. I tell you you're the only woman I've been able to think of—you with your wonderful understanding of a man, you who're such a thorough good sort—"

"Listen," interrupted Louisa. "Listen carefully. I know that's my reputation, but I'm through. I've had enough of being a good sort. I've had enough of being man's best friend. From now on, they'll have to take Airedales. I'm sorry to disappoint you, and thanks for my tea."

She brushed the cake crumbs from her fingers and rose. (She really felt adequately fed until next morning.) She powdered her nose standing, and moved definitely towards the door.

"Louisa!" cried F. Pennon desperately.

She knew better than to turn. He would be looking too much like an abandoned Sealyham. How infinitely preferable if he were!— then she could simply take him home.

"It's not only on my account," implored F. Pennon desperately, "it's on Enid's. I know she's a married woman—"

Louisa paused.

It suddenly struck her how extraordinarily few married women she knew. In fact she knew very few women at all, and those mostly of the Pammy type—without a wedding ring among them. Freddy's Enid had not only married once, but within the first months of widowhood was about to marry again. Louisa's own aim now being matrimony—if not with F. Pennon, then with another—it struck her that from a woman so eminently nubile she might well pick up a few tips.

"Oh, okay," said Louisa. "When do we go?"

VI

"You know what?" said the milkman. "That chap Ibsen's dead."

"I know," said Louisa.

"I didn't; my Auntie told me," said the milkman. "Also while never chaining herself to railings she did once black a gentleman's eye."

"Those were the days," said Louisa.

The milkman considered her with more attention.

"Since you mentioned it yourself, you do look a bit jaded. What about another spot of cream?"

"No, thanks," said Louisa. "In fact, you needn't leave anything for a week."

"Saving money or going on holiday?" inquired the milkman.

"Neither," said Louisa. "Summer school."

—She hesitated. Whether as a buffer between old Freddy and his beloved, or as a picker of that beloved's brains, she was pretty well assured of a week's good grub. She was still resolved to give Number Ten the go-by; she simply recognized that the idea of his peering fruitlessly outside the door each morning might spoil her appetite; and on second thoughts ordered yoghurt as usual.

Chapter Four

I

"And this," said F. Pennon, "is Miss Datchett, who's staying with us for a bit."

Was he flushed with triumph, or merely feeling the heat? The afternoon was so warm, Louisa couldn't decide—and indeed spared him but the briefest glance, so eager was she to observe the woman he'd worshiped for twenty years, and whom he'd just been to fetch from Bournemouth West station.

Enid Anstruther was small, slight, blonde and faded. Her age was more difficult to be precise about: on the facts, Louisa had worked her out at about forty, at which age a woman today is still young, and Mrs. Anstruther in manner at least was positively girlish; but this very girlishness had the effect of making her seem older. As she jumped out of the car, and ran up the loggia steps, Louisa, observing these pretty, girlish movements, had to tell herself not to be a cat.

"But how *nice!*" cried Mrs. Anstruther warmly.

—At least it was big of her, or at any rate she was a very quick thinker. A small gloved hand flew out and patted at Louisa's in a kind little gesture of acceptance. The latter, always dispassionate about her own appearance, was uncontrollably reminded of a recent First Prize Amateur Snap; of a robin making friends with a lurcher.

"Name's Louisa.—You'll get on together," promised F. Pennon optimistically. "Now then: Enid's had a long journey, she'll want to lie down."

Mrs. Anstruther turned to him gratefully.—She turned; and Louisa saw her profile.

No tropic heat, so ravaging of skin and hair, affects the profile. Enid Anstruther's had remained exquisite: low, straight forehead, straight, delicately cut nose, short upper lip and delicately rounded chin. It was a profile out of a Victorian keepsake—Grecian softened to prettiness. It was a profile, there was no denying, for a man to remember with devotion even after eighteen years.

Lying down being apparently the order of the day, as soon as Mrs. Anstruther had been shown her room, Louisa went and lay down too.

II

The bedspread, which she carefully turned back, was of pink brocade. Upon the floor a deep pile carpet, slightly darker in tone than the quilt, fitted from wall to wall. Curtains patterned with enormous pale green leaves framed a view of pine trees and sea. It wasn't even the best bed-room—that had Mrs. Anstruther lying down in it—but it was still so very different indeed from Louisa's room in Paddington, when she woke in it that morning she felt like the chimney sweep in Buck House.

Freddy had driven her from London the day before. (In his custom-built Rolls: his own luggage stowed in matching suitcases, Louisa's in a variety of air-line giveaway bags. Actually Freddy didn't drive himself, there was a custom-built chauffeur.) Louisa enjoyed the trip thoroughly, even though Freddy grew progressively more taciturn. ("And why the hell not?" thought Louisa sympathetically. What a lapful awaited him!) She sympathized—but not so acutely that she forgot to loll. Novel though the experience was, in Freddy's Rolls Louisa discovered that she could loll as to the manner born.

Halting for coffee, halfway through the morning's run, she didn't even descend, but let a cup be obsequiously carried out to her. Halting for lunch, at a famous and fabulously expensive inn, she just accepted the necessity of putting foot to ground. Then they had everything most expensive on the menu.

"I could, don't you think, make a woman comfortable?" suggested F. Pennon.

"Unless she's off her head," said Louisa warmly.

They reached Bournemouth about six: the big house above a famous chine awaited them in apple-pie order. "Evening, Karen," said Freddy casually. "Got any cocktails for us?" A large and smiling Swede indicated the tray. ("What she must be paid—!" thought Louisa.) Some sort of understrapper of the chauffeur's carried in their bags, and a dinner to recruit Arctic explorers was served at eight. Freddy was still taciturn, and what slight conversation took place concerned the desirability, or otherwise, of Louisa's accompanying him to meet Mrs. Anstruther's train.

"Just to break the ice!" pleaded Freddy.

"Not I," said Louisa. "You've got to take the plunge."

"I tell you, I've told you, it's exactly just at first I'll want you there."

"Yes, but not just at first as all that," said Louisa. "Not on the *platform . . .*"

As has been seen, she won her point, and Freddy went to the station alone.

III

Louisa pummeled the pillow into a sausage under her nape. It was an uncommonly warm afternoon, but she couldn't sleep. To sleep at such an hour was unnatural to her; naturally, or customarily, she'd have been developing film in Rossy's basement.—Louisa put the thought of Mr. Ross aside; as she saw now, she'd been over-impulsive in her confidences to him. She had also been over-impulsive in her confidences to Hugo, and was only thankful she hadn't said anything to Number Ten.

"All the same," thought Louisa uneasily, "I'm going to have a hell of a lot of explaining to do when I get back . . ."

She pummeled the pillow again. Its linen slip was pale pink, so were the sheets, and blankets. Impulsively Louisa stripped down the nearest corner for a look at the mattress. It was pink too.

"At least I'm on velvet for a week," thought Louisa.

It struck her that a week seemed to be the natural term of any luxury for her. It had been for a week that she'd luxuriated at Cannes . . .

Her thoughts veered to Mrs. Anstruther. Brief though their meeting had been, in Louisa's opinion it sufficed to form a judgment.

"She's nothing," thought Louisa, "she's a nonentity. She just happened to be born with a profile . . ."

But just that profile, that echo from a Victorian beauty-book, was going to put Enid Anstruther on velvet for the rest of her life.

IV

If Louisa had been thinking about Mrs. Anstruther, so, evidently, had Mrs. Anstruther been thinking about Louisa. It was only natural—as it was only natural that she should have cut short her siesta to stroll with Freddy on the broad gravel walk under the bedroom windows.

"Freddy dear, who exactly *is* Miss Datchett?" murmured Enid Anstruther.

Louisa had no scruples about eavesdropping in such a case as this; but sat up to listen better.

"Gel I've known all my life," said Freddy. "That is, knew her people all my life . . ."

There was a slight pause.

"I don't remember any Datchetts at Keithley?" mused Mrs. Anstruther.

"Came from Leeds," said Freddy instantly. "After you deserted me and went to Argentina. It's eighteen years, y'know."

"You've changed so little, I forget," sighed Mrs. Anstruther.—The next moment she rippled with pretty laughter; she was very volatile. "And *I* feel just a slip of a girl again," confessed Mrs. Anstruther, "with my chaperone! Kind Freddy, to take such care of me! I wonder what made you ask Miss Datchett."

"Convalescing after mumps," said Freddy. "Thought I'd kill two birds with one stone."

Louisa's outraged ear caught a delicate babble of alarm. Then—

"No, of course she ain't infectious," said Freddy. "I told you, she's convalescing. Building up."

V

As in completion of the circuit—

"Well, now you've seen her," inquired F. Pennon, "what d'you think of her?"

He and Louisa were waiting in the spacious, galleried entrance hall for Mrs. Anstruther to come down to dinner—Freddy in black tie, Louisa, to keep her spirits up, in toreador pants.

"She's got the most beautiful profile," said Louisa sincerely, "I've ever seen off an Afghan."

"She has, hasn't she?" said Freddy eagerly. "It's what I've always remembered about her—that little nose, and the way her lip curls . . . she hasn't changed in the least. She says I haven't either."

"In fact the water was quite warm," said Louisa.

He looked at her suspiciously.

"What water?"

"The plunge. In off the deep end, up with your pockets full of fish," said Louisa, who was feeling rather disagreeable. "Why the hell did you have to give me mumps?"

"It just came into my mind.—D'you mean to say you were listening?" retorted Freddy.

"Naturally, in this heat, I had the window open. You should be more careful, on that path."

"Well, what would you have liked me to give you?" inquired Freddy sulkily.

"Appendicitis," said Louisa. "If you had to give me anything, appendicitis would have been classier. I suppose I'm lucky you didn't think of pinkeye."

"You haven't much regard for my feelings," said Freddy, "if when I want to talk about Enid you start talking about pinkeye."

Absurdly, they were almost quarreling. With genuine remorse, for she really was fond of F. Pennon, Louisa pulled herself up.

"Okay, let's get back to her," said Louisa. "Her profile's smashing, and I'm only too glad, Freddy, honestly I am, everything's gone so well. In fact, if you'd like me to leave any sooner—" It cost her a slight effort to say this, a week's velvet being always a week's velvet; but she said it—"I've a kennel of dachshunds on ice, and you've only to give me the word."

There was a slight pause. On the gallery above a door opened.

"Don't think of it," said Freddy hastily.—"Enid, my dear, are you ready for dinner?"

VI

Mrs. Anstruther, wearing gray lace, flitted mothlike down the stair and came to rest at Freddy's side like a butterfly on a buddleia. Her soft gray glance flitted momentarily towards Louisa's pants, and as swiftly flitted away again. Louisa acknowledged a possibly justified criticism, and at the same time diagnosed short sight and a reluctance to appear in glasses.

—"Stop being a cat!" Louisa adjured herself.

But it was almost impossible not to be a cat, Mrs. Anstruther being so like a moth, or a bird, or a butterfly; for of all three, it was plain, did her nature partake.—It wasn't only, Louisa had to admit, her profile: there was a softness and fluffiness and a featheriness about her which one could well imagine irresistible to the tougher type of male. As Mrs. Anstruther slipped a hand through Freddy's arm, Louisa saw their common destiny inevitable; and the presence of a temporary buffer as much a luxury as—a pink mattress.

Chapter Five

I

During the days that followed, this opinion was confirmed. How Mrs. Anstruther and Freddy behaved when alone together Louisa of course didn't know; in public Enid had certain possessive little ways with him—the hand slipped through his arm, occasionally she straightened his tie—but Freddy accepted such attentions rather warily, and Enid was discreet enough to go no further. The most overt sign of their relationship, and in the circumstances a conclusive one, was the way she at once slipped into place as mistress of the house.

She did it so neatly, so smoothly, an earlier judgment of Louisa's had indeed to be revised. There was a brain behind that profile—or at least there were formidable instincts. Mrs. Anstruther immediately perceived that the woman to make an ally of wasn't Louisa, but Karen; and directed upon the latter the full force of what could only be called her ladylikeness. Her manner was at once sweetly incompetent and perfectly assured; taking it for granted that Karen ran the house, she also took it for granted that Karen now did so under her, Mrs. Anstruther's, authority. Within forty-eight hours Louisa saw with admiration the new routine established: at ten o'clock each morning there was Karen with the day's menus—for Mrs. Anstruther's approval.

"My dear, I'm *used* to having servants!" explained Enid mildly. "In Argentina, even when poor Archy's business went so downhill, I always had at least *three. . . !*"

It appeared that Karen, in Sweden, had been used to having a mistress. Within forty-eight hours Karen added to her duties as housekeeper those of lady's maid. Louisa, furtively, washed her own gloves and stockings; not so Mrs. Anstruther. Karen washed for her.

Only a woman used to having servants—and Enid, a rarity in the England of her generation, was so used—could have pulled it off. At the same time, she could have done so only in the full consciousness of Freddy's backing; and her handling of Karen betokened this so complete, any other sign of her empire over him would have been superfluous.

In point of fact, Mrs. Anstruther and Freddy weren't alone together very much. Unexpectedly, it was Mrs. Anstruther and Louisa who were alone together.

Immediately after breakfast Freddy went for a good long walk. ("Too hot for you gels!" declared Freddy, stepping briskly forth.) The girls stayed behind in the shady garden, under the pine trees, turning over the daily papers. (Mrs. Anstruther also embroidered. Louisa sometimes did a bit of weeding.) The siesta occupied the afternoon, and when the girls descended for tea Freddy would be found to have gone off again; then they simply waited for him to come back. It was an extraordinary sort of life to Louisa, but Mrs. Anstruther seemed to find it quite natural, and stitched away, or did nothing at all, with every appearance of content.

("I suppose you weren't ever in a harem?" asked Louisa impulsively.

"My dear, what things you think of!" exclaimed Mrs. Anstruther. "Of course I know you're only joking.")

In theory, of course, Louisa was at perfect liberty to go for a walk herself—or go for a swim, go into Bournemouth to look at the shops. Unfortunately she was also, in theory, convalescing, and

Enid Anstruther, now firmly in the saddle as hostess, was as strict as kind. "Freddy would never forgive me," explained Mrs. Anstruther earnestly. "I've promised him *faithfully* to see you take a proper rest!—To think," she added, "to *think*—you poor dear!—of having appendicitis *as well!*"

Louisa was only half appreciative of Freddy's well-meant addendum: after mumps and appendicitis combined, caution was obviously sensible. Under the pines each morning, in the drawing room before dinner, Louisa continued to sit—condemned to harem life with Mrs. Anstruther.

Her function as buffer came into play chiefly at meals. F. Pennon took his food seriously, but Mrs. Anstruther pecked like a wren; it fell to Louisa to praise, discriminate, and tuck in.—She had often observed that men commonly like women to eat well; as though still Turks at heart, haunted by the full-moon image of beauty, however much they praise a lissom figure they dislike actually witnessing the abstinence so often involved. Mrs. Anstruther's resolution in sticking to a diet was thus an additional sign of her confidence, but Louisa's appetite was nonetheless useful, keeping Freddy company in greed, also promoting conversation.

"But aren't you *terrified?*" exclaimed Mrs. Anstruther uncontrollably.

"What of?" asked Louisa.

"Putting on weight."

"I don't seem to," apologized Louisa.

"Take some more sauce," said Freddy.

It was Cumberland sauce; on baked ham. Louisa took some, also another roll.

"My dear, you really *shouldn't!*" cried Mrs. Anstruther. "I knew a girl in the Argentine, every bit as thin as you are, who thought she could eat anything she liked, and quite suddenly, at about thirty, she became simply *enormous!*"

"What happened to her?" asked Louisa.

"Well, in the first place, she couldn't ride any of her horses."

"That won't bother me," said Louisa. "But of course you're quite right. I've seen it myself: one day a woman looks like a string bean, the next she looks like a cantaloupe."

"But she needn't!" cried Mrs. Anstruther. "If she's on her guard!—Oh, see what kind Freddy's got for *me!*" cried Mrs. Anstruther. "A pineapple!"

After dinner Freddy liked to play chess. Enid—how confident she was!—at once proclaimed her incapacity; but Louisa, grateful for so much good grub, admitted to knowing the moves. "That'll do, give you a queen," said Freddy; so after dinner he and Louisa played chess. Of course Enid sat beside them. Also beside them was a tray with brandy, ice and soda, cigarettes and cigars, for F. Pennon believed in making himself comfortable. Mrs. Anstruther had her own little table with lime juice and peppermint creams. Louisa was free of either.

"You wouldn't play badly," said Freddy, "if you concentrated."

"*I* think Louisa's very clever to play at all!" declared Mrs. Anstruther.

Actually Louisa rather enjoyed these sessions. Both she and Freddy played hard: dogged as an old Sealyham he bent his hairy eyebrows above the board—having given Louisa a queen, he gave her no quarter—while Louisa, concentrating, could sometimes force a draw. Sometimes they were both so absorbed they forgot Mrs. Anstruther altogether. She for her part always let them finish a game before rising to go to bed; generally she let them have two.

Louisa always went upstairs when Mrs. Anstruther did, because Mrs. Anstruther was her hostess. The time was usually no later than eleven, but Enid emanated such a force of feminine conventionality, Louisa went up too.

II

On velvet as she was, Louisa, idle, and alone for the chief of the day with another woman, could soon have become extremely bored; fortunately their long tête-à-têtes offered her the very opportunity she sought, to pick Mrs. Anstruther's brains.

Chapter Six

I

"Freddy tells me you've such a fascinating career!" mused Mrs. Anstruther—under the pines, in the grateful shade. "How *I* should have liked one too!—But then I married straight out of the nursery."

"How did you manage it?" asked Louisa interestedly.

Mrs. Anstruther rippled with gentle laughter.

"My *dear!* I didn't 'manage' it, it just happened! Of course I *was* rather pretty—"

(She paused automatically for Louisa to say *Oh but you still are!* Louisa said it. It wasn't her nature to want something for nothing.)

"—and when poor Archy came home on leave, he simply put me in his pocket! That's how poor Freddy missed his chance," explained Mrs. Anstruther, "he thought of me as still a child. I shall never forget his tragic face, when I told him I was engaged."

"Yes, but go back a bit," said Louisa. "What were you doing when you met Archy?"

"Why, I was just at home," said Mrs. Anstruther, surprised. "I was an only daughter. I just stayed at home."

"Where?" asked Louisa.

"My dear, in the *depths* of the country. Keithley! But of course you know it," added Mrs. Anstruther.—For the moment however Louisa was too absorbed to take the reference.

"And Archy just came along like one of those radar-fitted moths?"

"His people were neighbors," explained Mrs. Anstruther. "Of course we knew several families.—And really, looking back, it seems quite strange: so many of the daughters *had* careers, and went off to London and so on, quite often when the *sons* came home I was the only girl left! Archy had to stand up to quite fierce competition!"

It was an exchange to leave Louisa discouraged. How early, it seemed, had she missed the way to matrimony! There were of course disparities: Louisa's original home was the strictly non-rural London suburb of Broydon, and none of the neighboring youths had people, they just had Mum and Dad. (With some Louisa skylarked about the roads on bicycles; the meeting place for intellectuals was the Free Library.) Nor could Louisa "have stayed at home if she'd wanted to; she'd been apprenticed to a local photographer not as any gesture towards a career, but for the sake of the pound or so a week she brought in. To set up on her own—to cut and run and set up on her own—had been a positive achievement . . . Mrs. Anstruther's next remark brought her sharply back to the present.

"*You* must have come quite soon after I married?" remarked Mrs. Anstruther. "I mean, to Keithley. I wonder if I know the house?"

"I shouldn't think so," said Louisa. "It was new."

—If Freddy could improvise, so could she; evidently this was a lucky hit.

"One of those they were building on the Ridge?" asked Mrs. Anstruther eagerly.

"That's right," said Louisa.

"And was it nice?—I remember what an interest we all took," said Mrs. Anstruther, "because some were going to be quite hideously modern—all glass and concrete roofs.—Oh, dear, I hope *yours* wasn't one of the modern ones?"

"I'm afraid it was," said Louisa—happy to see a way of quitting Keithley as soon as possible. "I simply hated it. In fact, it was that horrible modern house that drove me from home."

"How you do put things!" cried Mrs. Anstruther, laughing. "You mean you were impatient, just like all the other girls. But if you'd *stayed*, who knows that an Archy mightn't have turned up for you too?"

On the side, as it were, during these conversations, Louisa learned something more about F. Pennon. His money derived originally from coal; when Enid Anstruther first knew him he still lived at Keithley, outside Sheffield, in an enormous Victorian-Gothic mansion known locally as Pennon's Pile. (Freddy himself enjoyed the joke as much as anyone, recalled Mrs. Anstruther; he always had a splendid sense of humor.) Why he sloughed off both Keithley and coal together she didn't quite know—perhaps because the place seemed so empty without her, or perhaps it was something to do with nationalization? In any case, the year the Labor Government got in found Freddy shifted to London and with a seat on the Stock Exchange. Mrs. Anstruther personally rejoiced, Freddy seemed to be doing very nicely on the Stock Exchange, and a house outside Bournemouth appealed to her far more than Pennon's Pile. Sheffield, even in her time, had been reaching out its tentacles—as witness those new houses on the Ridge!—and Keithley today, feared Mrs. Anstruther, was little better than a dormitory suburb . . .

"What became of Pennon's Pile?" asked Louisa curiously.

"I believe Freddy sold it rather well," said Mrs. Anstruther, "to some sort of agricultural college. One still can't help feeling a little sad, remembering all those lovely tennis and garden parties . . ."

Louisa saw the picture easily: the tennis and garden parties at Pennon's Pile, Freddy the industrial squire of the community hospitable to, amongst others, an Enid in white linen and her first bloom. What age must *he* have been, then? About forty? "—No wonder!" thought Louisa, telescopically.

She was still much more interested in picking, as far as possible, Mrs. Anstruther's brains. The trouble was that they each started out with such different preconceptions.

"Did you always *expect* to get married?" asked Louisa—under the pines, in the grateful shade.

"Why, just as all girls do!" smiled Mrs. Anstruther.

But in Louisa's experience, all girls didn't. Pammies, for instance (to employ a convenient group-term), she honestly believed thought of nothing beyond their artistic careers—on the stage, or as painters, or as novelists—and took any love affair primarily as an enrichment of artistic experience, or as an insurance against sexual repression. Of course Pammies as a genus were very young—but didn't that put them all the more in Mrs. Anstruther's category of girls?

"What about the ones you knew yourself?" objected Louisa. "The ones you told me about, who left Keithley and went off to London for careers?"

"*They* were impatient," explained Mrs. Anstruther calmly, "just as you were. They couldn't wait quietly at home. Of course no one took their careers seriously! Though I must admit that for a *plain* girl, training to be an architect, for instance, was a very sensible idea. The men students outnumbered them by I believe about twenty to one. Of course I couldn't help knowing *I* was pretty—"

("You still are," said Louisa automatically.)

"And besides," added Mrs. Anstruther, with a touch of roguishness, "I was always very fond of men!"

Louisa absolutely started. How extraordinarily different, again, their angle of vision! To Louisa, being fond of men implied unpaid nursing and the peddling of beechnuts; to Mrs. Anstruther, apparently, marriage and being supported for life.

"I'm fond of men too," said Louisa, "but it hasn't got me anywhere."

Mrs. Anstruther considered the point, and Louisa, with ready interest. (She enjoyed, Louisa realized, *talking shop.*)

"Now I wonder why that is?" meditated Mrs. Anstruther. "You've certainly an appearance, though rather *dashing . . .* Probably an older man—"

"Would be less likely to be scared off?" prompted Louisa.

"—would be more suitable," corrected Mrs. Anstruther. "A *young* man, with his way to make, doesn't want a *dashing* wife, he wants a wife who'll just make herself agreeable and let herself be taught the ropes. I learnt that at once," said Mrs. Anstruther, "when I first went out to the Argentine. Luckily it came very naturally to me—*I'd* never been anything but a daughter at home! Whereas you, my dear, have such a strong personality—"

"You mean it's the boss or nothing?" said Louisa uneasily.

"Perhaps," admitted Mrs. Anstruther. "To anyone *at the top*, I believe you'd make a very good wife indeed. You'd keep all the other wives in order! And of course, marrying an older man, you could get a better settlement."

The very word was novel to Louisa—as her look betrayed.

"Pin money," glossed Mrs. Anstruther. "Say ten or twenty thousand—"

"What, *pounds?*" demanded Louisa, startled.

"My dear, I hope we're not on the dollar standard *yet!*" cried Mrs. Anstruther patriotically. "I admit I got nothing from poor Archy, but then I was so young, and so much in love! Some women get a great deal *more.*"

It was all news to Louisa. In Louisa's experience (though admittedly she knew very few married couples) husband and wife contributed equally to the common stock; both painted, or both acted, or both taught; sometimes it was the wife who contributed most. In fact, the notion that a woman should get a lump sum down, for marrying a man due to keep her for the rest of her life, struck Louisa as really almost immoral. Possibly her look betrayed her again.

"A man rich enough to *make* a settlement," instructed Mrs. Anstruther patiently, "doesn't want his wife to be continually asking him for money. You surely see that!"

"Couldn't he give her an allowance?" suggested Louisa.

"Yes, and suppose something goes wrong?" retorted Mrs. Anstruther sharply. "Suppose he *loses* his money? Then what would she do?"

"Well, I suppose she'd give it him back," said Louisa—a trifle behind, her mind still occupied with the idea of settlements.

There was a slight pause. Then—

"Exactly," said Mrs. Anstruther. "Which makes it a kind of insurance as well!"

Louisa went off and did a bit of weeding with much to digest.

II

"I told you you'd get on together," said Freddy complacently. "Enid was always full of chat."

Chat didn't seem to Louisa quite the right word, for Mrs. Anstruther's purposeful theorizing; perhaps her converse with Freddy was on slighter topics. For the moment, indeed, he seemed rather noticeably ready to forego it, at least for any stretch of time.

"After eighteen years, I should have thought you'd want to be chatting to her yourself," observed Louisa.

"Don't worry about that," said Freddy self-sacrificingly. "There'll be plenty of opportunities. You go ahead and enjoy yourself."

III

About mid-week Louisa telephoned Mr. Ross. She had left unposted, in the hurry of departure, a set of proofs of My Handsome of York—sired by My Lucky out of My Winsome, possibly apt to follow in My Lucky's victorious tracks, and therefore by no means (now that Louisa's prospects had changed again) to be treated with any casualness.

"Listen, Rossy," called Louisa, "those proofs of My Hansome—"

"Now, that's what I like," said Mr. Ross warmly. "Not giving a client the go-by just because you're in the money. I've sent 'em.—All going well?"

"Fine," said Louisa, "and thanks a lot. What was the postage?"

"Sevenpence ha'penny," said Mr. Ross. "It can wait. I just thought there was no sense your leaving an unintended poor impression."

Even over a telephone, the kindness and knowledgeableness of his personality were wonderfully marked.

"Listen, Rossy," said Louisa again, "when your sister married—"

"Which one?" asked Mr. Ross. "I've got three."

"The one who married into a chain store.—Did she get a settlement?"

"You bet your sweet life she did," said Mr. Ross. "Has that come up on the *tapis?*"

"In a way," said Louisa.

"Have your own solicitor," advised Mr. Ross, "and congratulations again . . ."

Too late, Louisa once more recognized a lack of discretion.

IV

Naturally Louisa's conversations with Mrs. Anstruther didn't deal solely with her, Louisa's, matrimonial prospects; Enid Anstruther had her own matrimonial prospects—which indeed formed a far more cheerful topic.

"Poor Archy would be so happy too!" mused Mrs. Anstruther, emerging from a pleasant daydream. "He and Freddy thought the world of each other. I feel that makes it so nice!"

"I can see it must," said Louisa. "Has he any idea when it's to be?"

Mrs. Anstruther looked candid.

"One *should*, I know, wait a year; or if one's superstitious, a year and a day; and I'm sure I'm the last woman in the world to flout convention! But in such rather special circumstances—"

Louisa took this to indicate that Freddy's hours as a bachelor were numbered. She wondered whether Freddy knew. But whether he did or he didn't, she now hadn't the slightest doubt of Enid's ability to get him to the church on time.

"And it's not as though I needed to collect a trousseau—all *that*," said Mrs. Anstruther simply, "can wait till later. Poor Archy left us in April . . . do you think *July?*"

"As he and Freddy thought so much of each other," agreed Louisa.

"And of course very, very quietly."

"In church?"

"My dear, naturally," said Mrs. Anstruther. *"Always* get married in church—if you *can*," she added delicately. (Louisa took this to indicate that men at the top were sometimes also divorcés.) "I believe some of the registrars, in London, do it really very nicely!—But of course I shan't wear white; probably a very pale hyacinth blue."

Trousseauless though she would be (until later), Enid was already giving her wedding garments serious thought. The very pale hyacinth blue (possibly wild silk?) was to be topped by a very small toque of hyacinths. With some surprise Louisa found herself taking quite a keen interest in these details, and of her own accord suggested a very small eye veil.

"With perhaps a sequin or two?" reflected Mrs. Anstruther. "Just to give a tiny sparkle?"

More than surprised, absolutely dismayed, Louisa discovered that she was envisaging herself as a bridesmaid in pale green.— So *en rapport* were they at this moment, Mrs. Anstruther almost apologized.

"If I were having any bridesmaids at all, naturally I should think of you at once," said Mrs. Anstruther. "Though your coloring would set quite a problem! You couldn't wear green; green, even a very pale green, would be out of the question, with my blue."

"What about coffee?" suggested Louisa—surrendering herself to fantasy. "I've a coffee-colored linen—"

"No. I'm sorry," said Mrs. Anstruther firmly. "Not coffee. It would be a flat note. Perhaps a very pale *amber*—My dear, we're as bad as a couple of girls," cried Mrs. Anstruther, laughing, "sitting up in bed after a dance planning our weddings! *How* Freddy would laugh, to hear us!"

Maybe Archie'd laugh too, thought Louisa; but was chiefly appalled, as she came to her senses, by her vulnerability to the appeal of bridal millinery. It was something quite new; hitherto, as has been said, Louisa's reaction to a church wedding was purely professional, she just wondered who'd get the job of photographing it. In any bridal party, only a Pekingese in a white bow really caught her eye. Now, she felt that if Mrs. Anstruther came across with an amber shantung, she, Louisa, would jump straight into it. (Possibly a very small toque of tea roses. . . ?) Promoting herself to lead, she envisaged the full glory of white from top to toe. Of if (as Mrs. Anstruther tactfully warned) she had to pick up her settlement at a registrar's, why not, thought Louisa, that very pale green after all?—Even while appalled by them, such thoughts ran uncontrollably through Louisa's mind; as though some essence of femininity had been rubbed off, from Enid's mothlike wings, upon her own hard-wearing lurcher's coat . . .

"I'll tell you another thing," said Mrs. Anstruther abruptly. "Marry the life, not the man. *I* did, with poor Archy—though heaven knows where I found the sense! Even at our very poorest, in Argentina I never had to wash a cup."

"It's lucky Freddy can give you the same sort of life over here," said Louisa absently.

"Yes, isn't it?" smiled Enid—gay and heedless again as a bird, or a moth, or a butterfly. "Isn't it *lucky*, that I answered his letters?"

V

Undoubtedly Louisa learned a lot, from intimacy with Mrs. Anstruther. Sometimes she felt like a tenderfoot sitting over a camp-fire with an experienced trapper. And Mrs. Anstruther enjoyed instructing her; it might almost be said that they enjoyed—as Freddy had prophesied they would!—each other's company. By the sixth day, the Sunday, however, the fact that Louisa was leaving on Tuesday by no means damaged their relations.

"How I shall miss you!" exclaimed Mrs. Anstruther—with the sudden vivacity of one who sees a guest look at the clock. "Of course I quite understand you must be off, but my dear, *how* I shall miss you!"

She might be going to miss Louisa, but she wasn't going to let her have the car. On Tuesday—really too tiresome, when she knew Freddy *wanted* to send Louisa up by car!—some very very old friends had invited them to lunch at Poole. Louisa had learned so much, she didn't even wonder where those friends had been all week; but recognized that a man's car is so much a man's appanage, any prospective wife is naturally jealous of its loan.

"I'd much rather go by train," said Louisa.

"In this heat, how sensible! Karen shall pack you a nice lunch."

But if Louisa had been staying much longer, it was doubtful whether she'd have got a sandwich.

She had stayed long enough. Whether as buffer or chaperone—and it was remarkable how completely the point of chaperonage had been dropped—Louisa had stayed long enough. She'd learned all Mrs. Anstruther had to teach; moreover, she was getting soft—and not only physically. (To Louisa, indeed, the discovery that she was susceptible to white tulle was almost as alarming as a discovery that she was susceptible to asthma.) Since there was no sense, as Rossy said, in leaving a poor impression, she wasn't going to beat it; but— "Roll on Tuesday!" thought Louisa.

She had stayed long enough. With Freddy, discussing her departure, she almost quarreled.

"Naturally you want to be off," said Freddy sulkily, "but you needn't go like a bat out of hell. Ain't you comfortable here?"

"Of course I am!" cried Louisa impatiently. "I'm on velvet! I'm so on velvet it's making me soft—like the Romans at Capri."

"Capua," corrected Freddy disagreeably.

"I bet they got soft at Capri too," snapped Louisa.—How absurd it was! It reminded her of the day of Enid's arrival, when they'd quarreled over mumps and pinkeye. As then, she pulled herself up. "I've never been so comfortable in my life," said Louisa formally. "I'm very glad you persuaded me to come, and thank you for asking me."

"And when you've nothing to do in town," said Freddy, "you might read a bit of Roman history."

Chapter Seven

I

The Monday was extremely hot. Bournemouth had already lived up to, and even beyond, its brochures: to the slight constraint that attends all interruptions was now added a heat positively oppressive. Freddy was crosser, Mrs. Anstruther wan, and Louisa so restive she early declared her intention of catching the 8:20 next morning.

"No one need get up," added Louisa. "I'll have breakfast on the train."

"I shall get up of course," said Freddy irritably, "but it's an ungodly hour."

"Louisa wants to avoid the heat," said Mrs. Anstruther.

"Then she'd much better let me send her by car."

Both Louisa and Mrs. Anstruther ignored this.

"And of course I'll be down too!" promised Enid kindly.

This was about ten: there were still twelve or so hours to be got through, and their usual program had mistakenly been abandoned—because it was Louisa's last day.

"I'm going for a swim," said Louisa, "if it kills me."

"I'll come with you," said Freddy. "It'll probably give me rheumatism."

After some discussion, it was agreed that they should all drive to the beach together, where Freddy and Mrs. Anstruther would watch Louisa from the shore. Even this mild scheme, however, failed; Louisa had scarcely entered the water before Freddy was calling urgently from the edge of the surf.

"What's up now?" called back Louisa.

"Too hot," called Freddy. "Enid's got a headache."

"Give her an aspirin!" called Louisa.

"She's had one. She wants to go home."

"All right, take her!" called Louisa. "I'll walk."

He mouthed something more, but Louisa swam further out.— Actually it was all she could do to stay in until the car moved off again; the sea was colder than it looked. Louisa emerged goose-pimpled and blue, with no other consolation than that she'd killed the morning.

Luncheon equally lacked *entrain*. Mrs. Anstruther, determined to make amends—for she really wouldn't be a wet blanket, on Louisa's last day!—chatted with resolute vivacity; but the effort it cost her was obvious, and their whole conversation as a consequence highly artificial.

"I believe they use 'em for smoke signals," offered Freddy.

"Use what?" asked Louisa glumly.

"Wet blankets. Red Indians. Dip 'em up and down over a fire . . ."

"What a boy he is still!" cried Mrs. Anstruther.

The siesta killed the afternoon. Tacitly, they all agreed not to omit the siesta. Karen, sensitive to the prevailing atmosphere, brought up cups of tea all round, as in a hospital or nursing home; even this attention was distressing to Louisa. "I suppose I'll have to give her something," thought Louisa uneasily.—She had never before stayed in a private house, and though pretty confident that a vail would be acceptable, and indeed expected, had no idea of any appropriate sum. "I wonder what's the *least*?" thought Louisa—heaven knew she wasn't mean, but Karen was undoubtedly the better fixed; and there was a ticket to buy in the morning. As she sipped her tea Louisa's calculations ranged from five bob up to a pound; then they ranged down again. It was a last minor irritation—not indeed unknown to many another parting guest, but in Louisa's case particularly poignant. She hadn't worried about money for a week . . .

"I'd better get back into the habit," thought Louisa bleakly.

There were other habits she'd have to get back into: the habit of working, the habit of stretching meals. Whether at Capua or Capri, she'd stayed long enough to make the prospect bleak.

"I suppose it's got to be at least ten bob," thought Louisa, and piled four half-crowns on the dressing table before she weakened. Paper would have looked better, but no doubt Karen could add.

Cocktails before dinner produced a slight fictitious cheerfulness, though only Freddy and Louisa partook of them. Dinner at least killed the next hour. Mrs. Anstruther made another effort. She was really looking ill, her headache was evidently genuine; gallant, fragile and animated, she nonetheless chatted on—displaying a touch of the professional entertainer Louisa was forced to admire. In her own way Enid was a good trouper: give her a dinner table and she'd animate it, even though her head split. "It's still lucky she's got Freddy," thought Louisa. "There still has to *be* a dinner table . . ."

Freddy too was watching Enid solicitously. As they at last rose—

"Enid, my dear," said Freddy, "go straight to bed."

She looked at him uncertainly.

"I feel so dreadful about Louisa—!"

"Louisa will understand."

"Of course I do!" cried Louisa, with genuine compassion.

Mrs. Anstruther still looked towards Freddy, but the quality of her gaze changed. It was now a wifely look—frank in submission to a husband's better judgment.

"If you really think so—" she began—and only then turned to Louisa. "Freddy always knows what's best for me!" confessed Mrs. Anstruther. "Wise old Freddy, and lucky me!—You can still give him," she permitted, "a last game of chess . . ."

II

So after dinner Freddy and Louisa adjourned to the chessboard in the drawing room. The heat had scarcely abated, but like two old campaigners they made themselves comfortable: by leaving open all windows, and the door to the hall, achieved a good through draft, and saw there was plenty of ice. Freddy removed his dinner jacket; Louisa kicked off her shoes. Without Enid there, the atmosphere wasn't exactly public bar, but it was definitely smoking room.

"Give you queen and move," said Freddy.

"Too much," objected Louisa.

"It's your last night."

"Okay," said Louisa.

They played two games, and Louisa won both. She didn't suspect Freddy of deliberately letting her, but he wasn't concentrating. Louisa found it fairly hard to concentrate herself—there is a melancholy about anything final, even a final game of chess; she nonetheless won.

"What about another?" suggested Louisa. "As it's my last night?"

"Too hot," said Freddy restlessly.

He pushed aside the board and got up. He was restless. Though the tray of drinks stood convenient to his elbow, he got up and walked about the room a bit before refilling their glasses. (They were drinking brandy on the rocks.)

"Steady on," said Louisa. "Remember I've a train at 8:20."

"I'll get you there.—You're quite sure you won't stay a bit longer?" asked Freddy abruptly.

"Of course I'd love to," said Louisa, "but I've put off a kennel of dachshunds already." (She wasn't going to be led into the Capua-Capri argument again.) "Otherwise I honestly couldn't be enjoying myself more. I don't know where you get your brandy—"

"I'll give you a couple of bottles to take back with you."

"Thank you very much," said Louisa warmly. "And if I'm too busy to come to the wedding, I'll drink your healths in it."

There was a brief pause. Freddy walked once or twice again about the room before coming back to his seat.—The chessboard, between them, recording the last moves of an endgame . . .

"It's not actually settled, y'know."

"The date? I don't suppose it is," said Louisa. "But as Enid won't have to collect a trousseau—"

"I mean the whole thing," said Freddy. "I haven't actually . . . popped, yet."

"It's taken for granted," said Louisa.

"I don't even know Enid'll have me."

"You can take that for granted too," said Louisa encouragingly. "My dear Freddy," she added (it really seemed time to say something of the sort), "I hope you'll be very, very happy!"

"So do I," said Freddy.

Louisa looked at him. There was a note in his voice she could only define as—unsuitable; not exactly a note of doubt, but rather of resignation. The expression on F. Pennon's face was also unsuitable; not exactly sulky, but certainly not as joyous as one would expect, on the face of a man at last about to wed the woman he'd worshiped for twenty years.

"We're going to miss you," stated Freddy.

"Nonsense," said Louisa.

"I know I am. At meals," said Freddy. "It's been a real pleasure, Louisa, to see you eat."

"That's because I've no chat," said Louisa. "Give *me* a dinner table, and you'd hear nothing but munching."

"We could always bring books," suggested Freddy. "I know chaps say it's an insult, to decent food and wine, but we needn't bring anything heavy. With a couple of detective stories—"

He broke off, as well he might. The picture he had been painting was in the circumstances uncommonly odd. Where, for example, was Mrs. Anstruther in it? Evidently he realized this himself; though too old to blush, he looked uncommonly embarrassed.

He looked also, the moment after, suddenly relieved—as might a steeplechaser who finds himself over a first formidable fence before he has had time to think about it.

"It's happened before," said F. Pennon hardily.

"What has?" asked Louisa.

"A chap due to marry one woman, and then finding, well, another who suits him better."

There was no mistaking his meaning. He was now regarding her with a fixed, urgent appeal. He might be embarrassed, but he was determined—to give himself a chance. He was ready to undergo any amount of awkwardness, face any number of painful scenes, if only Louisa, not Mrs. Anstruther, would marry him.

As once before in Gladstone Mansions, Louisa sat perfectly still: taking it in.

There was so much to take.—Literally, so much! House and income (let alone a settlement), car and chauffeur, three square meals a day—so much, all at once, that though it was no more than she'd deliberately set out to bag, from the first moment of reading F. Pennon's letter, now that it was actually within her grasp Louisa needed a moment to draw breath.

As once before in Gladstone Mansions—

"Don't we get on uncommonly well?" suggested Freddy.

There was that too: she liked him. She didn't love him, as probably he didn't love her; but they liked each other, they got on, as he said, uncommonly well. Even their slight bickering adumbrated a free and easy, friendly companionship. To become genuinely fond of F. Pennon as a husband would be the easiest thing in the world. "A week ago, I'd have been a straight gold-digger," thought Louisa, "but not now. Now, I'd almost marry him just for the company . . ."

He hadn't taken his eyes from her face. He put out his hand on the chessboard and let it lie there, palm up—spilling bounty. It wasn't a young man's hand, but it was hard and scrubbed, perfectly acceptable.

"What about it?" asked Freddy urgently.

He was too much absorbed to hear the very slight sound from the hall, but Louisa heard. She glanced across at the open door, and beyond perceived not Mrs. Anstruther, but Mrs. Anstruther's reflection. Enid Anstruther believed herself hidden, standing so close behind the jamb; only a big mirror opposite betrayed her.

III

Louisa could see her quite plainly; and quite plainly she had been eavesdropping. Now she stood with her handkerchief pressed to her mouth, and above it her eyes fixed in an expression of such helpless dismay, she looked like a frightened child.—Not like a bird, or a moth, or a butterfly; like a frightened child.

It took perhaps an instant, no more, for Louisa to fix the image in every detail; her eye photographed even the lace on the handkerchief, a wisp of hair fallen across one cheek, before she looked swiftly away from the tragic sight.

For it was tragic.—Only pitifully, not tragic in the grand manner, but nonetheless authentically so. The triviality was of detail only. (The lace on a handkerchief, the ribbon roses on—for heaven's sake!—a boudoir cap.) Enid Anstruther's face, ravaged by incredulous dismay, was authentically tragic.

"And why not?" thought Louisa.

For what on earth would become of her, without Freddy?—A woman so completely unfitted to face the day and age without a husband?—A woman with neither a penny to her name, nor the least idea how to set about earning one? Nubile and nothing more was Enid Anstruther, even with her profile . . .

"She can't look after herself, and I can," thought Louisa. "Even if I don't pick up a settlement, I can look after myself . . ."

Oddly enough in one so fond of men, she considered F. Pennon scarcely at all. *He* could look after himself too. He'd always have Gladstone Mansions as a blow-hole . . . The point lay, as Louisa saw it, between herself and Mrs. Anstruther; and to scoop up old Freddy away from Enid would be too much like robbing a blind man . . .

Regretfully she shook her head.

"I'm sorry, Freddy dear . . ."

"If you're thinking of all the fuss and commotion—"

"I'm not. I can take any amount of either," said Louisa. What she was thinking of now was Mrs. Anstruther's resolute vivacity, while her head split, at a dinner table. "I'm just sorry," said Louisa.

Again there was a silence. It was a regret again to Louisa that she couldn't see the effects of her heroism, but she didn't dare look back. She just took as long as possible, rattling the chessmen into their box, to give Mrs. Anstruther time to get upstairs.

As once before in Gladstone Mansions—

"Louisa!" implored F. Pennon desperately.

"I'm sorry," repeated Louisa. "You'll just have to be brave." And whether she addressed herself or F. Pennon, she really didn't know.

IV

The farewells, next morning, in fact called for a good deal of courage all round. The situation was complex: Mrs. Anstruther knew of Freddy's treachery—or rather of the treachery he'd aimed at; Freddy didn't know she knew, as neither was Mrs. Anstruther aware that Louisa knew she knew. Each one of them had thus to play a part— Freddy in the suit of unsmutched loyalty, Enid sugared with confident proprietorship, and Louisa disguised as a gay career woman. They all pulled it off.

"Good-by, Louisa," said F. Pennon—a trifle huskily, no more.

"Dear Louisa, good-by!" breathed Mrs. Anstruther affectionately. "You will, won't you, let us hear from you soon?"

She slipped one little hand through Freddy's arm, and held out the other to her chum.—Louisa, accepting it, couldn't forbear looking into Mrs. Anstruther's face. Would there be any sign there of gratitude? It wouldn't have been, all things considered, misplaced!

But for once the soft gray glance wasn't vague at all, and Louisa had no difficulty in reading it: Mrs. Anstruther thought her a damned fool.

PART TWO

Chapter Eight

I

"Have a nice time?" asked the milkman.

"No," said Louisa.

"You still look better for it," said the milkman.

"The food was all right," admitted Louisa.

"Summer schools must've changed since my Auntie's day," observed the milkman. "According to her, they fed mostly on prunes. According to my Auntie—"

"Look," said Louisa, "I've got a busy day. I'm due at a kennels in Surrey—"

"I can take a hint," said the milkman.

He glanced at his nest of cream jars, then back, speculatively, at Louisa; but something in her face told him this was no morning for cream.

II

All the same it was a piece of luck, and Louisa thoroughly felt it so, that she had been able to retrieve the dachshund job for the very morrow of her return. She not only needed the fee, and to have her mind occupied, she was also thankful to remove, however briefly, from her usual haunts. Only to Hugo and Mr. Ross had she actually spoken of her approaching marriage, but each, she was well aware, would have hastened to spread the glad news: Louisa was perhaps supersensitive, in feeling that she couldn't cross a street without meeting either a Pammy (and being congratulated) or one of the boys (and being advised as to settlements); but so she uncontrollably did feel, and even one day's grace was welcome to her.

There was no doubt about it, Louisa had returned from Bournemouth considerably changed. Her reactions were far nearer what Enid's would have been, to a broken engagement, than to what her own would have been even a week before.—With a hand on the receiver to telephone Hugo, why did Louisa refrain? Because she didn't want to have to *tell* . . . and only as she dropped the receiver back remembered that she was in any case giving him the go-by.

Upon this point her resolve was stiffened. No more sympathy did Louisa intend to waste upon the off-beat, bronchial and indigent. Henceforward, following Mrs. Anstruther's advice, she intended to reserve it strictly for men at the top. She hoped she'd meet one soon; though probably it wouldn't be at Kerseymere Kennels . . .

III

Indeed the bus proposed in Mrs. Meare's letter of instructions bore Louisa some five miles from Dorking station to an establishment very unlike either Gladstone Mansions or the villa at Bournemouth. Fifty years earlier, when it was built, Kersey Cottage might have been trim; fifty years hence, might tumble down to picturesqueness; in the meantime, it was simply dilapidated. From the palings by the gate to the curlicues under the eaves, every inch of woodwork needed repainting; the brickwork needed repointing, and several tiles had dropped off from the roof over the porch. A sizable garden exhibited the same characteristics: in the house agent's term mature, it was also unkempt without being overgrown. (No head-high *berceaux* of Gloire de Dijon roses, no mysterious gloom of ancient trees; the flower beds just needed weeding, an elm lopping.) Wherever the eye rested, in fact, the need for a bit of money spent was so obvious, what on earth induced the Meares to buy a couple of plaster dwarfs Louisa couldn't for the life of her imagine.

But there the dwarfs were, one on each side of the gate, and there the Meares were too. On the head of each dwarf was a scarlet cap; the Meares wore Panama hats—Mrs. Meare's with a Liberty scarf round it, her husband's with a plain black band; both equally recognizable, from the tint of the yellowed straw, as hats not bought, but inherited. They looked about the same age as the Meares' cottage.—So did Mr. and Mrs. Meare themselves, though they'd worn better: achieving between youth and decrepitude (unlike their hats and their house) a comfortable middle age . . .

"Miss Datchett? We've the chaps all ready for you," said Mr. Meare. "Or would you like to see—"

"The kennels first?" said Mrs. Meare.

Looking straight over their heads—for she was a good deal taller than either—Louisa perceived a dachshund-shaped weathervane (probably stuck, since in the light westerly breeze it pointed due north) attached to some sort of outbuilding. It didn't exactly beckon, but the Meares so obviously wished to show her round, she gave the polite answer.

"We thought you might!" said Mrs. Meare. "Be a little careful of the whitewash, will you?—Ted only finished it this morning."

As Louisa by now anticipated, it wasn't much of a kennels. Compared with the splendid York establishment starred by My Lucky, My Winsome, and now My Handsome, Kerseymere was practically amateur. (So was Mr. Meare's whitewashing amateur: streaky above, coagulated below.) The lying-in room had obviously been a toolshed, the puppy-run adjoined a cabbage patch; Mrs. Meare frankly did kennel maid herself. ("It's so nice that we can manage everything between us!" she observed happily. "Teddy's a vet, you know.

Of course I have to let the garden go a little!") But the dachshunds themselves were all right—clean-bred and sturdy, classically colored, alert and gay; and before Sebastian the Third of Kerseymere Louisa at last unslung her camera with genuine relief. She had by this time a feeling that her fee had been saved up in a piggy bank.

"If we can only get him into *Country Month!*" sighed Mrs. Meare. "I don't mean in an advertisement—though we *have* advertised, once—I mean among the proper photographs!"

"Don't worry," said Louisa absently. "He's about the best dachs I've seen yet. Anyway, I know the editor . . ."

For the next hour she was completely absorbed, as upon the rough grass obediently paraded Sebastian, Viola and Orsino of Kerseymere. The Meares' handling of them was impeccable; indeed, only a minimum was required. (The poodles at Cannes had been more of hams, but strictly on their own temperamental terms.) "These must be a gift to show," said Louisa appreciatively. "Who shows them?"

"Molly does," said Mr. Meare. "A woman catches the judge's eye," he added seriously.

—Louisa glanced at Mrs. Meare's weatherbeaten cheek under the Panama hat, and continued photographing Sebastian the Third. As though reading her thoughts, he glanced severely back at her; Louisa got a rather good shot. Her last, a trickier one, was of a tumble of Viola's offspring; then she packed up, but only because she'd run out of film.

"What trouble you've taken!" exclaimed Mrs. Meare gratefully. "Now you must have tea and a nice sit-down!"

IV

At least Louisa, at this period, was getting a good many free meals. Calibrating a cup of char with Rossy as one extreme, and tea at Gladstone Mansions as the other, tea with the Meares, which they took out of doors, came about halfway. There was no solid silver, but there were clean plates, and the milk wasn't poured from the bottle but from a jug with a Devonshire motto on it. (Referring actually to cream: *O Devonshire cream, like Devonshire lasses/For richness and beauty the world surpasses*—a souvenir of the Meares' honeymoon.) There were no scones, but there was brown bread and butter; and if no plum cake, rock cakes, homemade.

"Molly makes 'em," munched Teddy Meare.

"I'm afraid these got a little burnt," apologized his wife.

"Personally I like 'em a bit burnt," said Teddy.

"So do I," said Louisa sincerely.

Between them they cleared the plate; when only one rock cake was left, and Louisa couldn't be persuaded to take it, the Meares wordlessly divided it between them . . .

As she sat back replete, her mind no longer on her job, Louisa considered the Meares with more attention.

Her first, hasty impression had been simply that they were rather like a couple of dachshunds themselves. It has often been remarked that any long-married pair tend to resemble one another, as do also dog-owner and dog; in the case of the Meares, both factors seemed to have worked in conjunction. Plump, sleek Mrs. Meare was but nearer chestnut, her husband nearer tan. As they jumped up into their basket-chairs for tea—or rather, as they sat down; it was the two canine patriarchs of the establishment who jumped up beside them—Louisa could have offered each a lump of sugar. Now, she began to see the flippancy misplaced.

There was a peaceableness about them. What peace and content, indeed, lay over the whole shabby house, the whole shabby garden! And what did it spring from, if not from the relation between the Meares themselves?—Another thought struck Louisa: that in Teddy Meare, for almost the first time in her life, she'd met a man who made no demands on her sympathy.

If Teddy Meare wanted sympathy, he'd get it from his wife; and wasn't that a very right and proper thing?

Unconsciously, Louisa sighed.

"You're tired," said Mrs. Meare kindly. "Why not stay a little? There's another train at six, and if you'll wait till Ted's watered the cabbages—"

"I'll run you to the station," said Mr. Meare.

Louisa hesitated. She wanted to stay, but she didn't know whether they wanted her.

"Won't it be a nuisance—?" she began uncertainly.

"Not a bit!" cried both the Meares together.

V

Off stumped Teddy to uncoil the hose. Mrs. Meare went indoors and fetched her knitting. One of the dachshunds packed itself comfortably behind Louisa's ankles. She began to feel like a neighbor who had dropped in for a quiet, customary chat.—But such evidently wasn't the view taken by her hostess.

"Ted's going to *enjoy* driving you to the station," confided Mrs. Meare. "You look so Londony! I expect half the village, tomorrow, will be asking who you are!"

Obviously one of Louisa's newly acquired notions needed adjusting. A man's car being so much a man's appanage, shouldn't a wife, even more than a prospective wife, be naturally jealous of it? Mrs. Meare didn't sound jealous in the least: she sounded gleeful.

"It does him so much good," she explained, "to cut a little dash now and again! (Just give Sebastian a push, if he's annoying you.) We live," added Mrs. Meare unnecessarily, "such a very quiet life."

Louisa felt she could hardly imagine a quieter, if driving herself to the station constituted cutting a dash. Yet it evidently suited Mrs. Meare; Louisa had never seen a woman more content . . .

Had she married the life, wondered Louisa suddenly, or the man? It seemed important to find out.

"Did you always," asked Louisa—going a bit roundabout— "mean to breed dachshunds?"

"*Some* sort of dog," agreed Mrs. Meare innocently. "We settled on dachs because they're so easy. Even when we show, I just rub them over in the car with a loofah glove . . ."

For a moment Louisa was tempted to visualize the Meares at Cruft's; they probably looked as though they'd been rubbed over with a loofah too. But she was becoming more and more in earnest.

"Well, did you always mean to live in the country?"

"I suppose so," said Mrs. Meare, more vaguely. "Not that dachs take up much room. But of course Teddy being a vet—"

("Ah!" thought Louisa—feeling her hand on a clue. The life, not the man: if you want to breed dogs, marry a vet.)

"—the country seemed obvious. Of course, I didn't *know* he was a vet," added Mrs. Meare. "When we met, in the war, he was heavily disguised as a gunner! Actually we bought the cottage out of his gratuity . . ."

She looked affectionately over her shoulder towards the peeling paint, the unpointed brick; glanced fondly at the plaster dwarfs. Louisa found a compliment surprisingly easy to produce.

"It's so peaceful," said Louisa. "It's quite marvelous . . . Would you mind going back a bit? How did you know—or didn't you know?—it would work out so well?"

"I saw Ted was steady," said Mrs. Meare simply. "That's all a woman wants, don't you think? I mean, surely it's the *basis?* We'll never be rich, but Ted has a wonderfully steady little practice; and if he wasn't a vet he'd be something else steady!—Now I've just talked about myself," said Mrs. Meare remorsefully, "and there he is with the car!"

VI

Mr. Meare was a bit damp about the trousers, but he'd changed his jacket; in place of leather-patched tweed he now sported, Louisa was touched to see, an ancient gunner blazer. He meant to cut a dash indeed, he meant to drive her to the station in style! With what looked like an old pajama leg he carefully dusted the car seats; turfed out a bundle of old newspapers and a dog-odorous blanket. He even gave a swift polish to the door handles and headlamps, before inviting Louisa to enter.

Louisa entered looking as Londony as she could.—Casting her mind back to Cannes, she even tried to look cosmopolitan. (Or like a model; Louisa was so long-limbed, she practically achieved it—the elegant stretch of leg, the final loose-jointed subsidence.) A glance in the driving mirror confirmed her hat at a suitably cosmopolitan angle, and powder and lipstick both sufficient. As a final gesture of good will she impulsively got out her eyebrow pencil and drew a slight bistered streak up from the corner of each eye.

"I *say!*" exclaimed Mr. Meare, in candid admiration. "I'll feel I'm driving a film star! D'you mind if we slow down through the village?"

"Not a bit," quoted Louisa, "so long as I catch my train."

"There's plenty of time, I've allowed for it," said Mr. Meare. "May as well give the natives a treat! Sure you're quite comfortable?"

"Perfectly," said Louisa.

"Then I'll just get Molly," said Mr. Meare.

Louisa heard him calling all up the garden. From the house, she heard his wife call some protesting reply. But whatever argument took place within, in a matter of moments Molly joined them.—Not in the least like a model looked Mrs. Meare, in her Panama hat, a woolly cardigan thrown hastily about her shoulders; but her beaming smile made her a very agreeable sight.

"This is all wrong!" she complained happily. "How will anyone take Teddy for a wolf, with me in the back seat?"

"You do our neighbors an injustice," said Mr. Meare complacently. "They'll think you have to keep an eye on me.—We'll stop at the local on our way back," he explained to Louisa. "It's not often I get Molly out on the spree!"

The parting at the station was genuinely affectionate all round. The Meares waited to see Louisa's train draw in, and then draw out. Her last glimpse of them was as they stood waving vigorously—Mr. Meare to the left, his wife to the right; it had to be thus, because they were also hand-in-hand.

VII

The train drew out. Louisa, alone in her compartment, sat reflective and—envious.

She hadn't envied, or not much, Mrs. Anstruther and F. Pennon. Louisa might have envied all the good grub going, but she didn't envy the (prospective) Pennons in their personal relation. They'd probably do well enough—he acquiring a profile and an accomplished hostess, she a gilt-edged meal ticket; no doubt some slight festooning of sentiment, under Enid's expert hands, would soften the transaction to acceptability. The Meares were something else. In the Meares, Louisa saw something she envied not with her appetite, but with her heart.

They were just so damned fond of each other, Molly Meare didn't even see how the paint was peeling. Ted Meare was so fond of his Molly, driving a Londony glamour girl to the station became an innocent domestic joke. ("Which is going to last them for years," thought Louisa perceptively. For years Molly Meare would remind her husband of that wild excursion!) On a railway platform they stood as unselfconsciously hand-in-hand as a couple of teenagers— more so; with the Meares it was evidently a matter of habit. Louisa pictured them hand-in-hand still, at the local; sitting close together on a hard bench, having a devil of a spree over small sherries.

"I've been on the wrong tack," thought Louisa. "I don't need a rich husband, I need a husband like Teddy Meare . . ."

On either side of the line, now, small back gardens ran up to small houses. In more than one, a man was digging, or mowing the lawn; in more than one, a woman had come out to bear him company. Louisa fancied a breath of contentment rising up from them, as the scent of limes might have risen, the train running between an avenue of lime trees.

"What do *I* want with a lot of money?" thought Louisa. "I can't want it badly; if I did, I'd have collared old Freddy. It was my subconscious damn well right as usual," thought Louisa, "I don't want someone rich, I want someone steady . . .

"Who do I know who's steady?" thought Louisa.

She had to think a long way back, all the way to Broydon, to the days when she'd skylarked about the evening roads with boys on bicycles. But it wasn't one of these Louisa at last recalled; against the more sober background of the Free Library—sniffing again the mingled odors of dust, bookbindings, and her own Phul-Nana perfume—she saw the figure of Jimmy Brown edge shyly round from Ceramics to Biography, as she, from Biography, edged round to Ceramics.

VIII

Louisa was the only girl who paid much attention to him. She was already so fond of men, Jimmy's gangling figure and pebble lenses didn't put her off, they rather roused her sympathy; she quite often kept a date with him at the Library even if it wasn't raining. Her reward was an earnest, awkward devotion, which if Louisa didn't particularly value, she allowed no one else to make game of.

Contemplating it, and Jimmy, now, she was more appreciative. He mightn't have been much to look at, but he was steady as a rock.

He had even, or very nearly (in Mrs. Anstruther's phrase), people. His father was an optician, and on the Borough Council. His mother had been a schoolteacher. From the rare occasions when she visited them Louisa recalled an upright piano and bound volumes of the *National Geographic* magazine. She recalled also their quiet pride in the fact that Jimmy was taking a full-time course at the London Polytechnic. "He'll be better qualified than his father," said Mr. Brown, "when the time comes to take over!"

"Louisa ought to go to the Poly too," said Jimmy earnestly. "She's got a very good brain, Dad; she has really."

But both elders looked at Louisa's fiery hair and long legs.

"Louisa's found her career already," said Mrs. Brown kindly. "How are you liking it, dear, with Mr. Hughes?"

Mr. Hughes was the local photographer. Louisa, a sulky if not idle apprentice, said he was all right.

"In my opinion, it's still a waste," stated Jimmy.

"In *my* opinion," said Mr. Brown heartily, "Louisa'll find herself married to one of her many admirers before she can turn round!"

Well, he'd been wrong. It wasn't marriage that took Louisa away from Broydon, it was her own initiative. And after an interval of ten years, if Jimmy himself hadn't married in the meantime, that same initiative was going to take her back.

The conclusion was as swift as when she decided to marry F. Pennon; but it will be seen that Louisa, from that same disappointing episode, had learned a modicum of prudence. Jimmy Brown was in fact still a bachelor; but she made sure of it in advance.

Chapter Nine

I

"Is that the optician's?" asked Louisa, over the telephone.

She'd already checked in the directory that it was listed under James, not Henry, Brown; fortunately Jimmy hadn't been named for his father. (Was his father dead, or merely retired? In any case the circumstance was propitious.) Propitious too was the answering voice—not Jimmy's, but evidently that of a female assistant.

"Actually it's *Mrs.* Brown I want to speak to," said Louisa cunningly. "Mrs. James Brown. Could you possibly put me through to her?"

"I'm afraid there's some mistake," said the assistant. "There is no Mrs. Brown."

Louisa thought rapidly. She had learned all she needed, but didn't wish the conversation officiously reported . . .

The voice sounded conscientious—and prim.

"I suppose you wouldn't be interested yourself, in a new type of foundation garment?"

"Certainly not!" snapped the assistant, and rang off with her lips effectually sealed.

II

Newly prudent, newly cautious Louisa! (*Che va piano va sicuro;* also softly-softly catchee monkey.) A night's reflection had convinced her that this time she should not only look before she leaped but should also, so to speak, establish some solid base for unhurried operating. Steadiness has its limitations; however glad to see her, if she simply blew into the shop Jimmy was quite capable of letting her blow out again before he realized, too late, all of gladness the future might hold in store.... Only a semi-permanent relation (say a week) would give him time to get his hocks under him; and a week Louisa was fully prepared to devote.

Fortunately she had an extremely accurate memory for dogs. (This not in the circumstances an irrelevance; far from it.) After leafing through only two back numbers of *Country Month* Louisa picked out Ivor and Ivan Cracarovitch, owner Mrs. Arthur Brent, of Broydon Court. The aristocratic address was misleading; even in Louisa's day Broydon Court had declined to a residential hotel; Mrs. Brent was the proprietress.

She lifted the receiver again.

"Mrs. Brent? This is Miss Datchett speaking," said Louisa, "Datchett Photographer of Dogs. May I tell you I think your borzois are quite magnificent?"

A flattered unsuspicious babble answered her.

"It's just a shame," continued Louisa, "that they've been photographed so badly. I've Ivan in front of me now; one doesn't get the least idea of his quality."

"Oh, don't you think so?" cried Mrs. Brent, distressed. "What's wrong with him?"

"He looks like a camel colt."

"I'm sure he doesn't!" protested Ivan's owner.—But she sounded shaken nonetheless.

"Ivor," continued Louisa remorselessly, "isn't even standing properly. He's carrying his tail too high. Really, one could weep."

"I didn't think so very much of Ivor myself," confessed Mrs. Brent. "But then of course I'm not an expert. I'm not *breeding* them, you know; I just want to sell them."

"That makes it worse," said Louisa. "Have you had any inquiries?"

"Well, no," admitted Mrs. Brent. "I can't say I have. All the same"—a slight suspicion had evidently infiltrated at last—"I'm afraid I can't afford to have them taken again . . ."

This was no blow to Louisa. What she was working on was the presumption that Broydon Court, as so often in the past, lacked its full quota of residents.

"Look," said Louisa, "I'm so impressed I'm not even asking a fee. What I *would* like is time. I'm prepared to spend if necessary a week—getting to know them, letting them get to know *me*, waiting to catch exactly the right moment. Then we'd have something really worthwhile.—And as it happens I've just got a week free; if you can put me up."

Mrs. Brent fell for it.

III

A certain caution informed all Louisa's actions, that morning. She hadn't seen the milkman; she'd been in the bath. She didn't see Mr. Ross either; though she spent a couple of hours in his Soho hangout, she was there by ten and gone before he put in an appearance.—Not conscientiousness alone sent her there, she was sincerely grateful to Mrs. Meare for putting her on the right track, and wanted to have done an extra good job for Kerseymere Kennels; almost every negative promising success, she streaked back to Paddington with an easy mind.

The only other thing that held her up was an unfortunate encounter with Number Ten.

Louisa did her best to avoid it; perceiving his door half-open, she approached her own almost furtively. But he was evidently on the watch, and even as she slipped her key into the lock, emerged.

"Miss Datchett!"

"Hi," said Louisa, "I'm in a blazing hurry."

"Only to say, Miss Datchett—"

"Not now, d'you mind?" snapped Louisa—remembering amongst other things that Number Ten was due for the brush-off.

He brushed off very easily. He didn't argue. He didn't say anything at all. He just stood there, dumb and humble—with the box of beechnut-jewelry in his hand.

All arranged neatly on fresh cotton wool; six boutonnières, six brooches, and what looked like, however improbably, a sort of tiara or carcanet. Attached to each was a very small price tag, meticulously (and humbly) figured in green ink.

The edges of the box itself had been lovingly bound with green *passe partout.*—The only thing lacking, thought Louisa bitterly, was the one label more: *All My Own Work.*

Number Ten moistened his lips.

"It looks nice, Miss Datchett?"

Louisa swallowed a curse and lied.

"I thought you might like to see," explained Number Ten. "Not to bother you!" he added carefully. "There is no hurry!"

It had been Louisa's intention to reach Broydon Court by lunchtime and get in a first free meal; but she'd probably be late as it was . . .

He made a little joke.

"I do not suppose them *waiting* for these, at the shops!"

Louisa spent half the afternoon peddling beechnuts. Fortunately she had no doubt where to offer them—only in the most homespun, the most arty and crafty of *boutiques* would they be so much as looked at. Louisa took a bus to Chelsea. Fortunately again, in each of the establishments she had her eye on she found a man in charge; Louisa with true nobility let it be assumed that her horrible wares were of her own fabrication. (Actually, against a swatch of tweed or hand-woven linen the boutonnières didn't look so bad; the potential tiara or carcanet Louisa wisely wrote off altogether.) She returned with the box half-emptied and twenty-one shillings in cash; banged on Number Ten's door, thrust remainders and takings into his hands, refused to be played to on the flute, and at last got down to filling, once again, her airline giveaway bags.

Thus she didn't get any lunch at all; and didn't reach Broydon until nearly five.

IV

It was a queer sensation, to Louisa, to be staying at Broydon Court.

In her youth, the Court had been an ultimate symbol of luxury. Once a fine seignorial mansion, and still removed by the breadth of the Common from Broydon's more commercial paths, the Court was widely believed to accept no inmate under the rank of retired colonel. (A genuine retired admiral set the tone.) To book a table for dinner there the local aspirant required certain influence. Naturally neither Louisa nor anyone she knew had ever set foot inside the place; its glories were bruited among the commonalty by such other infra dig characters as chambermaids or tradesmen, from whom a fascinated public learned that each bedroom had its solid mahogany suite, that the kitchen used a pint of cream a day, and that the cellars were kept full of champagne.—A gardener with a boy under him, too grand in the ordinary way for gossip, mentioned to his friend the chemist not only vineries, but pineries; and though this might be a harking-back to the past, the exotic odor of pineapple undoubtedly persisted, haloing Broydon Court with a quite uncommon aura.

Thus to find the whole establishment slightly tatty was to Louisa at once a relief and a disappointment.

"Miss Datchett? How prompt you are!" exclaimed Mrs. Brent.

"I'm fitting you in," explained Louisa.

They passed through the lounge.—It was so large, and so gloomy, it reminded Louisa of Gladstone Mansions. But there are shades of gloom—the chiaroscuro of a Rembrandt, the murk of a bad family portrait; the gloom of the Broydon Court lounge definitely reflected the latter. Only one resident was visible, and she an ancient dame playing patience at a balding card table.

"Haven't you still got the Admiral?" asked Louisa impulsively.

Mrs. Brent looked surprised.

"Admiral Colley? Do you know him?"

"Not *well*," admitted Louisa. "I'd still like to see him again."

"So you will," said Mrs. Brent, regarding her with new respect. (Perhaps things hadn't entirely changed, at Broydon Court.) "Though I'm afraid you'll find him," she added, "rather inclined to say things he doesn't *mean*. Rather *silly* things, you know, about the food . . ."

Evidently the grub had gone off too, thought Louisa regretfully; it would still be free.—There was mahogany in the bedroom all right. There was so much mahogany, indeed, Louisa had hardly room to turn round. But she recognized her slightly ambiguous status, and after all could have been put a floor higher. She was only on the third.

"And as soon as you come down," promised Mrs. Brent, "I'll have Ivor and Ivan ready to meet you. You'll find their kennel at the back—"

"Splendid," said Louisa.

Mrs. Brent paused. Between the moment of Louisa's telephoning, and the moment of her arrival, Mrs. Brent had had time to think; and like many other people who had anything to do with Louisa, had perhaps discovered a need for—fuller explanations.

"Do you *really*," asked Mrs. Brent, "need a whole *week*? Just to photograph two dogs?"

Louisa smiled.

"Just to *snap* them, of course not. What *I'm* after—besides of course the straights—is probably the most difficult damn shot on earth. If I can get your dogs in action, together—romping together—we can have a full-page spread in any paper you like. I'm not sure *Country Month*'s even good enough—"

"*I* only thought of getting them in at all," said Mrs. Brent, quite astonished.

"I'm not sure they couldn't be syndicated," mused Louisa.

"Syndicated?"

"Which would do me a lot of good too," said Louisa frankly. "And *that's* why I'm prepared to give a week."

She pulled it off all right. Whether or not perfectly convinced, Mrs. Brent was at least silenced; Louisa had successfully established her base.

V

The next step was obviously to reconnoiter.—It must be said at once that Louisa had no intention of wasting the next precious hour on Ivor and Ivan. What she intended was to catch Jimmy Brown just before he shut up shop—say at ten to six; it was now nearly half past five, and she reckoned on a twenty minutes' walk to the High Street. The situation presented certain difficulties, however; though she could probably avoid the kennels (at the back), what further fuller explanations would be needed, of her truancy!

Yet she couldn't endure to wait. She had only a week—and was besides naturally anxious to see what Jimmy looked like.

After a little thought, Louisa hit on a bright idea. It involved her slipping away at once, without even renewing her make-up; it involved her reencountering a long-lost love while carrying a parcel of liver: but strategically speaking, it was pretty bright.

Chapter Ten

I

From an island in the middle of the High Street, parcel of liver in hand, prudent Louisa first took a good look at the shop.

There could be no doubt of its prosperity. Fresh green paint framed the large window, and on the fascia threw into bold relief the name of James Brown painted in white. Behind immaculate glass the range of spectacle frames, limited in Louisa's day to gold, silver and tortoise shell—or hadn't even steel its humble place?—now displayed the laminated in every color, the *diamanté* and even the bamboo. The sign that jutted from above was still the traditional pair of spectacles; but here too, what advance! The lenses weren't merely, in broad daylight, illuminated; the light went on and off . . .

Two customers came out while Louisa watched.

She waited however a moment longer. It was almost six. A head-scarved, plumpish figure—"Honestly, she could *do* with a foundation garment!" thought Louisa—emerged and made off towards a bus stop. Behind the glass door a taller, a masculine silhouette reached up to pull the blind.

Louisa's hands felt slightly damp—but it might have been the liver. She completed the crossing at a run, and found the door—could it be symbolically?—still unlocked.

II

The years had improved him. He still wore glasses, but no longer so pebble-lensed, and framed with appropriate dignity. His long gangling figure had filled out, giving his height importance. ("Taller than I am!" thought Louisa gladly; she wouldn't have to wear flat heels.) In sober but well-cut suit—shirt fresh and tie positively fashionable—there stood Jimmy Brown, all, and far, far more, than Louisa had hoped.

The blind rattled up.

"Louisa! For heavens' sake, *Louisa!*"

"Hi," said Louisa.

It had been an anxious moment for her; but there was no mistaking his pleasure. It equaled, it overtopped his astonishment, as he stood beaming down. Louisa was so rarely beamed down on, this alone, if he'd been a perfect stranger, would have attracted her to him at once.

"This is amazing," declared Jimmy Brown earnestly. "I was thinking of you only this lunchtime, passing the Library.—And now, dammit, it's Thursday!"

Louisa thought fast. Actually for the last twenty-four hours she'd been so living in the past, she picked up both reference and implication almost instantaneously.

"Ibsen night?"

"What a memory you've got!" exclaimed Jimmy admiringly. "Actually we're reading *Pygmalion;* I'm Higgins. But never mind that now! What are you *doing* here, Louisa?"

Even before she answered—and never was answer readier—her thoughts had raced again. Reading circles, naturally, go round in circles: ten years earlier, Jimmy'd been no more than a Bystander. Now he was Professor Higgins! Yet with this increased stature went no diminution of steadiness; steadily he'd stuck to the Circle, steadily, now, in the midst of whatever emotional excitement, he recalled the evening's commitment . . .

"It's a job," explained Louisa (how truthfully!). "I'm photographing Mrs. Brent's borzois. She's putting me up at the Court."

"I *say!*" marveled Jimmy. "I always knew you'd do well, Louisa, but I'd no idea you were such a swell as all that!—How long for?"

"Perhaps a week . . ."

"Then that's all right, I shan't have to chuck Higgins. Can you give me tomorrow night instead?"

"I'd love to," said Louisa.

"Then we can talk. Now, I'll just have a look at you!" said Jimmy Brown.

Feeling positively nervous, Louisa advanced into the shop and turned to face him.—It was so lined with mirrors, his little shop, from every angle a Louisa was reflected back; as were also a couple of gleaming counters (on one of which she hastily deposited the packet of liver) and three or four smart little chairs with yellow seats and chromium legs. The days of H. Brown's fumed oak and steel rims seemed dead indeed . . .

Which reminded her.—Louisa had been if anything rather fond of old Mr. Brown, but how infinitely preferable that Jimmy should be his own master!

"Your father—?" she suggested delicately.

"Passed on. Both," said Jimmy. His tone was exactly right; he sounded sad, but not heartbroken. His eyes were still on her fiery head. "And your own people here, Louisa?"

"Passed on too."

His glance dropped to her bare, ungloved left hand.

"No, I'm not married yet!" smiled Louisa.

"That's rum," said Jimmy seriously. "I've always thought of you as married. In fact, I shouldn't have been surprised if you'd been married two or three times."

Louisa felt a momentary dismay.

"Do I look as dashing as all that?"

"To be frank, yes," said Jimmy. "As you always did, Louisa! I suppose you just haven't been able to make up your mind."

Well, there were advantages in looking dashing after all, thought
Louisa. (She'd have liked to point this out to Mrs. Anstruther. Or
did Jimmy count as a man at the top? In Broydon, probably yes;
a circumstance to please her too.) But there was now a question she urgently needed to put herself; though she knew Jimmy
wasn't married either, it suddenly struck her, considering his altogether improved appearance and personality, that he might well be
engaged. Even after a week's tuition from Enid, Louisa had still a
few scruples; she couldn't see herself cutting out some dewy-eyed
fiancée . . .

She chose her words with care; not to betray what information
she already possessed.

"If it comes to that, what about you?"

He paused so long before replying, she had time to envisage
the dewy-eyed in detail—petite, brunette, with slightly promi-
nent front teeth; probably due (being both ladylike and a bit
silly) to read Miss Eynsford Hill to his Professor Higgins. But
how groundless her fears! He was actually fabricating a witty
compliment.

"I've been waiting for a girl with red hair and long legs," said
Jimmy. "They don't seem to grow here any more.—Will you call for
me again tomorrow, Louisa?"

"You bet," breathed Louisa.

He hesitated.

"If I don't walk back with you now, it's because I do rather want
to run through my part," said steady Jimmy Brown.

III

In the drive of Broydon Court, as Louisa had half anticipated, stood
Mrs. Brent flanked by Ivor and Ivan Cracarovitch.—At this, her first
view of the latter, Louisa was immediately and favorably struck by a
resemblance: not between dogs and owner (Mrs. Brent, unlike Mrs.

Meare, was obviously in the wrong class), but between Ivor and Ivan and Kurt and René at Cannes. The soft cravats of hair about their throats, their long, elegantly loose trousers, recalled so distinctly the appearance of René and Kurt under wraps after bathing, Louisa felt on terms with them at once.

"My dear Miss Datchett—" began Mrs. Brent ominously.

"Liver!" said Louisa.

Was it René she addressed, or Kurt? Louisa couldn't at this point distinguish. In any case, both nosed appreciatively at her hand.

"Say you want it!" instructed Louisa.

Two plumy tails quivered avidly.

"Then you shall have it!" said Louisa.—"My dear Mrs. Brent," she added smoothly, "*never* be introduced to a strange dog empty-handed! I've been all the way to the High Street, I've been to two shops, but I'm sure you'll agree that it was time well spent!"

She pulled it off again.

Louisa was in fact to get on very well with Ivor and Ivan Cracarovitch; even though she never bought them any more liver.

IV

There was still half an hour to go before whatever semblance of dinner Broydon Court still offered. (Louisa had been warned, however incautiously, by Mrs. Brent herself; Admiral Colley made silly remarks about the food.) To fill the interval Louisa nosed about her room; idly pulled open the drawer of a mahogany bureau, and within discovered, like a relic of better days, a few sheets of engraved note paper, a few envelopes to match . . .

They were of such good quality, it seemed a pity not to write to someone. Louisa recalled a neglected duty: she'd never sent a bread and butter letter to F. Pennon. Impulsively she sat down and filled a sheet with her big untidy scrawl.

Dear Freddy

Thank you for having me. I must have put on about three pounds. And thank you for being so sweet, that last evening. But I feel you'll be even happier, at any rate I hope you will, and if my very best wishes can help, they're all yours.

Affectionately,
Louisa

Both these episodes, however—her encounter with the dogs, her writing to old Freddy—were but parenthesis; to be mentioned simply because they occurred.

V

Louisa's mind was made up. She had been prudent, she had been thorough, she hadn't rushed things; she was in possession of every relevant fact—nothing left to fancy, or in memory's rosy shade. Enid Anstruther would have been proud of her. And the upshot was that she'd found in Jimmy Brown not only the precise husband she sought, but one practically in the bag already. After those fifteen minutes between five to six and ten past, Louisa naturally felt all time lost, merely a parenthesis, until she sighted the quarry again.

Once more, she cast an affectionate thought towards Colonel Hamlyn trailing his wildebeeste, towards C. P. Coe on the track of his moose . . .

Chapter Eleven

———— ❉ ————

I

Given Louisa's basic disposition it was nonetheless impossible that she should hold entirely aloof from her fellow residents at Broydon Court.—Or from four of them; the great majority were away all day—how had the standards of the Court declined!—at business; only four of the *vieille roche* remained, to keep Louisa company between the hours of nine and six, but three were men. Besides Miss Wilbraham (the patience player), there were Admiral Colley, Mr. Wright and Mr. Wray; all in leaf so sere as to be scarcely yellow, but rather dun.

The Admiral was by far the liveliest. Evidently alerted by Mrs. Brent, he cocked upon Louisa, that first night after dinner, a definitely lively old eye. It reminded her a little of F. Pennon's.

"I don't remember ye," stated Admiral Colley. "That means I've never seen ye. A head of hair like that, let alone those legs, I'd remember distinctly. What the hell did the woman mean?"

"It was my fault," apologized Louisa. "I told her *I* remembered you."

"Ye did? And how?" demanded the Admiral. "When to the best of my recollection—and my memory's pretty keen—I've never seen those ankles before?"

"I lived in Broydon when I was a little girl," explained Louisa. "You don't realize what a famous character you are . . ."

"In Broydon," grunted the Admiral. "Dear God, in Broydon!—But it'll be a pleasure to have ye about, just for the sake of those remarkable ankles."

By contrast, the reactions of the other three, to Louisa's presence, were rather reserved. Mr. Wray, retired from managing a bank, and Mr. Wright, retired from an insurance company, each seemed to regard her with faint alarm. Miss Wilbraham offered but a few nervous *politesses*. ("How nice," began Miss Wilbraham, "to have another lady here! Good Mrs. Brent being hardly—" There she broke off, evidently perceiving that Louisa was hardly too.) Yet upon one point all four equally stretched out a hand: it being a well-known fact that all elderly persons, resident in private hotels, cherish certain personal possessions, or treasures, upon which from time to time they need the reassurance of an outside opinion.

Before lunch next day Louisa had seen them all.

Admiral Colley's was a lacquer pagoda, about five feet high, scarlet picked out with gold, the very thing to terminate a vista in some stately country house. Even in a fairly spacious drawing room it wouldn't have been out of place; in the lobby of a super-cinema, could have competed successfully with the decorations. The Admiral had to keep it jammed between his bed and his wardrobe.

"Picked it up in Shanghai," explained the Admiral. "Got it home, believe it or not, in a destroyer. Dare say today it's worth thousands. What d'*you* think?"

"Honestly, I can't tell lacquer from nail varnish," confessed Louisa. (But she had a pretty good idea of what the pagoda would fetch in the Portobello Road: say four pound ten.) "Anyway, I'm sure it's *rare*," said Louisa politely.

"And I mean to hold on to it," said the Admiral. "It's my sheet anchor, d'you see. At a pinch I can always send it to Sotheby's—but till then I'm holding on to it."

II

Miss Wilbraham had silhouettes.

She had a whole gallery of them—single profiles, full-length figures, an ambitious family group showing ladies in crinolines and little girls in pantalettes. Dotted about her bedroom walls they produced a curiously nursery effect: objects too long in a family to be thrown away, but not wanted any more downstairs . . .

"Done in *India*," explained Miss Wilbraham, "by such a clever young man! Actually I believe he came out to Railways—but what a talent! That's my grandfather."

"He looks as though he's in uniform," said Louisa.

"My dear, he was in Harrowby's Horse.—The young man had to make six attempts, before he succeeded with those sabretaches; he was such an artist, he wouldn't use Indian ink."

Louisa scrutinized the portrait more closely.

"Not even for the whiskers?"

"Not even for the whiskers," said Miss Wilbraham firmly. "That's what makes it so valuable.—I suppose you've never seen any at Sotheby's?"

Louisa said she hadn't.

"I always watch the *Times*," explained Miss Wilbraham, "to see if any other silhouettes ever come up there; but I might have missed the right day. *These*, if I ever send them, I dare say will cause quite a stir!"

III

It was quite a relief to Louisa that Mr. Wray treasured no more than a poster advertising bullfights. Actually it made a much better effect, pinned over the inevitable mahogany bureau, than either the Admiral's pagoda or Miss Wilbraham's silhouettes, and at least he had no

illusions as to its worth.—Mr. Wray's illusion was that he had personally fought bulls. To Louisa this seemed extremely improbable,
since his single visit to Spain was admittedly by way of a Cook's tour;
it was so long ago, she thought his memory must have betrayed him.
But she spent quite a cheerful half-hour, while he demonstrated
veronicas with a counterpane, before proceeding to Mr. Wright's
collection of shrapnel.

Modestly, Mr. Wright admitted to having had unusual opportunities: he had been an air raid warden in 1940. No fewer than two
hundred and sixty specimens, nesting on cotton wool, filled his top
bureau drawer, each with date, and, if room, place, neatly inscribed
in white paint ("Downing Street, 14. x. '40"; "St. Paul's, 29. xii. '40").
"That alone's been quite a job," said Mr. Wright, modestly. "Some I
had to take a magnifying glass to. At the time, of course, I just used a
bit of red pencil." He pulled out the drawer below in demonstration:
Louisa beheld what looked like hundreds of fragments more, each
indeed faintly scrawled in red.

And on the washstand, Louisa noticed the little tin of white
enamel, the fine brush, the magnifying glass . . .

"I think it's the most wonderful hobby I ever heard of," said Louisa warmly; and tried to cheer herself up by reflecting that at least
he didn't imagine he was insuring against penury. It wasn't cash Mr.
Wright was after, but glory.

"I intend to leave 'em to the War Museum," he confided. "To be
kept together as the Arthur Wright Collection. I wrote a letter to
the curator there only the other day; and I must say I got a very nice
reply."

IV

It will be obvious that the morning had been wet. (Among the
many contrasts between Louisa's week in Broydon and her week
at Bournemouth—the most marked being in the quality of the

food—was to be this, that whereas the weather at Bournemouth was consistently and remarkably fine, at Broydon it was consistently and remarkably bad.) The afternoon, however, cleared sufficiently for Louisa to exercise Ivor and Ivan on the Common. ("Are you taking your camera?" suggested Mrs. Brent hopefully. "Not in *this* light," said Louisa. She wasn't by any means reluctant to start photographing, but to shoot away for a whole week would be damnably expensive in film. It wasn't till later that she hit on the idea of employing, under Mrs. Brent's eye, a camera without any film in it.) Once fairly on grass Louisa let the dogs off their leads and sent them to race in freedom; they bowled over an infant with a hoop, Louisa was rebuked by a keeper, but otherwise the walk passed without incident.

So the parenthesis wore away, until at five o'clock she began to get ready, and at six had her sights once more on Jimmy Brown.

V

"Where are you taking me?" asked Louisa.

"Not," said Jimmy, "to the Bon-Bon."

How it all came back! The Bon-Bon, in their salad days, had filled a place somewhere between a sandwich counter and an espresso bar: innocently muraled with sugar-plum cottages and gnomes in chef's hats, strictly dry, but nonetheless, in Broydon, possessing a certain aura of dash. Louisa went there quite a lot.

"D'you mean to say the Bon-Bon's still going?" cried Louisa nostalgically.

"Yes, but I'm not going to take you there," repeated Jimmy. "I'm going to take you for a cocktail first, and then dinner at the Theater Club."

He couldn't quite keep the pride out of his voice; Louisa looked suitably impressed.—Indeed, she was impressed; there'd been no Theater Club in the old days; there hadn't even been a theater.

"Broydon Rep," explained Jimmy casually. "It's in the Old Assembly Rooms. I believe there's a rather interesting piece on. If you like, we might go one night. We might go tomorrow."

Nothing could be more welcome to Louisa than to have a second date already in view; it made her able to relax. She had warned herself most carefully against rushing him—against ducking him, so to speak, too impetuously (so that he came up gasping) into the deeper waters of the sentimental past; now restraint would be almost easy. *Che va piano va sicuro!* As they walked past the Free Library, Louisa merely inquired how he'd got on with Higgins.

"The Ibsens seemed to like it," said Jimmy carelessly. "I only wish *you'*d been there, Louisa, to give an honest opinion. I can't think now why I didn't ask you—though of course you'd have found us a terribly amateur bunch."

"Who read Miss Eynsford Hill?"

"Oh, one of the girls. We don't only read Shaw either, you know," added Jimmy. "Last week we read Dylan Thomas. *Under Milk Wood.* It was a struggle, but I made 'em."

"Did they enjoy it?" asked Louisa interestedly.

"Not particularly. But someone's got to take the lead . . ."

With this same new assurance he propelled her before him into the Theater Club cocktail bar and ordered a couple of dry martinis.—Once again, as outside the Free Library, Louisa could have given sentiment rein: the bar was at one end of the old supper-room; in Louisa's youth devoted to charity bazaars, of which her Aunt May had been a great supporter; Louisa never got further than washing up teacups—was never given license to rove with lavender bags or buttonhole carnations—but did Jimmy too remember, she wondered, the time she dropped a whole crashing trayful just as the Mayoress began to speak? Single-handed he'd helped her clear the mess—being indeed the only one of her swains steady enough to be present. . . . "I come here quite a lot," observed Jimmy (though obviously in a different context). "It's about the most civilized place in Broydon."

Louisa had noticed that as the bar began to fill several people recognized him. They also took a good look at herself. She was wearing a rather striking black sheath, bought secondhand, via the *Times* personal column, from Model Disposing of Wardrobe, and her flaming hair fell naturally into the fashionable chrysanthemum mop. For a moment she felt uneasy, also glad she hadn't her toreador pants on; more than once had an escort complained of being made to look conspicuous. But Jimmy's aplomb was unshaken. It even verged on the complacent.

Hardily, Louisa quoted Mrs. Meare.

"I dare say tomorrow everyone will be asking who I am!"

"Oh, I don't think I'm all as important as that," said Jimmy seriously. "Though I must say," he added, "you make me feel as if I were." He paused. "As you always did, Louisa! Remember?"

He'd taken the header of his own accord.

VI

"All the same, from what *I* remember," said Louisa honestly—a little later, over dinner, "it was *you* who were rather grand . . . I mean compared with the rest of us. Yours was much the grandest house. I still remember the piano, and all those bound volumes of the *National Geographic.*"

"I had to get the scouts to cart 'em away," said Jimmy wryly, "at a Bob a Job.—No, I was out of things; you don't know what it meant, having a popular girl like you take notice of me."

"Well, we were friends," said Louisa modestly. (*Che va piano va sicuro!*)

"Not that I saw much of you," recalled Jimmy Brown. "You were always larking about with boys on bicycles."

"*You* weren't always there at the Library," Louisa reminded him.

"I had to be home for supper," explained Jimmy seriously. "You still made me late once or twice—waiting in case you turned up. Did you ever know, Louisa, how I felt about you?"

Softly-softly catchee monkey!

"I'm not sure what I knew," murmured Louisa. "Now, I'm just remembering . . ."

It turned out that they remembered, jointly, a great deal. An hour over dinner insufficient, the long light evening found them strolling across the Common—identifying an oak tree Louisa used to climb, a nook where once bloomed honeysuckle amid a tangle of blackberry bushes. (At least Louisa identified it; with some other swain than Jimmy, it seemed, had she plucked honeysuckle. It didn't matter; the error merely aroused, or so she hoped, a slight retrospective jealousy.) Both unhesitatingly, fondly, recalled a regulation Sunday walk—as far as the pond, once round and back again—after church, for Jimmy Brown, and chapel for Louisa. They'd neither of them been so fond of that walk at the time—Jimmy Brown flanked by his parents, Louisa tagging in the wake of Aunt May; but distance lent enchantment, and there is nothing so agreeable as sharing old memories.

"How splendid that you're here for a whole week!" exclaimed Jimmy, as they parted at the Court gate. (Certain Broydon conventions were still strong in him, for all his new sophistication; automatically he left Louisa at the gate. Nor did Louisa, either, ask him in for a drink; certain Broydon conventions reviving in Louisa also.) "You'll let me see as much of you as you can, Louisa?—Though I don't suppose I'm very exciting company," added Jimmy humbly, "for anyone so glamorous as you are now . . ."

All the way up the drive, Louisa glowed with pleasure. Only once, hitherto, had she glimpsed even the possibility of being glamorous: at Kerseymere Kennels. There Teddy Meare's fixation on his wife had canceled it out—and heaven knew Louisa wouldn't have wished anything else; but she was happy indeed, as well as surprised, to appear glamorous to Jimmy Brown.

VII

Actually Louisa began to feel pretty glamorous all round. Against the sub-fusc background of Broydon Court, she sometimes felt practically dazzling. A couple of little typists were pretty, one of the men away all day was reputed a successful architect, but Louisa's dash and *savoir-vivre*, and what she had no difficulty in presenting as a glitter of worldly success, set her—glamorously—apart. The only sales-resistance came from Mrs. Brent, who tried to boost the architect in opposition; explaining to all who would hear that though at Broydon to supervise a mere block of flats, Mr. McAndrew—"Surely you know the name?" exclaimed Mrs. Brent. *"Andrew* McAndrew?"—commonly specialized in the restoration of stately homes. "I suppose there's hardly a stately home in England," exclaimed Mrs. Brent, "he hasn't restored at some time or another! I think we should all feel quite honored." It was no use. Louisa just left lying about that old number of the *Tatler* in which appeared an Italian film star, plus two poodles, photographed by Datchett Photographer of Dogs. Compared with film stars, stately homes were just so much old rope.

Louisa also slammed down Mr. McAndrew whenever possible.

She might have been less successful, professionally, than she gave her new public to understand; but in the new field of glamour her star undoubtedly ascended.

Chapter Twelve

I

The Saturday morning offering a gleam of sun, Louisa comman-
deered both Admiral Colley and Mrs. Brent for a session of pho-
tography. Between them, under Louisa's instructions, they carried
out an old ping-pong table, draped a dark rug over a clotheshorse
behind, and induced first Ivor, then Ivan, to stand firmly in profile. (There is always one peculiar difficulty in photographing any
long-nosed dog such as a borzoi: taken head-on, too much nostril.
Nostrils like enlarged snail shells fill the lens.) Mrs. Brent hadn't
anything of Mrs. Meare's knack as a handler, but the Admiral, accustomed to command, was a tower of strength; before the rain came
down again, Louisa was pretty sure of having enough straights on
film to make a reasonable showing.

In the afternoon, she went to look at her old home.

II

Even as she entered Telscombe Road her motive was still obscure.—
Not from the bosom of any loving family had Louisa lit out for
the metropolis. An uncle and aunt merely accepted, on Christian

principles, responsibility for a niece, Louisa's parents having met their deserts (or so the circumstance was presented to her) when the local *palais de danse* stopped a buzz bomb. Louisa was if anything glad, despite Aunt May's prognostications, to think they'd been having a good time—and together, Dad back from Africa; but learned to keep her tears, like her opinions, to herself.

No doubt Aunt May and Uncle Thomas believed they were doing their best for her, in apprenticing her to Mr. Hughes for a pound a week, and taking back eighteen shillings of it for her keep.

Louisa halted: there it stood, the small, mean-proportioned, semi-detached prison of her youth. (But be fair!—at the age of fourteen also her refuge.) The narrow front garden however was now neglected, the window curtains less than immaculate; Number 34 had so evidently changed hands, Louisa was able for the first time in her life to walk up the path without a sinking of the heart.

She knocked. The woman who opened was stout as Aunt May had been lean, florid as Aunt May had been pale, also, halfway through the afternoon, still in curling pins.

"Tell me if it's inconvenient," said Louisa, "but I used to live here. Would you let me just look round?"

Again, a change! Though it had been Aunt May's oft-proclaimed boast that her domestic arrangements lay open night or day to inspection by the Queen of England, no one else appearing suddenly on the doorstep had the slightest chance of admittance. Now, after but one shrewd glance—

"So long as you're not from the hire-purchase," said the woman warmly, "look anywhere you like. Come in, dear."

The door closing behind her, Louisa sniffed. It was at this point that she had been used to feel definitely guilty; a feeling associated with a certain smell, of floor-polish combined with wet mackintosh . . . the mackintosh admittedly her own, thrown down in a heap under the stairs, not even properly hung up, before she dashed out again after school to skylark with boys on bicycles. "I must have been a headache!" thought Louisa—guiltily. But the disquieting moment was brief; all she could smell now was fried fish.

"Can I go upstairs?" asked Louisa.

"Anywhere you like," repeated the woman. "I won't come with you on account of my weight, but you go anywhere you like, dear!"

Louisa mounted the familiar stairs. Certain fittings had evidently gone with the house; the stair carpet was familiar too. But the stair rods weren't bright any more, and Louisa, whose Saturday task it had been to polish them, stepped over each tarnished bar with increasing confidence.

She pushed open the door to what had once been her attic-bedroom. It was still, inevitably, an attic; but now housed chiefly empty beer bottles.

"Found the cellar?" called the woman cheerfully. "A joke, ain't it? Only we haven't a cellar, and my hubby never seems to take 'em back, and I can't abide waste, so there they go, and one day we'll have to have a lorry.—Don't tell me that's what used to be your bedroom, dear?"

Louisa put her head over the banister and nodded.

"Then I'm really sorry," said the woman. "I truly am. But it's just that there's nowhere else to put them."

"Don't worry," said Louisa.

"If you'd like to stay up there a bit—revisiting, like on the telly—just shift a crate off the chair."

"Thanks, I've seen all I wanted," said Louisa. "And thank you very much for letting me."

Only when she was out in the road again did she realize why she'd come. She had been laying—and how satisfactorily!—a ghost.

With no black spot to be avoided, no street she couldn't tread unapprehensive, her happiness in Broydon would be unflawed. Louisa's last, subconscious doubts had in fact vanished as she looked into her old room; even though she didn't realize it until she was outside again.

III

That night Jimmy took her to the Rep.

"It's very advanced," he warned her. "Some of the Ibsens haven't been able to make head or tail of it. But I dare say it's just up your street."

In fact Louisa, observing the curtain already raised on a gallows, a bicycle, and what looked like a sewing machine wreathed in straw, felt at home at once; it being the type of décor to which contact with Hugo Pym had accustomed her. Three muffled thumps (evidently borrowed from the famous *trois coups* of the French) heralded an action equally, in a way, familiar; complex, symbolic and gloomy, with a few music-hall jokes thrown in. Louisa didn't wonder that the Ibsens had been baffled; but she also formed the opinion that the admittedly sparse audience was enjoying itself—partly perhaps from a sense of intellectual daring, and partly, perhaps, because all that took place on the stage was so extremely unlike anything that took place in Broydon. The atmosphere was still one of hard-breathed mental endeavor.

("I imagine that chap in the diving helmet's Fate?" muttered Jimmy. "Just let it flow over you," advised Louisa . . .)

No curtain descended at the interval; the house lights simply went up again as a couple of black-costumed handymen (probably borrowed from the Chinese) appeared to reset the stage. Some of the audience kept their seats, under the impression that the play was going straight on, but to the waverers Louisa gave a useful lead.

"Interesting, isn't it?" said Jimmy, as they emerged. "Of course you're perfectly right; one must let it flow over one . . . Would you like a lemonade?"

The foyer bar was unlicensed, but nonetheless thronged; as after a stiff examination paper, everyone was thirsty. Watching Jimmy's progress, how fortunate Louisa felt herself! He was not only game for symbolic drama, he was also the tallest man in sight.—The next moment her thoughts were violently diverted, as she beheld purposefully forging towards her Hugo Pym.

IV

"Dear Louisa, what a friend you are!" cried Hugo. "Is that him?"

Louisa had to think rapidly back over the past fortnight, before she picked up the allusion, now so outdated, to F. Pennon. She had to think even before putting two and two together and realizing that this must be Hugo's Outer London rep. (Though she might have guessed it, from the performance just witnessed.) The situation was still too complex to be immediately disentangled.—Indeed, Louisa had no intention of disentangling it; she merely smiled consciously and asked after Hugo's bronchitis.

"Better," coughed Hugo.—"Would he like to come backstage? They do, you know; the chaps who put up money. Why not bring him round?"

Louisa glanced towards Jimmy Brown still patiently in line for lemonade. She thought he might indeed enjoy going backstage; but the situation held too many awkward possibilities.

"Just leave it to me," said Louisa.

"Probably you know best," admitted Hugo. "Though it does seem an opportunity . . . I must say he looks younger than I expected," observed Hugo Pym. "In fact he looks very nice. A bit *de province*, perhaps—"

Just as she'd resented his tone on behalf of F. Pennon, so Louisa resented it now on Jimmy Brown's.

"Don't be so damned superior," said Louisa sharply.

"Darling, you *must* be in love!" noted Hugo Pym. "What a lucky girl you are! All that cash as well! But thank you very much, dear, for bringing him; and I'll hope to see you both very soon."

To Louisa's extreme relief he cocked an eye at the foyer clock— was it he who thumped those three thumps?—and slid away just before Jimmy returned.

"Who was that you were talking to?" asked Jimmy interestedly.

"Hugo Pym," said Louisa. "He's the stage manager."

"What fascinating people you know!" marveled Jimmy. "I say, could he take us round backstage?"

"Not tonight," said Louisa. "He's got bronchitis, he wants to get home."

The encounter did her no harm, however; far from it. It made her in Jimmy's eyes all the more glamourous.

Chapter Thirteen

— ❋ —

I

Full of confidence for the future, also living free, these were happy days for Louisa. Materially, indeed, she had been better off at Bournemouth, especially as regards food, but at Broydon Court there were more men about, and Louisa, though thoroughly determined to stop being fond of them, was far happier in the company of an admiral than in that of Mrs. Anstruther. Actually the Admiral was a slight chink in her new armor; his situation struck Louisa as truly tragic, and she so much admired the rakish spirit in which he faced it, it was impossible not to grow *slightly* fond of him; but Mr. Wright and Mr. Wray she just liked seeing around in trousers, and otherwise remained quite indifferent to. Louisa had at least become fond of only one man out of a possible three—while with Mr. McAndrew she was practically at daggers drawn.

It lent an interest, even though the engagement was rather one-sided; Mr. McAndrew simply came up for punishment. He was a large, quiet-spoken, entirely personable Scot, and Louisa indeed would have had nothing against him if Mrs. Brent hadn't so persisted in building him up. Jealous for her own position as center of interest, however, Louisa slammed him down whenever possible. Thus—

"Working up and down the country as I do," suggested Mr. McAndrew mildly, "I run into quite a few hounds myself. Maybe you've photographed some of them?"

"Actually no," returned Louisa, willfully misunderstanding. "Meets are rather local-talent stuff, don't you think? I'm a professional . . ."

Mr. McAndrew, divided between wanting to say that he'd often seen staff-photographer photographs of meets in the *Times*, and that he hadn't been referring to meets at all, muttered something about not that kind of hound in particular, not the foxhunting sort, just country sorts of dogs in general, the kind you found around country houses. "I'm so sorry, I thought you said *hounds*," apologized Louisa sweetly. The two typists—this particular exchange took place at breakfast—began to giggle. Though all Scots are naturally argumentative, Mr. McAndrew looked at the girls, looked at Louisa, and held his peace—slammed down again.

Another point on which Louisa preferred Broydon Court to the Pines was that she got more exercise: wet or fine, Ivor and Ivan Cracarovitch were like herself always ready for a walk.—Sometimes the Admiral came too, and once had a really exhilarating row with the Common-keeper. ("The lady's to exercise her beasts as she damn well pleases!" roared Admiral Colley. Ivor had bowled over a tricycle.) Each day until six o'clock, though still a parenthesis, passed really agreeably; and at six Louisa called for Jimmy at the shop.

She had no fears now, of too impetuously reviving old memories. It was Jimmy himself who suggested a pilgrimage to the Free Library.

II

Slightly to Louisa's disappointment it had been rather smartened up— gay wrappers off new books pinned to a board in the lobby, a positively enticing Children's Corner arranged in the Reading Room; a couple of cases of Stone Age bric-a-brac had vanished altogether. ("Where's the mammoth's tooth?" complained Louisa—it used to have a third, a special case to itself: vanished too.) But back in the stacks, between B for Biography and C for Ceramics, something of the old gloom lingered; and something of the old sentiment as well.

"D'you remember, Louisa?"

"Do I not!" sighed Louisa nostalgically. "You'd be surprised how much biography I picked up . . . waiting about."

"*I* picked up a good deal about ceramics—waiting about."

"You practically taught me to open a book," said Louisa.—"I had to do *something*," she added honestly, "waiting about."

"I can't see why you waited for me at all. It wasn't always," said Jimmy, rather perceptively, "raining . . ."

"I suppose I liked you," said Louisa.

"Even with my pebble lenses and my spots?"

"I didn't notice them."

"That I don't believe," stated Jimmy. "Everyone in Broydon noticed 'em. You were just kind, Louisa—as you are still . . ."

It was the most on-coming conversation they had yet had; but *che va piano va sicuro!*—Entering the Library, Louisa had had some idea of being kissed by Jimmy, in the stacks between B for Biography and C for Ceramics. If she'd at that moment offered her cheek, he quite probably would have kissed her. But *che va piano va sicuro!* Mrs. Anstruther might have been at her elbow, as Louisa laughed and led the way out.

III

On another occasion, before dining as usual at the Theater Club— (As usual! How precious a phrase!)—Jimmy took Louisa to see what he'd made of his own semi-detached heritage.

"Of course it's freehold," explained Jimmy seriously, "so I didn't mind spending a bit. But what d'you think of it, Louisa?"

Louisa beheld changes no less startling than those at Telscombe Road. But they were of a different sort—not from austere to easygoing, but from dowdy comfort to absolute elegance. She gazed about in unfeigned admiration. Where was now the over-furnished, slightly stuffy parlor? One wall at least must have been knocked down: between back and front windows stretched a relatively spacious apartment, made to appear all the more spacious by a glass door that separated it from, without concealing, a kitchen papered with cabbage roses. Where was now the upright piano, where now were all those bound volumes of the *National Geographic?* Louisa remembered: the scouts had carted them off. Had the scouts carted off the piano too? In any case, in its room now stood a handsome radio-gramophone; as the emptied bookshelves now housed longplaying records . . .

There was almost no furniture at all, save for one long, low divan covered in Picasso-influence linen, and a bamboo coffee table. This was in the front part of the room. In the dining alcove to the rear, Jimmy had gone Regency.

"I didn't care for it much either," said Jimmy, watching her, "as it was. You weren't the only one, Louisa, to have ideas!"

If he was surprising her more and more, each surprise was a pleasant one.—Louisa would have liked to see the bedroom, but really felt she could take it on trust.

IV

This was on the Sunday; Louisa had already been five days at Broydon Court, and was thoroughly aware that the Wednesday must put a period to her stay. (Dining out each night hadn't exactly saved her bacon, with Mrs. Brent, but it was just as well that she did.) The ill luck of losing one last evening out of two with Jimmy, however, so far from depressed her, she returned alone to the Court, on the Monday, in excellent spirits.

To discover a common taste for bamboo and theater-clubs had been truly delightful. What Louisa still desired most from a husband was stability; and nothing could have better confirmed her belief in Jimmy's basic steadiness, than his reason for letting her down.

"I clean forgot," apologized Jimmy—Louisa calling for him as usual—"but I've an appointment with the dentist. Until I looked at my diary just now, I'd clean forgotten. And as he's taking me after hours, as a bit of a favor, I don't like to cry off."

"I wouldn't want you to," said Louisa warmly.—She was naturally disappointed, but even more struck by such a proof of sterling character. Having toothache, Jimmy made an appointment with the dentist; having an excuse for postponing it, he refrained. In Louisa's experience, getting a man to the dentist's was like getting a cat to the vet's.

"I suppose you don't want me to come with you?" suggested Louisa tentatively.

"Good heavens, why?" exclaimed Jimmy.

In happy contrast Louisa recalled practically doping Number Ten with gin, before inducing him to benefit by the National Health Service. If it had been not a dentist's but an electric chair she was haling him to, he could hardly have shown more reluctance; and that after six sleepless nights in a row . . .

"Are you having anything out?" asked Louisa hopefully.

"Just one at the back."

"Wisdom?" pressed Louisa.

"Actually it's impacted," said Jimmy casually.

Louisa sighed with pleasure. She wasn't unfeeling, she simply rejoiced in his solid worth. And as if this wasn't enough happiness—

"But tomorrow night," said Jimmy earnestly, "I want you to do something you haven't done yet. I want you to have dinner with me at home."

V

So on this penultimate evening Louisa returned to the Court alone, but by no means low-spirited. On the contrary; the evening in prospect, domestically tête-à-tête, offered exactly the circumstances she would have chosen for springing a matrimonial trap. (Louisa had ceased to identify herself with Colonel Hamlyn, or C. P. Coe. She didn't want Jimmy bagged like moose or wilde-beeste. It was rather with that skilled trapper Enid Anstruther that she now identified herself. In either case, quite honestly, she didn't see Jimmy standing a chance.)

Loping back across the Common, Louisa recapitulated in sober contentment his many admirable qualities. Of all the men she'd ever met, he was the best able to look after himself. (This mightn't have been an attraction to some women, but it was to Louisa.) He might have clean forgotten an appointment—but only until he looked at his diary. (Most of the men Louisa knew didn't even possess diaries.) Fondly her thoughts returned to their first re-encounter, when even in the excitement of her presence he hadn't forgotten Ibsen night . . . steadily attended over how many years? If ever there was a steady man breathing—a man able to look after himself—it was Jimmy Brown.

Passing the tangled thicket where once honeysuckle bloomed, Louisa noticed that the path alongside had been asphalted. But she'd never picked honeysuckle with Jimmy, and wasn't asphalt far more practical?

Soberly content, gratefully optimistic, Louisa regained Broydon Court; and there stationed before the door beheld F. Pennon's Rolls.

Chapter Fourteen

I

She backed into the rhododendrons.—The movement was purely instinctive, an instinctive recoil before all the complications of the past. Fond of men as she was, and particularly fond as she was of F. Pennon, Louisa backed so abruptly into the rhododendrons she scratched her nape on a protrusive twig. But she had to come out again. Mrs. Brent, who had evidently been lying in wait, hurried breathless down the drive.

"You've a visitor!" panted Mrs. Brent, in urgent but congratulatory tones. "He's in the lounge. He wouldn't have tea. In fact—I'm afraid I counted him as a *resident!*—he's ordered a bottle of champagne."

At least Freddy was in his usual form, thought Louisa; and the idea of a glass of champagne wasn't unwelcome to herself. Mrs. Brent hurried her on, pausing only to cast an admiring glance at the Rolls. ("He hasn't *said* anything," panted Mrs. Brent, "but if he *should* want to stay, I could have a bedroom ready in an hour.") At the lounge door, however, with a movement of irritating discretion, she drew back. Louisa rubbed the scratch on her nape, hardened her heart, and entered, warily . . .

There was Freddy with his bottle all right, neighboring Miss Wilbraham's patience table. A slight circumstance to touch her: a glass foamed among the patience cards too. Freddy had never liked to drink alone, but for Miss Wilbraham, what a treat! Still warily, however—

"Hi," said Louisa.

"*You've* been a hell of a time," complained Freddy at once.

"Did I know you were coming?" retorted Louisa.

She advanced, and sat. (Miss Wilbraham hiccoughed gently.) There was a third glass set ready, but a glance at the bottle was discouraging. Freddy and Miss Wilbraham between them had almost polished it off.

"There's another on ice," Freddy reassured her. "Probably among the corpses," he added. "What extraordinary places you do find, Louisa!"

"Actually I'm here on a job," said Louisa repressively. "I know you've never realized I'm a professional—"

"Probably run in and out on slabs," elaborated Freddy. "Ever seen the Paris morgue?"

"At any rate you seem to have revived Miss Wilbraham," snapped Louisa.

"Coming along nicely," agreed Freddy complacently. "Now we'll see how the old allez-oop works . . ."

Incredibly, at Broydon Court, he clapped his hands. (Echoing the *trois coups* of Hugo's stage management!) Louisa still wasn't deceived; Freddy was being too larkish altogether. That old Albert the waiter immediately appeared with a fresh bottle of champagne gave him a temporary build-up; but he definitely wasn't his usual self . . .

Old Albert, with a flourish of dirty napkin, poured. Miss Wilbraham gently hiccoughed again. An absent, almost unconscious movement of her hand (which had just laid a red nine on a red ten) slid her glass across the ace of spades in Albert's general direction. ("Fill her up!" said Freddy.) In the short silence that followed Louisa took a welcome mouthful, and waited.

"Well, don't you want to know why I'm here?" asked Freddy at last.

"No," said Louisa.

"That's a hell of a welcome, when I've driven all the way from Town."

"Why aren't you at Bournemouth?" demanded Louisa.—For one alarming moment it crossed her mind that he had simply run away, that he was going to demand to be *hidden* . . . But at least it wasn't as bad as that.

"I shall probably drive back to Bournemouth tonight. I've come up to see my lawyers."

"Ah!" said Louisa. "Settlements?"

"That's it. I don't know how you guessed, but you're right. Enid's going to marry me next month," stated Freddy—with a sort of heroic detachment.

"And why not?" said Louisa. "I think you're both being very sensible, not to wait. And if you've driven all the way from Town just to tell me, I think it's very sweet."

He hesitated.

"As a matter of fact, that isn't the *only* reason," said F. Pennon.

This time Louisa refilled her glass herself.—Indeed, she had refilled it twice, before Freddy came to the end of his remarkable proposition.

II

It was such as only a very rich man, and a very uninhibited rich man, could have even contemplated. F. Pennon was preeminently both; but perhaps the most surprising point of all was that he didn't appear to see anything unusual in it.

"It simply occurred to me," explained Freddy, "and the deuce knows why I didn't think of it before—while I'm *making* settlements, why don't I make one on you too?"

Louisa gaped. At this point, she could say nothing at all.

"Say three or four hundred a year," proceeded old Freddy reasonably. "Just pin money, y'know; because of course you wouldn't have any expenses.—I suppose you haven't changed your mind about the other thing?" he hazarded, almost in parenthesis. "I mean, marrying me?"

Louisa shook her head.

"I thought not. And you're quite right; I'm too old. I respected you, Louisa, for turning me down, even though I took a knock. So I've thought of this," continued Freddy, more cheerfully, "because we did, didn't we, get on uncommonly well?—all three of us?—and at the same time you wouldn't care to take a salary. A settlement would look after everything."

Although by this time Louisa realized that what he had in mind was nothing short of a permanent *ménage à trois*, at least she had the sense not to feel insulted. He was old, was old Freddy, and beginning to know it; he wasn't seeking a mistress, he was seeking, rather pathetically, a friend. Of course he wanted a buffer too; but as he sat gazing at her across the card table Louisa read in his wistful glance chiefly a desire for her friendship. Nor did she accuse him of trying to buy it: his standards were such that he quite probably imagined her earning far more than three or four hundred a year (pin money) already. He simply didn't want her to lose on the deal.

"If you're thinking of Enid—" began Freddy again.

What a thought was *there!* For a moment, fascinated, Louisa contemplated its full beauty: pin money, settlement, even in a sense a man at the top—the very booty Enid had described, and all looted from that experienced trapper's own trap!

"I don't see anything to laugh at," said Freddy stiffly. "As I was saying, if you're thinking about Enid, she'll be as pleased as I shall. She told me to tell you—"

"You mean she *agrees?*" asked Louisa, startled.

"Of course. I may not know much about women," said F. Pennon complacently, "but I always knew you and she'd get on. Naturally Enid agrees."

Louisa thought rapidly. Her first astonishment over, it struck her that Enid was an experienced trapper indeed; it struck her also that Mrs. Anstruther was gambling on a certainty. To Mrs.

Anstruther's mind, if such a proposal could tempt Louisa at all she'd have grabbed at it already—when it included absolute matrimony. Mrs. Anstruther was evidently gambling on the certainty that she, Louisa, was still a damned fool.

III

"As perhaps I was," thought Louisa, "when I hadn't found Jimmy again . . ."

She admitted it to herself: she had been over-chivalrous, a female Quixote, that night at Bournemouth. (Or say she had behaved too much like a gentleman; always Louisa's weakness.) It was easy enough, now, not to be tempted, since she so genuinely preferred what Jimmy Brown could offer; but Enid would have run more risk than she knew, if Louisa had found him already preempted by that dewy-eyed fiancée!

As it was, she had only to spare Freddy's feelings.

"Dear Freddy, I'm sorry," said Louisa. "I like you so very much—and Enid too," she lied. "I hope you'll tell her from me I haven't words to express what I think of her." (There was a pleasing ambiguity about this; Louisa hoped Freddy'd get it right.) "But the fact is—"

She paused. She had learned so much discretion, she wouldn't say she was going to get married. Instead—

"I'd miss photographing dogs," explained Louisa.

The conclusion was weak, and she knew it. Was it *fair* to Freddy, to be so discreet?—As the lounge door swung open, how much Louisa would have given to see Jimmy himself advancing towards her, to make all plain by his earnest, devoted looks! But it was only Admiral Colley.

"If that's all, we'll buy a few," said Freddy readily. "Buy as many as you like! I'm fond of a dog myself."

Louisa saw she must be blunter. (The Admiral, reconnoitering

Miss Wilbraham's card table, dropped anchor. Miss Wilbraham gently hiccoughed.)

"Dear Freddy, it just wouldn't be the life to suit me," said Louisa. "Fond of you as I am—and of Enid too—I can't think of anything likelier to send me up the wall."

"You might at least think it over."

"I don't need to, and it's much better to have it settled."

He paused in turn. Then he did something very nice. He refrained from offering her more money.

"If that's your last word, I suppose I must just take another knock," said Freddy sadly.

Louisa offered all the consolation she could. It wasn't much.

"At any rate stay and have dinner, Freddy."

"Thank you, I'll just be getting along," said F. Pennon.

"As far as the grub goes, you're probably right," agreed Louisa heartily.—But she was now feeling almost as sad as he was; she cast desperately about for some fresh, some gayer topic to carry them over the mournful moment.—It was a relief to catch Admiral Colley's eye; though the Admiral wasn't looking particularly cheerful either, the mere presence of a third might help . . .

"Who's that poor old feller?" asked Freddy.

"Admiral Colley," said Louisa.—"Admiral, this is Mr. Pennon."

"Have a glass of champagne," said Freddy gloomily.

IV

Two hours later, what a change!

What a party!

It was an evening such as Broydon Court had never known before and never would again. Freddy's carte blanche for champagne all round released every inhibition.—What extraordinary experiences Miss Wilbraham related, of the siege of Lucknow!—No doubt her grandmother's experiences; to Miss Wilbraham nonetheless so vivid, she absolutely cowered behind a sofa, out of the way of sepoy bullets. No one thought this in the least surprising; Mr. Wright was extinguishing fire bombs on the dome of St. Paul's, Mr. Wray fighting bulls at Malaga. As for the lesser fry of residents, returning one by one to find practically an orgy going on, it was remarkable how quickly they forgot their surprise and entered into the spirit. Only Mr. McAndrew held slightly aloof: the two typists actually nipped upstairs and changed into evening dress—this after Mrs. Brent began to play the piano.

Who let in Ivor and Ivan Cracarovitch? There they were too, getting between people's legs, nosing into the champagne buckets. Mrs. Brent played the piano, old Albert was run off his feet, jest and jollity burgeoned; while at the calm center of this happy whirlwind F. Pennon and the Admiral were swearing an eternal friendship based on the Admiral's luckless devotion to a dear little woman at Malta.

"She'd the most charmin' profile—" mourned the Admiral.

"You don't say so!" exclaimed Freddy. "My dear chap, this is amazin'!—So's Enid's."

"Not Enid; Marion—and a way of peeping up at one that made one feel about eight feet high."

"Protective?"

"Exactly. A chap felt he wanted to lay down his life in her defense."

With happy astonishment, Louisa heard Freddy reply that this described Enid to a T.—It might be the champagne in him speaking, but couldn't he always afford champagne?

Who turned the lights out in the middle of a Paul Jones? The lid was off Broydon Court with a vengeance! From the amount of giggling that ensued Louisa guessed that the typists were being kissed; and the next moment was kissed herself. The lights went up again, she encountered on one side an extremely dour look from Mr. McAndrew, on the other the over-innocent gaze of Mr. Wray. "He must have stood on his toes!" thought Louisa kindly, and allowed him to lead her into a tango. (That Mrs. Brent was playing a waltz was neither here nor there; Mr. Wray had learned to tango in Spain, and tango he would.) Mr. Wright cut in, stately exponent of the slow fox trot; one of the young men took over from Mrs. Brent and launched a cha-cha. (No one had any thought of dinner—indeed there was no dinner, that night, at Broydon Court; Freddy's bounty overflowed, via Albert, to the cook.) More than once it crossed Louisa's mind to telephone and summon Jimmy, it seemed a shame he was missing such a good party; but the thought of his aching tooth restrained her; he was probably in bed. Actually the hour was no more than about nine, but Louisa, like everyone else, had lost count of time . . .

Freddy and the Admiral at least, however, followed the classic rhythm of party time. About halfway, they began to get sad. Admiral Colley was the sadder—as he had reason to be: not for him, as for Freddy, reunion at last with his little woman!

"Don't think I grudge it you," said the Admiral earnestly, "but by God, it's hard!"

"It's leaving the old Mansions I'm going to feel," mourned Freddy. (Not on champagne now; brandy.)

"I'm in the sunset of my days," stated the Admiral, "and what's it look like?—You've heard of a D.B.S.?"

"Distressed British Seaman," supplied Louisa, who had paused beside them in sympathy.

"That's right. Consuls have to send 'em home. Well, I'm a Distressed British Admiral," stated Admiral Colley, "and no consul will ever send *me* home, because I haven't got one. I lie rotting in this unspeakable crab-infested dock—"

"Morgue," corrected Freddy. "Run in and out on slabs."

"—waiting to die in my damned uncomfortable bed. How's that for a bloody sunset?"

"Horrible."

"But what else can I do? Isn't one damned lodginghouse just like another damned lodginghouse? A wife—don't think I grudge you, old chap, I don't. Let the best man go in and win!" exclaimed

Admiral Colley, a trifle obscurely—"a wife sees to things. Goes to the butcher and gets a nice cut. Whereas here I lie rotting—"

It was at this moment that Louisa had the inspiration destined to be so valuable all round.

V

The air outside struck fresh and cool; bright moonlight lent Freddy's Rolls an almost supernatural beauty. Behind its wheel sat Hallam the chauffeur.

—Louisa spared a moment to admire him. A custom-built, Rolls chauffeur, after three hours waiting he had but removed his cap and permitted himself a cigarette—and was obviously ready to don the one and extinguish the other at a moment's notice. Even at Louisa's (not his boss's) approach, he performed both these actions simultaneously. It was a real pleasure to be recognized by him.

"Nice to see you again, madam," he said kindly.

Louisa hesitated. She was feeling extraordinarily clearheaded, only the moonlight on the bonnet slightly dazzled her.

"Look," said Louisa, "are you really driving straight back to Bournemouth?"

"If Mr. Pennon so decides, madam. The roads will be nice and clear."

"Look," said Louisa again, "it's just possible Mr. Pennon may have someone with him."

"There are plenty of rugs, madam."

"The difficulty may be the pagoda. Would it go in the boot?"

"How large a pagoda, madam?"

"About five foot."

"In sections?"

"I don't know," confessed Louisa. "Maybe you could lash it to the roof?"

"In any case, just leave it to me, madam."

"Thank you very much," said Louisa warmly; and hastened back into the lounge.

VI

Most fortunately, the Admiral had just been called upon to steady Miss Wilbraham with news from Delhi. (Though not Army, he was eminently Service.) Louisa dropped into the vacant chair beside Freddy's, and refused a brandy.

"Honestly, isn't he tragic?" sighed Louisa.—Freddy had no doubt of whom she spoke; they were both of them gazing in the same direction, the eyes of Freddy at least practically filled with tears.

"You know what, Louisa?" said Freddy solemnly. "My heart bleeds for him. He tells me he ain't had a decent glass of claret in years."

"And how he'd appreciate one!" sighed Louisa.

"Not a doubt of it.—You weren't here, Louisa, but on claret he's sound as a bell. We could have gone on talking, just about claret— we never even touched on hock—for hours and hours . . . What I'd give," exclaimed Freddy pathetically, "to have a chap like him at Bournemouth!"

There it was, in solution, the whole beautiful answer to Freddy's need for a buffer, the Admiral's need for a home, Louisa's need to see them both happy. She stopped sighing and precipitated it.

"Well, why not?" said Louisa. "Why don't you take him," asked Louisa explicitly, "back with you?"

VII

From which moment things moved so fast that even she, their instigator, was slightly astonished. ("What about Enid?" suggested Freddy. "Won't Enid *love* an Admiral?" countered Louisa. "By

George, you're right!" agreed Freddy; and that settled Enid.) Admiral Colley received the proposition with enthusiasm, also sailor-like readiness.—As Louisa had foreseen, his one anxiety was for his pagoda. "Either in the boot or lashed on top," Louisa reassured him. A dozen willing hands helped him pack, while Freddy settled the bill. (It was so enormous, the slight sum due from Admiral Colley Mrs. Brent just slipped in. Louisa genuinely admired her, she had never liked Mrs. Brent so well, as the latter downed a hasty cup of coffee and proved she could still add. She might regret the loss of a resident later, but at the moment twelve five-pound notes rejoiced her heart.) Then the whole party went out to see Freddy and the Admiral off.

Of course they had all had a great deal of champagne.

The pagoda had to be lashed onto the roof after all; but Hallam swathed it carefully in a rug. An unexpected detritus of Oriental bric-a-brac cumbered the floor space; there was still ample room, in a Rolls, for Freddy and the Admiral. Hallam imperturbably lapped them too in rugs, as Freddy stuck his head out of the window for a last farewell.

"Sure you won't come with us, Louisa?" called Freddy.

But Louisa, thinking of Jimmy Brown, was quite sure.

Chapter Fifteen

———— ❀ ————

I

Breakfast next day was a rather subdued meal, at Broydon Court. Mr. McAndrew, who had left the party early, was the only guest who showed any appetite, except of course Louisa. Like the two survivors of a rough Atlantic crossing they ate in competitive silence—as Mr. McAndrew took a second slice of ham (there was no cooked breakfast, that morning, at Broydon Court), so did Louisa; as Louisa took a third, so did Mr. McAndrew. On toast and marmalade Louisa won hands down, if only because Mr. McAndrew's client came to pick him up; but she would probably have done so in any case, since nothing gave her such an appetite as having done good.

For once, a morning after brought no regrets, no misgivings. The more Louisa considered it, the more the shanghaiing of Admiral Colley rejoiced her. A villa at Bournemouth was the very place for him, a setting as appropriate and congenial—good quarters, first-rate messing, Air-Sea Rescue base at Poole—as could well be imagined; while as for his pagoda, Louisa already visualized it in position looking like a million dollars at the head of the Pines' broad stair . . .

And for old Freddy too, what a break! He wouldn't even have to make a settlement. As the third in a *ménage à trois* (which Louisa felt confident was what would result), almost any Admiral would have filled the bill—flattering to Enid's snobbishness yet no rival to her, sending up Freddy's local stock while still acting as Prisoner's Friend. Admiral Colley was in addition a man after Freddy's own heart. What sessions they'd have together, thought Louisa gladly, over the claret! With what sympathetic enthusiasm—and with what alacrity—would they embark upon the lighter topic of hock!—While after dinner Enid, in pretty profile, listened to the tale of the little woman at Malta, agreeably conscious of a transferred devotion . . .

It was a measure of Louisa's altruism that she foresaw this development too with pleasure. She could have had the Admiral in her pocket herself, and she was fond of him; her opinion of Mrs. Anstruther was low; but her recognition of how easily Enid would get her birdlike claws into him was coupled with the recognition that nothing would make Freddy more comfortable. "They'll be snug as bugs in a rug," thought Louisa—a bit vulgarly, but nonetheless altruistically . . .

"I shouldn't wonder if he gives her away," thought Louisa. "I wonder what's become of his full-dress uniform?—Anyway he can hire one," thought Louisa cheerfully; and finished up with a banana off Mr. Wray's empty table.

II

Quiet and still lay Broydon Court, nursing its hangover. Louisa had a fine time with Ivor and Ivan Cracarovitch.

For the first time in her career, after a morning of cautious stalking, she believed she'd got it—the shot she'd promised Mrs. Brent, the one shot every photographer of dogs dreams of: of two animals romping together.—Louisa at the crucial moment, almost flat in the grass; at the very best angle of all. If they'd been ballerinas, Ivan and Ivor, they'd have appeared to be leaping into the flies; through the lens of Louisa's camera, they leaped to the firmament . . . Louisa was so excited, she almost nipped back to Soho to develop at once; but instead—what a day it was to be!—spent the afternoon washing and setting her hair.

—The thought had been there, at the back of her mind, all day: behind her happy musings on old Freddy and the Admiral, behind her professional concentration on Ivor and Ivan; only for a split second, as she caught the dogs' leap to the skies, had Louisa, at the back of her mind, stopped thinking about Jimmy Brown.

Waiting for her hair to dry, she now thought of him deliberately.

It was time to plan the evening's campaign. Or safari.

With special reference to trap and bait: the enticing morsel in the pit, the treacherous, yielding branches spread above . . .

Pushing a hairpin back under the net, Louisa tried to recall all she'd learned from Mrs. Anstruther. How would Enid Anstruther set about it?

"Well, of course she'd flutter down like a moth," thought Louisa.

The image was slightly surrealistic; moths didn't dig pits, they flew into candles. To Louisa, however, it was clear enough—but also unhelpful. She doubted whether she could pull off a butterfly-on-buddleia either; even at bird-weight would be unconvincing. Mrs. Anstruther's entrenching tool was fragile helplessness; but if there was one thing Jimmy knew about herself, it was that she wasn't helpless. Also he'd seen her eat like a horse.

Louisa sighed, for she hated waste. She hated, now, having to jettison all those useful tips picked up under the Bournemouth pines. But as far as she could see, they were about as useful to her present aim as so much old rope.

She was relieved.

Sitting with her head bent towards the electric fire, seventeen hairpins under the net, Louisa recognized with relief that Mrs. Anstruther's tuition wasn't going to be the slightest damn use. She was justified in jettisoning them, all those useful, slightly distasteful tips . . .

Her honesty hadn't been entirely corrupted—in the shade, under the pines; it had only been nibbled at. Eager as she was to get married, and fully confident that Jimmy was the ideal husband for her, when it came to the point Louisa didn't want him trapped.

The electric fire abruptly died. Searching for another shilling—

"He can take as long as he likes," thought Louisa. "We'll still see each other, after I go back!" It would be running a risk; on her native Paddingtonian heath she would undoubtedly lose glamour; but wasn't that only fair to Jimmy too, to let him see her as she really was?

Mentally Louisa dismantled the trap altogether. She wasn't a natural trapper . . .

As things turned out, it seemed that she had no need to be. Lucky Louisa, to find honesty so undetrimental to her prospects! From the very first moment of that evening, it was apparent that the occasion meant as much to Jimmy as it did to herself.

III

The flowers in the vases were tiger lilies. Arranged in saucers on the bamboo coffee table were, besides olives, three kinds of nuts. (Almond, pecan and plain monkey.) There were cocktails ready in a shaker—thus a trifle watery, but properly cold. The table was already laid, with two candles on it. And all these preparations were evidence of something more striking still: that Jimmy for once in his life had come home early.

This wasn't a guess; he told her.

"Miss Lamb got the shock of her life," he added. "However, she's perfectly capable of making an appointment. Perhaps I should do it more often, Louisa?"

"Perhaps you should," said Louisa.

Despite every resolve, it was impossible to help feeling anticipatory. The candles alone—!

Actually the candles were a bit of a failure; they simply didn't give half enough light to eat by, and Jimmy had to switch a lamp on after the soup. (Cold vichyssoise, from a tin; but with chives chopped into it.) The main course was cold salmon, with mayonnaise not out of a bottle; Camembert cheese preceded the sweet: *glace pralinée*. ("Because he had the nuts," thought Louisa affectionately; the little touch of economy-combinded-with-chichi went straight to a heart already, despite every resolve, wifely.)—As though to pull her up, a moth chose that same moment to fly into one of the candles: Louisa somersaulted several images together—Enid not moth but flame, F. Pennon not buddleia but moth—and felt that not for worlds would she see Jimmy fall so singed . . .

"How's the tooth?" asked Louisa.

"Not bad at all," said Jimmy. He'd been eating on one side of his mouth—without complaint.

"Did you have penicillin?"

"I believe so," said Jimmy, vaguely.

It was by his motion, not hers, that for coffee they returned to the sofa by the low bamboo table. As he put out the lamp again, and produced a bottle of brandy, Louisa had even a moment of delightful nervousness, as of one in danger of seduction. "Just a spot," begged Louisa nervously—who with F. Pennon had knocked back glass for glass. However, a spot was all Jimmy poured.

He sat down beside her. Louisa didn't even let her hand lie where his would fall into it. She actually moved a little away.

"What a week it's been!" sighed Jimmy. "I can't tell you, Louisa, how I've enjoyed it!"

"So have I," breathed Louisa. It would have been sheer bad manners not to say so.

"I believe you have," said Jimmy affectionately. "That's because you've such a sweet nature. It must still have seemed a bit like slumming. Whereas for *me*—"

He broke off, searching for words; also regarding her with so exactly the old mixture of diffidence and earnestness, Louisa felt her heart beat.—It had never been used to beat, before that look, in the Free Library, or on the Common; but now she was ten years older.

"I don't know how to put it," continued Jimmy, "but somehow you've . . . pepped everything up for me. I mean, a chap may know he's doing pretty well, isn't exactly an oaf, but he'd like an outside opinion, so to speak; from someone with broader experience. Take the shop, for instance: I suppose if *you* needed glasses you'd go to Wimpole Street—"

"No, I wouldn't," said Louisa. "I'd come to you like a shot—and have bamboo frames."

"There you are: they've been in the window a month, and you're the first person to notice them. You've liked this place too; the Ibsens—for all they read Dylan Thomas!" said Jimmy wryly—"think it's a bit lunatic. *You* come along and back my judgment. Could you live in it yourself, Louisa?"

"Easily," breathed Louisa.

He hesitated.

"You're not just being kind? You mustn't be *too* kind," said Jimmy anxiously. "You wouldn't let me make a fool of myself?"

Louisa paused, but only for a moment.—It was still no trap she sprung! On the contrary, from sheer impulsive generosity she threw away a woman's most precious privilege: that of making the man declare himself first.

"If you asked me, perhaps I *would* live here . . ." breathed Louisa.

IV

They were words to raise him, in one instant, from the depths of faithful yearning to the topmost peak of fulfillment. Louisa's heart beat faster still, as she watched the changing emotions reflected in his face. Incredulity was, naturally, the first; after which came sudden illumination, followed by—plain terror.

Just as F. Pennon had done, the love of a lifetime at last zooming into his lap, Jimmy Brown looked, plainly, terrified.

And just as swiftly as in Gladstone Mansions, Louisa understood. How settled and well-organized the life of each, of F. Pennon the tycoon and Jimmy Brown the Broydon optician! For each certain sentimental memories (of a profile, of long legs and red hair) had sweetened the daily round; before the embodiment of which each, equally, flinched. It was no use F. Pennon's flinching, Enid Anstruther knew her feminine business too well; indeed her last remembered look urged Louisa not to be a damned fool. But Louisa, unlike Mrs. Anstruther, was fond of men.

She understood everything. In a flash, casting her mind back over the past week, she realized that it hadn't been even a last beautiful memory Jimmy wanted. What he wanted was an outside opinion—just like Miss Wilbraham with her silhouettes, and Mr. Wright with his collection of bomb fragments. Jimmy Brown had something more interesting to offer—his struggle towards sophistication; but the principle was the same. He didn't want Louisa to marry him, he just wanted her to give him full marks.

". . . if I hadn't to go back tomorrow!" finished Louisa.

So fast can thought travel (even while the expression changes on a face), the interval was scarcely noticeable. Jimmy's processes were a little slower, the peril he'd glimpsed had been unnerving; another moment passed before he could breathe quite freely; but what a happy breath he drew at last!

"That's the nicest thing you could possibly have said, Louisa. You really like *everything?*"

Now all she had to do was give him his marks.

"I honestly think," pronounced Louisa, "you've made something quite special here. (Why not have another brandy?" she suggested kindly.) "I mean, I've seen all sorts of bachelor quarters—not only in London, in places like Cannes as well—but this is really something special. Like the shop," added Louisa. (Here she had to pause and think; she could hardly make him believe she had a wide experience of opticians'. Fortunately the echo of an earlier remark helped her out.) "Those bamboo frames!" exclaimed Louisa. "I only wish I'd had *them*, at Cannes! D'you know you've grown very sophisticated, Jimmy?"

He glowed.

"It's made me a bit of a rare bird, in Broydon."

"That you must put up with," said Louisa firmly. "D'you know what you should do next? Make the Ibsens read Aristophanes in modern dress.—I mean in modern English," amended Louisa. (Naturally they'd be in modern dress; she was getting a little tired.) She paused; really she couldn't think of anything else. "And now as I *have* to go back tomorrow, it's time I went and packed," said Louisa, rising. "And so as this is good-by, Jimmy, you can give me a kiss."

It was their first, it was their last. Jimmy Brown put everything he knew into it; but what Louisa chiefly recognized was gratitude.

V

Awaiting her at Broydon Court she unexpectedly found a telegram. Louisa was almost too tired, and too downhearted, to open it; but an orange envelope demands to be slit.

ARRIVED SAFELY ALL WELL ALL THANK YOU STOP CONSIDER YOURSELF GOOD ANGEL ENID PERFECTLY COOPERATIVE LOVE FROM ALL AT BOURNEMOUTH FREDDY.

Louisa screwed it up and tossed it into the paper-basket.

She unloaded her camera. In the preoccupations of the day, she had omitted to do this earlier; now she discovered another omission. She had forgotten to put any film in. Accustomed to making play, under the eye of Mrs. Brent, with blank shot, then preoccupied with thoughts of Jimmy Brown, Louisa had labored all morning with her camera empty. Ivor and Ivan might indeed have leaped to the firmament—but unrecorded.

PART THREE

Chapter Sixteen

I

"So you've bin away again," said the milkman. "What was it like this time?"

"Disappointing," said Louisa; and shut the door.

She turned on a tap, filled the kettle, lit the gas, laid the table and reached down the coffee tin, all without moving her feet. Never before had she felt cramped, in her kitchenette-dinette; but after the gay, light spaciousness of Freddy's villa, after the gloomy but spacious dining room at Broydon Court, she felt cramped.

In the distraction, a week before, of peddling Number Ten's beech-nuts, she'd evidently forgotten to empty the sink basket. It smelt. She looked about for a paper bag. After a week—two weeks—without shopping, there wasn't one. Louisa found an old newspaper instead. Tea leaves and a stalk of spring onion leaked from the untidy parcel; it would still have to do, until she dressed and went down to the dustbins.

The kettle boiling, she made coffee and sat down. The striped oilcloth covering the table was still fairly clean, there was still an adequate supply of paper napkins advertising cider. No china had been broken in her absence—no one, during her absence, had come in to clean. Which was probably why the whole divan-bedroom-bathroom-et-cetera set-up looked so tatty . . .

She might have been a good angel to old Freddy, and a good angel to the Admiral, but if what she now sat down to was a good angel's normal breakfast, Louisa felt she'd been gypped.

In any case, she hadn't wanted a halo, what she'd wanted was a wedding ring.—The image of Admiral Colley sporting at Bournemouth was irritating enough, but before the image of Enid Anstruther in very pale blue Louisa could have wept with disappointment. For hadn't everything started so hopefully? Hadn't Jimmy been truly rejoiced to see her?—"And wasn't I made a fool of?" thought Louisa bitterly.

It was noticeable that she gave scarcely a thought to her disappointment over Ivor and Ivan. Rewarding though that final shot should have been, Louisa merely reflected that at least she had enough straights to keep Mrs. Brent from suing her. She wasn't interested in dogs any more, she was interested in husbands . . .

"Some women get three or four," thought Louisa enviously. "They must go in runs . . ."

She had in fact hit on a profound truth, and might have elaborated it: runs of the same suit.—It has often been observed, for example, that if a woman begins by marrying a millionaire, millionaires are what she will continue to marry, they have a great sense of solidarity, they won't let poor Nelly starve. Less fortunate women fall upon runs of invalids, or ne'er-do-wells, or plain crooks. Louisa, less fortunate still, seemed to have begun with Jimmy Brown upon a run of non-starters.

II

To make the next few days peculiarly trying, all the emotions she'd felt on returning husbandless from Bournemouth, now that she returned husbandless from Broydon, were doubled. It was absurd, and with one part of her brain Louisa recognized it, that she couldn't bear to encounter Rossy or Hugo Pym without either a square-cut emerald (F. Pennon) or a neat half-hoop (Jimmy Brown) on the appropriate finger; but so it was. Once again Louisa avoided her usual haunts; almost surreptitiously developed and printed the straights of Ivor and Ivan (and didn't dare send an order form with them); and when Hugo telephoned, hung up without answering.

Number Ten resumed his pleasant custom of a rhythmic aubade; Louisa didn't answer Number Ten either.

It was a strange, do-nothing, will-less period altogether, quite unlike any other in Louisa's life. By great good fortune, a firm of greeting-card publishers sent her a check for ten guineas: Louisa, reading the caption on the docket—"Bow-wows to Baby!"—didn't so much as check her files to see whether the bow-wow had been a poodle or a chow-chow. She should have been encouraged, she should immediately have set about borrowing a Kerseymere dachshund to pose for Greetings to Grandma; instead, she just cashed the check. She'd lost interest, in dogs.

She was just waiting for a run to break.

III

"You're losin' weight again," observed the milkman.

"Tell me something I don't know," said Louisa.

"Broodin' too much on Ibsen, p'raps?" suggested the milkman.

"Actually it's a name I never want to hear again," said Louisa.

He looked at her thoughtfully.—All milkmen know a great deal more about their customers than they let on: admire a bright young housewife's new washing machine while well aware that the new telly isn't paid for either, unblinkingly continue to deliver yoghurt for husbands missing but hoped back soon. It is a profession that calls for any amount of tact.

"Be that as it may," said the milkman, "you know what I b'lieve Ibsen'd do in your place?"

"No," said Louisa.

"He'd baby-sit."

"Sometimes I can't make up my mind," said Louisa, "whether you're trying to be funny or genuinely cracked."

"You do both me and His Whiskers an injustice," said the milkman. "What's wrong with three and six an hour, for nothing but watching the telly and eating supper?"

Louisa hesitated. She hadn't entirely gone to pieces, under disappointment. Her general indifference didn't extend to food, especially if free.

"You mean supper's thrown in?"

"Certainly it is," said the milkman. "Likewise char later on. Besides bringing tears of gratitude to the eyes of some pore distressed young wife and mother wishing to go out on the tiles."

"It's a sad picture all right," agreed Louisa.

"Such as Mrs. P., fr'instance," continued the milkman thoughtfully. "'Oh, milkman,' she cries (not half an hour ago; String Street) 'don't *you* know of anyone to help us out this evening?' She's that sort, see; won't have anyone not personally recommended. (And rightly, considering it's twins age four just like little angels.) 'No name occurs at the moment,' I told her, 'but if one should, in the course of the day, I'll get 'em to give you a tinkle.' 'Oh *do!*' cries she—"

"Look," said Louisa, "I know you're enjoying this, but you needn't go on. Just tell me the number."

Both money and meal would be welcome; the necessary concomitant of solitude was positively attractive. To sit alone and brood, though not on Ibsen, exactly suited Louisa's current mood.

IV

Unusually, however, as she rang the Peels' bell, Louisa was slightly nervous. She had no experience of baby-sitting.—She had no experience of children at all; moreover, during the course of the day,

try as she would to keep her mind on infancy's sweeter aspects—
"Where did you come from, baby dear?"—she kept remembering
far different lines from the Lays of Ancient Rome—"No child but
screamed out curses/And shook its little fist."

Nothing could have been more reassuring, however, than her
immediate reception. Louisa's first glance was naturally for the supper tray: there appeared to be at least a pound of ham on it, besides
trimmings—and the young Peels themselves welcomed her with
happy enthusiasm. They were in evening dress, they had already the
aura of celebration about them; she dark and pretty, he ugly and
engaging, the young Peels almost took Louisa into their arms, so
glad they were to see her.

"Miss Datchett? How good and kind of you!" cried Mrs. Peel.

"God bless our milkman," agreed her husband warmly.

"Because if we couldn't have found anyone in time—! There's
your supper, there's the television," exclaimed Mrs. Peel rapidly, "and
lots of books if you'd rather read, and of course the children are in
bed but we'll go and wake them up."

To Louisa this seemed a rash proposal indeed; why not let sleeping dogs lie? But Mrs. Peel—in a rustle of silk skirts, on a patter
of silver slippers—had run her into the nursery before she could
protest, and then Louisa saw the point. Switching on more candle-
power than the night lights afforded—

"Darlings," cried Mrs. Peel briskly, "this is the lady who's come to
keep house, just like the other ladies do, while Daddy and I go out.
Take a good look at her, so that if you wake up and she comes in you
won't be surprised."

Two infants, each in its cot, sat up and stared gravely.

"Hi," said Louisa—not quite sure of the right address. It seemed
acceptable enough, however; at least neither screamed out curses,
nor shook its little fist.

"She's got red hair," pointed out their mother. "(You don't mind,
Miss Datchett? It gives them a *clue*.) You'll see her nice red hair, and
remember she's the lady here to take care of you."

The children stared again, and accepted the situation with phlegm. Mrs. Peel embraced each in turn, popped each in turn under its covers with the offhand, expert gesture of a gardener bedding a bulb, switched off the lights again, and that was that. Evidently the Peels were a thoroughly well-adjusted family.

"I'll leave the door ajar," said Mrs. Peel, as she raced Louisa back to the sitting room, "and if you *do* hear anything, you might just look in. And if you should by any chance need to get in touch with us—"

"If the house catches fire!" said her husband affectionately.

"—you can phone us at the Savoy. We'll be in the River Room."

"Suppose anyone phones here?" asked Louisa.

"No one will," said Mrs. Peel confidently. "Everyone knows we're *always* out, on our anniversary!"

So that was it, thought Louisa: the reason for the evening dress and the River Room at the Savoy, and the general air of happy celebration. It was the Peels' wedding anniversary.

V

No circumstance could have afforded better food for brooding, but first things first; Louisa sat down to the supper tray. She was uncommonly hungry; she left a last slice of ham (disposed to cover as much of the dish as possible) purely for manners. Of the salad she left half a tomato, and of the long French loaf about four inches.

It must be admitted that the beauty and poetry of family life, by which Louisa was so soon and so forcibly to be struck, would have lost half its impact on an empty stomach. So square a meal left her unusually receptive to wholesome influences.

As she tiptoed through the nursery door (no stirring within had summoned her, Louisa was just being conscientious), the night-light-illumined room swam poetically before her gaze. The two small beds made blurs of whiteness like water lilies on a lake— within each its precious, golden-headed heart. There was the loving humor of poetry there too: a frieze of small stuffed animals, zebra and bear and panda, ranged in loving, humorous, nursery-rhyme order on the window seat . . .

Where Mrs. Peel no doubt sat to read fairy tales.

"Perhaps that's what does it," thought Louisa vaguely—envisaging Mrs. Peel, after at least five years of matrimony, silver-slippered and satin-skirted to celebrate an anniversary. "Not just having a husband, having a family as well . . ."

Thoughtfully she returned to the sitting room, and for the first time noted a dozen or more photographs, several silver-framed, displayed on desk and mantelshelf. She hadn't noticed them before because none were of dogs: they showed mostly the Peel infants from nappy stage onwards. But beside holiday snaps of their parents—and, yes, a wedding group!—stood as well, in the silver frames, photographs obviously of grandparents. "Something's been happening," thought Louisa. "While I've been nannying Hugo, and all the rest of that Bohemian bunch, something's been going on . . ."

Could it be that family life had made a comeback?

Could it be that what she really needed was a *family* man?

When she considered Mrs. Peel again, Louisa was sure of it.

"Only I'll have to find one soon," reflected Louisa uneasily. "As it is I'll be about fifty, before we've teen-agers . . ."

She pulled herself up. Temporarily at least she was a family's custodian, it was no time for dreams but a time to be alert and competent—apt to rout burglars, put out fires, or, alternatively, dash through smoke with an infant under each arm. Louisa in her new enthusiasm felt capable of any one of these acts—if possible would have made a shot at all three simultaneously. In fact, having nothing more to do than sit in a comfortable chair and watch television, Louisa felt slightly wasted. But she consoled herself with the knowledge that at least she brought peace of mind to affectionate parents out on the tiles.

—On second thoughts, she switched the sound off: in case she heard—or rather didn't hear—a noise. The resulting dumb-show was so eerie, she switched that off too; and on the blank screen instantly visualized a cigarette-end smoldering in a paper-basket, a man with his hat pulled over his eyes peering in at a window . . .

"Nonsense," Louisa adjured herself practically. "Isn't this the fourth floor?"

Also she hadn't been smoking. Nor had the Peels.

If it was probably mere prudence to turn off the television, there was no reason why she shouldn't read. Louisa selected from the crowded shelves what looked like a promising detective story, and put her feet up. It opened, the detective story, promisingly again, with an unexpected ring at a door.—The author would have been really gratified to see Louisa jump, as at that moment the flat door-bell rang too.

Chapter Seventeen

I

It rang again. Louisa hadn't moved. A ready and vivid imagination carries its penalties.

At the third ring she tiptoed into the lobby and listened. There was no sound of voices outside, no pleasant visitorish chatter. (Weren't the Peels *known* to be out?) Also there was no chain on the door. Belatedly telling herself not to be a fool, however, Louisa cautiously opened up.

On the mat stood a solitary man with his hat pulled over his eyes.

Obviously it was nothing in his favor, quite the contrary, that the sight of Louisa seemed to surprise him as much as he surprised Louisa.

"I thought there was no one in," said the man.

"Oh, you did, did you?" said Louisa menacingly.

"When there wasn't an answer. My name is Clark."

He gave it with some confidence, as though expecting it to be recognized; but this might have been just cunning, and Louisa stood her ground—not opening the door another inch.

"Mr. Peel's publisher," elaborated the man. "I've come for some corrected proofs. Ten days ago he assured me they were ready, my secretary has telephoned him constantly and fruitlessly since, now I have come to pick them up myself. Is he in?"

"No," admitted Louisa.

"Are you his secretary? Can *you* give them me?"

Louisa shook her head.

"They are probably lying somewhere ready to hand. If I might come in and see—"

By this time he had taken off his hat. The countenance revealed was middle-aged, kindly and conscientious. Certainly he didn't look like a burglar—but then what really dangerous burglar would? Louisa had no intention of reviving an hour later to find herself gagged and bound. Yet suppose he were speaking the truth? What if by offending him she did the Peels irreparable harm? In Louisa's world, publishers were practically father figures . . .

"Look," said Louisa, making up her mind, "actually I'm baby-sitting. Will you wait outside while I phone?"

To her surprise, his expression became positively approving. He stepped back of his own accord. Louisa shut the door and flew to the telephone already half-suspicious that she'd made a fool of herself indeed—but even so she would still need to get in touch with her employer, to ask where he'd put the proofs.—"If there are any!" thought Louisa, wavering again; for during the three or four minutes it took to locate him, look about as she might, at desk and table and the tops of bookshelves, certainly no bundle of galleys lay ready to hand.

"Miss Datchett? Is anything wrong?" called Henry Peel.—Evidently his wife had come to the phone with him. "Nothing's wrong with the children?" called Henry Peel.

"No, sound asleep," reassured Louisa swiftly. ("No, sound asleep," she heard him reassure in turn.) "Only there's a man here who says he's a Mr. Clark."

On an entirely different note—

"Oh, *Lord!*" groaned Henry Peel.

"Who says he ought to have had some proofs back from you ten days ago and now where are they because he's come to pick them up," finished Louisa, now quite confidently.

"Oh, *Lord!*" groaned Henry Peel again.

"It's no use groaning," said Louisa practically. "Tell me what I'm to do."

"Give him a drink."

"Can't I give him the proofs too?"

"No, because they aren't done," returned Henry Peel. "Just give him a drink and calm him down. I leave the matter entirely," said Mr. Peel blithely, "in your hands . . ."

For a moment, beside the silent telephone, Louisa paused to ask herself how they knew. How did men *know*, the moment they set eyes on her, that they could dump their problems in her lap? Couldn't she even baby-sit without having to calm publishers? Bitter indeed were the thoughts Louisa directed upon Henry Peel—now doubtless waltzing carefree round the River Room! From old habit, however, she did her best for him.

"Mr. Peel couldn't apoligize more," said Louisa, opening up again. "He's actually had a terribly punishing week, what with his mother-in-law's operation and the children's teeth. Now he asks me to apologize most sincerely, and says the proofs will be with you tomorrow, and he hopes you'll come in all the same for a drink."

Mr. Clark—indubitably Mr. Clark!—entered. Louisa took a better look at him. Why he pulled his hat over his eyes was explained by a slight baldness he was probably a trifle self-conscious about; the hair brushed back from either temple was still quite dark however, and very neatly barbered. His exceptionally well-shaven jaw was exceptionally firm, but his eyes, though shrewd, were also benevolent. Under his light spring overcoat he wore a dinner jacket. In short, Louisa at once recognized such worth and respectability, she felt impelled to apologize on her own account as well.

"I'd two children in my charge," explained Louisa, "and I'm all alone here.—Would you like a whiskey?"

"Thank you, a weak one," said Mr. Clark. "To my mind," he added kindly, "your reaction was altogether praiseworthy."

II

They got on like—a house afire.

The unusualness of the situation, the lateness of the hour, put Mr. Clark into such a pleasantly communicative mood, Louisa had little to do but listen.—She early formed the opinion that such an act as his descent on the Peels' flat was for him unusual indeed. "I shan't have been home so late in years," confided Mr. Clark. "Generally, after a typographers' dinner, I go straight back. But finding myself so near-by, and being I must say rather annoyed—"

"I don't wonder!" said Louisa warmly.

"—I took the step. But of course I've telephoned. My family won't worry," said Mr. Clark.

Everything he told Louisa, in fact, pointed to a life of beautiful regularity. Even his publishing business, it seemed, knew no ups and downs, being devoted to textbooks for schools. (Demands as accurately foreseen as punctually supplied, from Algebra through Zoology: the series being held up by Henry Peel covered Aeschylus to Zeno—which made the matter of proofreading all the more ticklish.) Half an hour passed before Louisa grew the least restive, and then only because she herself wanted to show off as a baby-sitter.

Admirable young Peels!—hitherto no sound had come from the nursery at all. But that didn't stymie Louisa. As Mr. Clark paused between the second and third editions of a Latin grammar—

"Hark!" said Louisa. "I believe I should take a peep at the little ones . . ."

It was remarkable how readily the phrase came to her; as though together with dormant family instincts she was discovering a dormant family vocabulary. And just as she'd intended—

"May I come too?" asked Mr. Clark. "I know, of course, the Peels have children, but I've never seen them. With three of my own," he added pleasantly, "I count myself a bit of an expert!"

Thus put on her mettle, Louisa stole noiselessly through the nursery door; efficiently, like an old hand, checked the night lights. (She'd have pricked down the wicks if she'd known how—dormant vocabulary again!—but in any case they looked okay.) Both young Peels appeared to be sleeping soundly; Louisa rapidly decided which was sleeping sounder, and bent over its cot in what she hoped was a becoming yet efficient attitude. The unconscious infant cooperated by remaining so; Louisa risked a maternal smoothing of the pillow.

"One can see you're fond of children," observed Mr. Clark.

"Hush!" said Louisa.—"Indeed I am," she added, stealing out again. She mightn't have been until a couple of hours ago, but she was now. She wasn't foxing.

"I don't wonder Mrs. Peel feels she can trust you," said Mr. Clark, stealing out behind.

"Actually it was the milkman—" began Louisa; and for once in her own interests held her tongue. What did it matter, that Mrs. Peel had never before that evening set eyes on her? Louisa would still have rushed through flame with the Peel infants; would still have attempted to crown Mr. Clark with a paperweight, had he been indeed the criminal of her imagination. Why not, for once, take the credit and let the explanations go? For once, Louisa did. As they stole back to the sitting room, and settled themselves comfortably again over Mr. Clark's half-finished whiskey—Louisa hoped he noticed she wasn't drinking anything herself—she simply basked in his approval without a word about the milkman. Instead she merely remarked, in a modest sort of way, that perhaps she *was* rather good with children . . .

"Mine are somewhat older," observed Mr. Clark.

"Have you their photographs?" asked Louisa eagerly.

With the pleasantly conscious smile of a fond parent who knows his weakness, Mr. Clark nodded.

"May I see?" begged Louisa.

He produced his wallet and extracted a sizable snapshot. Louisa received it with reverence.

"Catherine, Toby and Paul," said Mr. Clark. He paused; his expression grew melancholy. "Toby doesn't remember his mother at all, and the others scarcely more. They're all I have left," stated Mr. Clark sadly: "the children."

Louisa looked, she gazed. For there upon those few square inches was pictured the family of her new dream—*ready-made*.

III

They were rather older than from their father's tone she would have expected: two boys and a girl apparently in their later teens. (Just the ages she'd have chosen!) The girl stood tall and slim between her stockier brothers; otherwise little could be discovered of their looks—save by reflection from their father's face. Mr. Clark evidently thought them the world's wonders.

"And no mother!" sighed Louisa.

Sadly he nodded.

"I do my best to make them a home. But it isn't easy."

"Especially with a daughter."

"As to that, Cathy's a real father's girl," said Mr. Clark, whimsically. "They're all three very good children indeed."

"One can tell they are."

"But as I say, it isn't easy. Though Catherine is at home, the full burden of a household is too much for young shoulders."

"Indeed it is!" agreed Louisa warmly.

"And besides she has her own amusements. When the boys come in—they attend an excellent local grammar school—I'm afraid they all too often find an empty house."

"But that's terrible!" cried Louisa.

"Not that we haven't very competent daily help. When I say empty, I mean empty of any affectionate welcome, such as children have a right to expect. Even the most competent daily cannot make a house a home."

"That's one of the truest things I've ever heard," said Louisa.

"Friends have advised me to engage a resident housekeeper," mused Mr. Clark, "but there again difficulties present themselves. The truth is, Miss—"

He broke off to fix Louisa in surprise.

"Here I am telling you all my troubles," marveled Mr. Clark, "without even knowing your name!"

The circumstance was less extraordinary than he imagined it; its only unusualness lay in the fact that Mr. Clark's were troubles Louisa wanted to hear much more of. Hastily, not to break the thread, she said Louisa Datchett.

"The truth is, Miss Datchett, we need someone rather exceptional," continued Mr. Clark—and broke off again. Again he fixed Louisa; not this time in surprise, but with the expression of one upon whom an idea suddenly dawns. Possibly it was a surprising idea at that—at least to him.

"Someone to make a house a home?" prompted Louisa.

"Exactly. Someone with both a genuine love of children—or young people—and a genuine sense of responsibility. (Such as you showed yourself," added Mr. Clark, with a pleasant touch of humor, "when you made me wait outside!—Joking apart, that struck me very much; it did indeed.) But our essential want is for a person who could become so to speak one of the family—which without wishing to sound snobbish implies certain standards of education, and interests. How do I put all *that* to an employment agency, or into an advertisement? I admit it," confessed Mr. Clark, "I admit that I am baffled!"

A slight silence fell, and no wonder. Mr. Clark had probably never confessed himself baffled before. But from the mantelshelf the

Peel clock ticked peaceably, and from either side of it a Peel grand-
parent gazed benevolently down.—How glad Louisa was that she
hadn't met Mr. Clark in an espresso bar! Here every object breathed
of that cordial family life he so pathetically yearned after.

The benevolent influences did their work.

"This is going to surprise you," said Mr. Clark abruptly, "but
could I possibly persuade you, yourself, to come and give us a try?
Just for a week, say?"

Louisa, while her heart leaped, looked as surprised as she could.
She only wished he hadn't suggested a week. It was a period that had
lately been unlucky to her. Her hesitation did her no harm, however,
since Mr. Clark misinterpreted it.

"Naturally you'll want references—"

"Indeed I don't!" protested Louisa.

"You do—and rightly," corrected Mr. Clark. "I wouldn't wish it
otherwise. However your friends the Peels will I dare say vouch for
me. As to remuneration—"

"Wait," said Louisa.

For it was a moment to reflect. Louisa reflected. The photographed images of Catherine and Toby and Paul still lay in her lap—
the ready-made family of her new dream. Louisa dropped a loving
glance on them.—Loving already! Already Louisa's heart opened, to
Catherine and Toby and Paul. She had no doubts on their account,
she was prepared to do her damnedest to make them happy. But
that she was also prepared to marry their father by this time went
without saying, and in the circumstances she wanted to keep remuneration out of it.

"D'you know what I'd like best?" said Louisa at last. "I'd like to
come just as—well, just as a friend of the family. For. a week or perhaps more or less, just as it turns out. Then if we find we all get on
together, can't everything else be settled afterwards?"

"That's very generous of you," said Mr. Clark appreciatively.
"Perhaps you might have a word with your friends the Peels this
evening?"

It seemed that his eagerness to begin the experiment almost matched Louisa's. Before he left, it was agreed that if the Peels' account of him proved satisfactory he should drive Louisa home with him to Wendover after office hours next day.

IV

"Darling Miss Datchett, are we terribly, terribly late?" cried Mrs. Peel, at about two in the morning. "But we've kept the taxi for you—Henry, do look after Miss Datchett!—and were the children good?"

"Absolute angels," said Louisa warmly.

"How did you get on with old Clark?" asked Henry Peel, pressing paper into Louisa's palm. "Did you calm him down?"

"Well, I had to tell him he'd have those proofs tomorrow—"

"Oh, *Lord!*"

"—but I think he left," said Louisa, "quite happy."

And that was all she did say. She didn't want to rouse any scruples, in Mrs. Peel's maternal breast; Mrs. Peel might feel bound to telephone Mr. Clark and explain how very slightly her baby-sitter was in fact known to her. As for Mr. Clark himself, Louisa felt she could safely take him on trust.

Like a gambler who sees rouge turn up after noir, like an Arab watching rain fall after drought, she felt that a run had broken at last.

Chapter Eighteen

I

Louisa was no more superstitious than the next woman, but a benevolent star having at last directed its rays upon her, she was particularly careful, next morning, not to walk under any ladders. Indeed, her first impulse on waking had been to stay safely in bed until it was time to go and meet Mr. Clark; however she needed several articles of toilet, and there was a chemist's on the same side of the street (which reduced the risk of getting run over). It was manifestly impossible to refrain from any physical action at all; mentally and emotionally, though, Louisa determined to exclude every distraction, and just direct grateful thoughts upon her star, also encouraging telepathy towards Mr. Clark.

Thus only ineradicable habit led her to pick up a free lunch from—of all people—Mr. McAndrew.

She was just returning with her purchases, shortly after midday, when she observed him standing on the pavement immediately opposite her front door.—Or rather she didn't observe him, she bumped into him. She was rehearsing conversation with Mr. Clark. Fortunately the architect's substantial form made a good buffer; Louisa in full stride merely bounced off. (Number Ten she might have bowled clean over. Or Freddy.) "I'm so sorry, I beg your pardon—" began Louisa; and only then saw who it was.

"If you don't watch out, you'll be falling over your own feet," said Mr. McAndrew severely, "let alone losing all your wee parcels. It's to be hoped none's fragile."

"Not at all," said Louisa—saving a bottle of skin lotion just in time. Naturally she wondered what he was doing there, no stately home within miles; more pressingly, what did he think *she*was? Recalling the build-up she'd given herself at Broydon Court, Louisa would greatly have preferred to be encountered in Bond Street, or Park Lane; the peeling paint of her too adjacent door, let alone six dustbins in the area, struck a wrong note. "This is my favorite shopping district—away from the crowds," explained Louisa lightly. "I imagined you lived here," said Mr. McAndrew, checking the house number, "that is, according to the phone book." "My *pied-à-terre*," Louisa told him.—She could have wrung Number Ten's neck for creeping out just at that moment, in a tattered dressing gown, to empty tea leaves into one of the bins. He peered up through the area railings and tactlessly coo-ooed the first notes of a Brandenburg Concerto; Louisa felt almost a liking for Mr. McAndrew, as the latter took no notice.

"The fact is," said Mr. McAndrew, "I happen to be lunching in town; I thought you might join me."

This was where old habit came in. Ninety per cent of Louisa's mind might be fixed on her ready-made family, but the odd ten was still in a rut.

"Where?" asked Louisa uncontrollably.

"I had thought of Stack's in the Strand."

The mention of this world-famous chop-house settled it. Louisa had never fed at Stack's before—though she'd often wanted to: Stack's had the reputation, now almost historic, of providing second helpings gratis to any client capable of tackling one. However, she consulted her engagement book.

"Thank you, I believe I can," said Louisa, surprised.

"Then that's my car parked opposite," said Mr. McAndrew.

II

He was undoubtedly competent. If she hadn't been so preoccupied, Louisa could almost have enjoyed being taken out by him; regarded merely as a meal ticket, he was a very good one. At Stack's in the Strand he was recognized by both hat-check girl and head waiter; the latter immediately ushered them to a first-rate table. Seen at close quarters, moreover, across the starched white cloth, Mr. McAndrew proved better-looking than Louisa remembered him. (His sheer bulk was of course familiar: what she hadn't before appreciated was the really excellent shape of his skull. Also his sandy eyebrows, like his sandy head, showed quite noticeable tinges of russet.) But during the car drive Louisa had once more become a prey to superstitious fears, and was more than ever determined not to let her thoughts stray. Thus while McAndrew talked about restoring stately homes, Louisa, though preserving every appearance of attention, concentrated on Mr. Clark. She was so used to men, she could do this quite easily; put in just sufficient words to keep the flow going—such as, "But where did you find the right stone?" or, "What about the staircase?"—and in fact gave Mr. McAndrew a very fair opinion of her intelligence. Only over the saddle of lamb did she fall really silent, because she wanted to empty her plate in good time.

"Apple tart?" suggested the waiter.

"Thank you, I'll have a second helping," said Louisa boldly.

His look was genuinely admiring—also regretful.

"I'm sorry, madam; but not since the last war . . ."

Louisa's face fell.

"Are you quite certain?"

"The '14 war, madam . . ."

"Then just serve madam again," said Mr. McAndrew.

Louisa had to admit it was big of him. Not all men would have come up to scratch. Though she refused, she was appreciative. "Really it was just because I'd heard about it," explained Louisa, "and besides I don't often get the chance—" Here she broke off; what she'd been going to say was, "of a square meal," but just in time recognized this as much a wrong note as six dustbins in an area. Also it was no longer true; she foresaw the table presided over by Mr. Clark spread regularly with square meals. "—Of carrying on a tradition," finished Louisa. For the first time, however, she gave Mr. McAndrew a more than absent, indeed a grateful smile.

"I recall your appetite from the Court," observed Mr. McAndrew reflectively.

The smile faded. Any reference to Broydon Court still acted on Louisa's nerves like a dentist's drill on a sentient tooth.

"You left very unexpectedly," added Mr. McAndrew. "I was surprised."

You weren't the only one! thought Louisa—not bothering to examine his meaning. The recollection of how surprised she'd been herself, and how painfully, on that last evening spent in the company of Jimmy Brown, flooded back with almost unendurable poignancy. It didn't matter, now that she had Mr. Clark in view; but Louisa's affections, however easily rooted, were never just mustard and cress. During that week at Broydon she had become so truly fond of Jimmy, even the prospect of a ready-made family couldn't quite obliterate all regrets . . .

Happier thoughts of Mr. Clark notwithstanding, her appetite was quite cut. All she wanted now was to get away as soon as possible.—Attacking apple tart (merely because it was placed before her), she became dumb altogether; so did Mr. McAndrew. From time to time he looked at her thoughtfully, as though he had something on his mind; but Louisa had too much on her own to pay attention . . .

Such a silence might have been companionable, even cordial. For all her preoccupation, Louisa vaguely acknowledged it. She hadn't yet begun positively to dislike Mr. McAndrew again. There was indeed something in his quiet, trustable demeanor (as they scoffed down apple tart together) that made her almost forgive him his crime of having breathed the same air as Jimmy Brown, and if he'd had the wit to stay quiet they might have ended in amity. Unfortunately, a Scot with something on his mind is impervious to emotional climate.

"Who was yon old ruffian with the big car?" demanded Mr. McAndrew abruptly.

Louisa actually lowered a forkful untouched.

"If you mean Freddy—" she began indignantly.

"I mean he who drenched a decent hotel in champagne," stated Mr. McAndrew—in less than grateful tones.

"Didn't you have any yourself?" retorted Louisa.

"You mayn't have noticed, but I did not," said Mr. McAndrew. "What small amount of whiskey I consumed, in the course of the evening, I saw put down to my own bill."

"How very silly," said Louisa. "Will you tell me what we're arguing about?"

"Nothing at all," said Mr. McAndrew, "I hope. I merely inquired, in a perfectly friendly way, whether this Freddy—"

"F. Pennon."

"—whether this F. Pennon, apart from being old enough for your grandfather, happened to be a special, well, crony. I see now it may have been a misplaced question."

"Very," agreed Louisa, unplacated.—The term "crony" offended her particularly: it suggested—her imagination was always vivid—a couple of old-age pensioners sharing yesterday's newspaper on a park bench. How different indeed, what Freddy had offered! Louisa would have liked to go into this rather fully—beginning with the point that the car was a Rolls, sketching the villa at Bournemouth, referring back perhaps to junketings at Cannes; but she was even more anxious to disassociate herself from the first picture, even though it probably existed only in her own mind, and even though it meant rather *jettisoning* Freddy. (Her affection for him too no mere mustard and cress, but there are moments when pride prevails.) As it were putting the length of the bench between them—

"If you must know," said Louisa, "he's going to marry a friend of mine."

"Ah!" said Mr. McAndrew.

"A middle-aged widow," added Louisa—taking a swipe at Enid on the side. "Have you any more . . . misplaced . . . questions? Because if not, though I've enjoyed my lunch *enormously*, I've a rather important engagement for this afternoon."

Naturally she got no reply. She didn't expect one. Just as effectively as at Broydon Court, Mr. McAndrew was slammed down again. While he was checking the bill, moreover, Louisa managed to transmit, through her friend the waiter, so urgent a message to the doorman, there was a taxi waiting for her at the curb as they emerged. (Probably five shillings back to Paddington, but well worth it. "Cannot I drive you?" suggested Mr. McAndrew. "Thanks, I think this is mine," said Louisa—slamming him down again.) For so large a man Mr. McAndrew looked almost disconsolate, as Louisa abandoned him on the pavement outside Stack's in the Strand.

She wouldn't have been able to abandon F. Pennon so, at Gladstone Mansions—Enid or no Enid. At Gladstone Mansions, if she hadn't discovered the picking of Enid's brains an excuse, she'd undoubtedly have discovered some other, for not abandoning old Freddy. Since then, she'd learned sense. Not only did she abandon Mr. McAndrew (on the pavement, outside Stack's in the Strand), she immediately put him out of mind.

During what remained of the afternoon Louisa put Jimmy Brown out of mind too—along with Hugo Pym, Number Ten and even F. Pennon. It was a tour de force, but Louisa's subconscious achieved it, releasing her unhampered by past emotions to concentrate on Mr. Clark.

III

Their rendezvous was for five-thirty; Louisa was so afraid of being late, five-fifteen saw her lurking outside his office, weighed down by air-line giveaway bags, waiting for the nearest church clock to chime the half-hour. No less prompt was Mr. Clark however; as Louisa entered (on the dot), he emerged from the lift before she had time to summon it.

"My dear Miss Datchett," exclaimed Mr. Clark warmly, "what admirable punctuality!—May we perceive," he added shyly, "a good omen?"

Earnestly Louisa hoped so; but in fact recognized a good omen already, in his mere recollection of her. More than once, in the course of her career, had she been disconcerted by an overnight act of oblivion—had turned up for a film test, for example, to find all trace of the project washed by slumber from her sponsor's mind; and it may now be admitted (it was the first time Louisa admitted it herself, so painful the possibilities) that half her day-long anxiousness had been centered on this very point. Mr. Clark plainly remembered not only who she was, but also, so to speak, *why* she was; and Louisa regarded him with such open gratitude and admiration, the modest man looked quite surprised—though by no means displeased.

"I only hope you'll like the house," said Mr. Clark.

"I'm sure I shall!" said Louisa.

"And the children," added Mr. Clark. "I hope you'll take to *them . . .*"

"I'm sure I shall!" repeated Louisa.

"That they'll take to you I've no doubt," said Mr. Clark, confidently. "If that's all your baggage, shall we be on our way?"

Chapter Nineteen

I

The house was called Glenarvon.

It was a family house.—So estate agents, nine bedrooms on their hands, advertise a decaying vicarage; or failed private school; or any other interesting property needing repair. Glenarvon, though mid-Victorian, as kept up by Mr. Clark was so to speak the platonic ideal of their imaginings, and could probably have changed hands at seven thousand cash without a nail driven into a wall.

Mr. Clark led Louisa systematically over the entire ample accommodation. (None of the children were in, and however eager to meet them Louisa wasn't altogether sorry; the house was quite enough for her as a start.) With every step, her enthusiasm grew. There was a dining room and a drawing room and a morning room. There was a study—though Mr. Clark refused to dignify it by the name. "Just where I do a little extra breadwinning at night!" explained the modest man. Louisa peeped over his shoulder respectfully. There was a kitchen slightly larger than the whole of Louisa's flat—actually with a servant in it preparing dinner. Louisa was struck afresh; much more so than she'd been by anything at F. Pennon's. The Pines, in essence, was a small-scale luxury hotel, where one expected to find staff; to find a staff of even one, in a family house like Glenarvon, was far more remarkable . . .

"Mrs. Temple," introduced Mr. Clark casually. "Mrs. Temple, this is the Miss Datchett I mentioned to you at breakfast."

Just like the old family servant Louisa cast her for, Mrs. Temple darted a suspicious glance. "We'll see about that later!" thought Louisa, confidently.

Only at the doors of the children's bedrooms did she hang back a moment. "You're sure they wouldn't *mind*—?" began Louisa. "Dear me, no!" said Mr. Clark. "It will fall to your lot, I'm afraid, to try and keep them a little tidy . . . This is Cathy's."

Thus encouraged, Louisa looked inside; and beheld flowery, rosy paper, flowery, rosy chintz, a dressing table petticoated like a dancer, a thick white sheepskin rug—the bedroom of a young girl's dreams. That it was also indeed untidy gave her nothing but pleasure. How she would enjoy, if not making Catherine tidy, tidying *for* her!—The boys' rooms offered equal scope; both, just as boys' rooms should be, littered with fragments of ironmongery. Louisa wasn't quite sure how one got out oil stains, but she'd have a damn good try . . .

"Mrs. Temple," explained Mr. Clark fairly, "simply comes in to cook; also once a week performs what she calls a 'going over.' I'm told we're fortunate—but you see how much such a person as yourself is needed, to make us *pull our socks up!* Now shall we take a look at the garden?"

The garden was as spacious as the house. The front part had only a gravel drive and laurel bushes, and didn't count, but at the back there were practically grounds. First stretched a wide lawn, with beds of polyanthus roses; beyond, separated by a beechen hedge with a wicket in it, the rougher grass of a sizable orchard.—Mr. Clark and Louisa had quite a walk, before they reached the final boundary of a quiet, traffic-less road, upon which fronted, at the orchard's end, a couple of small outbuildings. Like everything else about Glenarvon they were beautifully kept up; as Louisa approached, she could see the pointing between the bricks.

Pausing at the first—

"Where the boys keep their Vespas," explained Mr. Clark. "They're at an age—as you must have gathered from the state of their rooms!—when they're mad about machinery. Of course both will eventually join me in publishing, but just at the moment they're mad about machinery."

"I suppose most boys are," said Louisa. "But they don't all get Vespas!"

Mr. Clark smiled, and led her on. Inside the second building, housed in a neat stall, stood what looked to Louisa a very superior pony.

Like the Queen of Sheba, she hadn't seen the half!

"Cathy's," said Mr. Clark. "Cathy's Tomboy. She takes care of him entirely herself. I should tell you," added Mr. Clark, with a pleasant mixture of pride and resignation, "that my daughter Catherine is mad about horses."

Louisa wasn't entirely surprised. She'd read in more than one newspaper article of the rising generation's passion for horses. But the kindness and understanding of Mr. Clark, in actually providing his daughter with a pony of her own, struck her with uncommon force, and she looked all the admiration she truly felt.

"One does one's best," said Mr. Clark simply.

"But *lucky* Catherine!" cried Louisa.

"I hope so," admitted Mr. Clark. "Tomboy certainly takes up all her time . . . I wouldn't wish it otherwise," he added—as it were defending his daughter from any breath of criticism—though heaven knew Louisa wasn't going to criticize—"isn't youth the time for enjoying oneself? I'm afraid you won't find Cathy as helpful in the house as she might be—but mayn't we forgive her, while she's young, and enjoying herself?"

Though he spoke no doubt unconsideredly, that word "we" fell like music on Louisa's ear. (Or perhaps because he *had* spoken unconsideredly?) As Mr. Clark put his hand in his pocket and brought out two lumps of sugar, as he gave one to Louisa, as Tomboy blew, and then gobbled, first into Mr. Clark's palm then into hers,

Louisa felt herself already on the verge of acceptance as one of the family.

II

Everything still depended on the children. For all her quick optimism, Louisa remained thoroughly aware of this. If her three potential step-children didn't accept her, from no mere self-indulgence would Mr. Clark allow his happy home to be disrupted. Thus it was with the most anxious expectation that Louisa, some half-hour later, observed from her new bedroom window the return of Catherine, Toby and Paul.

They all came back together.

It might have been by chance; nonetheless the impression Lou-isa immediately received was subsequently to prove correct: an impression of unitedness. Whatever they were discussing, so quietly and seriously, as they crossed first the orchard and then the lawn together, they were evidently in complete agreement. They looked as though they were always in agreement, as though they hadn't quar-reled since the nursery . . .

Catherine the eldest was tall, slim and blonde, and even in sum-mer dress and jersey characterized by a horsewomanly neatness. Her long fair hair didn't hang in the fashionable elf locks, but was combed back and plaited in a door-knocker behind—the very thing to go under a hard hat. Nor was her sweater the fashionably baggy sort; it fitted from beneath the turned-down points of a white col-lar to the ribbing at a trim waist. However disheveled she might leave counterpane and dressing table, Catherine's personal neatness was indeed so striking, Louisa instantly resolved to let the room go hang, in case it was a kind of compensation.

Of the boys, Paul already reached towards his sister's poise, Toby was still rough as a puppy. Paul appeared to use brilliantine, Toby had a double crown. (Louisa's heart fell in two parts like a cleft apple—just the slightly larger half towards Toby.) Though stockier in build, both echoed Catherine's coloring—as all three probably echoed their mother's, Mr. Clark being so noticeably dark. As the trio of matching heads bent together they made a really delightful picture; which Louisa would have enjoyed still more if she hadn't received a further impression: that Catherine and Toby and Paul, joined in such earnest conference, weren't merely discussing, but *plotting* something . . .

III

On the surface at least, their reception of her at dinner was quite perfect.

"Catherine, Paul, Toby," Mr. Clark introduced them cheerfully. "Children, this is Miss Datchett, who is going to see if she can put up with us, and keep us in order."

The eyes of all three turned intelligently towards Louisa. What the deuce they were thinking she couldn't guess.

"But how *nice!*" said Catherine warmly.

Had she or hadn't she kicked Paul under the table? In any case, both boys were ready on their marks.

"You'll find my underwear in absolute chaos," offered Paul. "To anyone who cares for darning, I'm an absolute gift."

"I haven't had a clean vest for months," offered Toby.

"Don't be silly, Toby," said Catherine sharply. "Of course it isn't quite as bad as that, Miss Datchett, but we do honestly need you like mad. Perhaps I should do more myself—"

"No, no," said Mr. Clark. "You have Tomboy to look after. Enjoy yourself while you can! Miss Datchett will see to things."

"That's what I'm here for," agreed Louisa brightly.

The three children looked at her again. Their eyes were really quite disconcertingly intelligent. *Yes; but is that ALL?* Louisa fancied each thinking, and to cover her nervousness plunged into chatter of pony clubs and praise of Tomboy.

"I'm told they're spreading all over the country," babbled Louisa. "What a lovely soft nose he has!"

"Yes, they are, and hasn't he?" agreed Catherine politely.

"I half expected to find you out on him this evening," observed Mr. Clark.

Catherine at once looked martyred.

"Tuesday's my first aid class, Daddy."

Mr. Clark glanced proudly at Louisa. Mad on horses as she was, his daughter Catherine attended first aid classes. What conscientiousness, what self-sacrifice, his look implied, with Tomboy waiting in his stall! Indeed, Louisa thoroughly agreed.

"I don't suppose you boys were exactly *kept in* either?" said Mr. Clark—as it were bringing forward Paul and Toby for their meed of praise. (Though Cathy was her father's girl, obviously he tried hard to make no favorites.) "What was it tonight—the scouts?"

"No, sir; overhauling our Vespas at the shop," said Paul.

"I'm glad to know you take such care of them," approved Mr. Clark. "Those infernal machines, Miss Datchett, are overhauled at least once a week! However, it doesn't affect their schoolwork; they both get very good marks indeed, and I expect great things from them at the University.—Now, children: shall we ask Miss Datchett to give us our pudding?"

Louisa flushed with pleasure as Mrs. Temple deposited before her an enormous Spotted Dick.—She still glanced warily at Catherine and Toby and Paul, alert for any sign of resentment. It was practically taking a mother's place already! But all three returned her look with perfect cheerfulness, Toby volunteering that he liked the middle; and Louisa sank a knife happily into the warm, rich, yielding, domestic duff.

Chapter Twenty

I

Next day was one of the happiest of Louisa's life. Mr. Clark went off to work just as a breadwinner should, the boys were to lunch at school and Catherine took out Tomboy and a packet of sandwiches. Louisa, as soon as she had the house to herself, plunged into domesticity with all the joyous abandon of a dolphin released in the waves.

She had more qualifications for domesticity than might be imagined. Long years of being fond of men had made her an expert darner of socks, washer of woolen underwear, sewer-on of buttons. Even at Cannes, a good proportion of her time had been spent on René's and Kurt's and Bobby's drip-dry shirts. Now with happy anticipation she went methodically through the linen basket and extracted all smalls.

("Laundry goes tomorrow," offered Mrs. Temple, pinning on her hat. They had come to terms over washing up breakfast. Louisa knew better than to attempt Mrs. Anstruther's method with Karen upon any true-born Briton coming in to oblige; instead, she let Mrs. Temple talk. Mrs. Temple dwelt in a Council house which some might look down upon but for labor-saving no more to desire, also being a bare ten minutes off was why she could nip in to do breakfast and dinner without inconvenience, apart from fighting her way through wind, rain and fog. Mrs. Temple also achieved the necessary shopping through wind, rain and fog; she was quite a byword for it. "What the trades people'll think to see someone fresh come in, I'm sure I don't know," said Mrs. Temple. "They won't see *me* come in," said Louisa cheerfully. "Mrs. Temple, you're a wonder!")

It was delightful, after the narrowness of Paddington, to have a whole separate kitchen to splash in.—Louisa's mood was such that she'd have rejoiced to find a copper; the kitchen at Glenarvon was too modern for that, but it wasn't modern enough for a washing machine: Louisa plunged to the elbows in authentic suds. She soaked, she squeezed; rinsed in two waters, rolled in towels; and at last staggered out with the clothes basket to peg in the open air of the orchard.

Only those who have perpetually dried smalls on radiators (or, at a pinch, above a gas ring) can appreciate the pleasure of pegging on an open-air clothesline. To Louisa, as she strung up the last sock—in the warmth of a summer morning, on green grass, under old apple trees—the moment was almost poetic in its beauty. Drops of moisture from Mr. Clark's long underwear sparkled on a dandelion like drops of dew; a gentle aroma of clean wool enhanced the scent of trodden grass. Somewhere up in the apple boughs a bird went tweet . . .

And every week it would be the same, thought Louisa happily.—She pulled herself up, with housewifely forethought: winter washdays would obviously be more rugged. But even on winter washdays she'd have a whole kitchen to dry in; would but exchange the scent of trodden grass for the warm smell of winter cooking. "*Where are the songs of spring? ay, where are they?*" thought Louisa—an echo from K for Keats in B for Biography. "'*Think not of them, thou hast thy music too!*'" Autumn was in fact quite far enough for her to look ahead; but she couldn't help seeing drops from Mr. Clark's long underwear sparkling upon—sugaring, so to speak—her first batch of mince pies.

"I'll put suet out for you!" Louisa promised the bird. She didn't know what sort it was, it might be the sort that wintered in

Africa—but in any case there'd be robins. "Just pass the word round!" Louisa adjured the bird. "Suet on the house!"

So soft and warm blew the drying wind from the west, Mr. Clark came home to find her seated before a big basket of clean mending.

"My dear girl—!" began Mr. Clark; and checked himself. "My dear Miss Datchett," he began again, "have you set to work already?"

"I'm enjoying myself," beamed Louisa.

Mr. Clark stood quite still, contemplating her.

"It's something I never thought to come home to again," he said solemnly. "I believe I'm going to be a very lucky man."

II

Lousia still wasn't going to hurry him. On this point her mind was made up quite firmly. If she'd at the last felt scruples about hurrying Jimmy Brown (as it turned out unnecessarily, but that wasn't Louisa's fault), how much more scrupulous should she feel towards a man so in every respect more deserving? Louisa had never been at close quarters with a breadwinner before, so perhaps her reactions were exaggerated; but as Mr. Clark set out each morning to win bread for three children and four adults—besides Mrs. Temple there was a part-time gardener—Louisa's respect for him was something quite uncommon.—His actual setting out no doubt a factor: F. Pennon, for example, supported both a villa at Bournemouth and a flat in Gladstone Mansions, also Karen and Hallam, and Hallam's understrapper and all the help Karen could get hold of, and would soon have Enid on hand as well: but he didn't set out, he sat back. Mr. Clark worked at breadwinning six hours a day.

("You should have a glass of sherry as soon as you come in," Louisa told him, firmly.

"You really think so?" said Mr. Clark.

"It's there ready for you," said Louisa, firmly.)

Actually it wasn't difficult, not to hurry. Every word and look of Mr. Clark's tacitly implied that the period of a week had become a dead letter.

All still depended, and Louisa knew it, on the children.

It was surprising how little they were at home. (Or not surprising, reflected Louisa uneasily? If they in fact couldn't stand the sight of her?) They seemed to keep roughly their father's hours; even Catherine departed daily with a packet lunch. Louisa was too wise to probe, but she was disappointed; with Cathy in particular she longed for nice cozy chats. As it was, as the days passed, she felt she knew her three potential stepchildren hardly better at all.

Only in the most general terms could she have summed their characters. Briefly, they were the opposite of juvenile delinquents.

Let it not be supposed for a moment that Louisa was disappointed. She would have been horrified and alarmed to find Paul and Toby carrying flick-knives, or Catherine smoking marijuana. But she did feel it would have helped her position had she been called on to smooth over some slight misunderstanding with their father, for instance, or to hear and soothe some tale of youthful frustration.—If Catherine hadn't owned a pony already, how eagerly would Louisa have pleaded with Mr. Clark to buy her one! The same went for the boys' Vespas: Louisa would have fought for the boys' Vespas tooth and nail—but there they were too, like Tomboy in his stall. In fact it was Louisa who was frustrated, no call made on her special *expertise;* and though this in a way was precisely what she wanted, after years of being a good sort she felt slightly lost.

So might the coxswain of a lifeboat feel, retired from service; or a fireman drawing his pension. It was wonderfully restful, but took getting used to.

Whenever the children appeared, their manners towards Louisa continued perfect. They expressed warm appreciation of everything she did for them. Paul and Toby came separately to thank her for darning their socks. Catherine exclaimed more than once how lovely it was not to find any chores waiting, when she came in from grooming and feeding Tomboy. Louisa, recalling how difficult this sort of thing is to adolescents, was both touched and heartened; but she recalled also the remarkable aptitude of adolescence for concealing its true sentiments.

Distasteful as it was to put herself in the position of her Aunt May, Louisa made the effort; and came to the conclusion that she really hadn't the slightest idea what the children truly thought of her.

—It didn't stop her looking ahead. Louisa devoted a considerable portion of her solitary hours to wondering what Catherine and Toby and Paul were going to call her after she was married to their father. "Mother" was out of the question—Louisa humbly, regretfully, set "mother" aside at once. The Victorian "mamma," which she believed currently fashionable among such sophisticated son-in-law types as Henry Peel, was unsuited to their age group. The appellation "mummy," on the lips of Catherine, would have made Louisa happy indeed—but hardly suited the lips of Paul and Toby. (The shorter version "mum" Louisa set aside as too common. She had traveled a long way already, from Paddington.) In the end, she mentally settled for the plain-spokenness of "stepmother."

III

Fortunately for a peace of mind thus sufficiently precarious already, Louisa's apprehensions as to Miss Lindrum were scotched almost before they took shape.

Miss Lindrum was Catherine's riding mistress, from whose pony club stables had been purchased Tomboy; so at least a business relationship existed, with Mr. Clark, and Louisa couldn't help asking herself, nervously, whether there existed any other. (To have no rival at all, for such a potential husband, struck her as too good to believe.) True, Mr. Clark did no more than once or twice pronounce Miss Lindrum's name, and then always in connection with Cathy's riding; but since he pronounced no other female name whatever, apart from that of a history don engaged on his Mediaeval Europe series, Louisa was very glad to have her mind relieved.

"There's Cathy back from her ride," said Mr. Clark, one evening just as he came in. "Shall we go and meet her?"

Of course Louisa accompanied him down the short gravel drive, to see Cathy pass the gate on her way round to Tomboy's stable; and Cathy wasn't alone. Beside her trotted Miss Lindrum on a stocky bay. It was a rather handsome animal, well up to weight; it had need to be—Miss Lindrum herself was well up to weight, as a pair of ill-advised white breeches emphasized. Nonetheless her bare, flaxen, Saxon head, and weather-ruddied cheeks, had a certain earthy attraction, and Louisa knew that some men liked big behinds.—She glanced swiftly at Mr. Clark. But obviously he had eyes only for his daughter. His greeting to Miss Lindrum was briefly courteous, no more. And Miss Lindrum merely waved her whip and trotted on . . .

Louisa still flew a slight kite, so to speak, watching Catherine rub down Tomboy in the stable. (Mr. Clark stayed only to see her unsaddle.)

"I dare say Miss Lindrum usually comes in for a drink?" suggested Louisa.

"What, our Lindy? Not on your life," returned Catherine absently. "She's never been inside the house."

Louisa hung about a bit, very willing to lend a hand if she could. But Catherine rubbed away with such fierce concentration, it was plain that any offer of assistance would only be resented.

Louisa didn't mind. She felt Catherine's fixation on horses entirely acceptable, so long as Catherine's father hadn't an eye for Catherine's riding mistress.

Louisa's nerves steadied. They were still daily over-stretched between enjoyment of the present and hopes for the future; but after this particular incident, they definitely steadied.

Which was just as well, considering what the very next evening held in store.

Chapter Twenty-One

I

Another instance of Mr. Clark's sympathy with youth was that Glenarvon possessed a television set. He himself disapproved the invention; as the telephone had killed the art of letter-writing, so television, according to Mr. Clark, would kill the art of conversation. (Louisa thoroughly enjoyed such pronouncements. She felt it was just the way a family man ought to talk.) But with a household of young people, acknowledged Mr. Clark—Louisa hanging on every word—to deny them the universal pablum would be like denying them bread and butter. Sometimes the family watched even *commercial* television, if there was a worthwhile program on some serious subject; thus on the Friday they all went down a coal mine, and though Paul for one came up again with a convinced prejudice in favor of oil, all agreed that it was a wonderfully interesting experience.

"But as for *this* rubbish—!" groaned Mr. Clark, as a first singing commercial replaced the fading pit-head. "Paul, or Toby, turn the thing off!"

"Can't we just see if it's the soap-bubbly one?" begged Catherine. "Miss Datchett, don't *you* like the soap-bubbly one?"

Louisa, her eye on Mr. Clark, hesitated. He gave back a

whimsical, understanding smile. "Though neither of *us* care for this sort of thing," that smile seemed to say, "I see you mean to side with Cathy!" He nodded; Louisa felt it a minor triumph . . .

Only what came next wasn't the soap-bubbly one, what came next was F. Pennon.

II

Old Freddy had evidently got himself up for the occasion. Though only his head and shoulders were on view, he was in dinner jacket. From its left lapel sprouted an outsize white carnation; his hand-kerchief was equally overdone—arranged to display two white peaks like the sails of a miniature schooner. Were his eyebrows powdered? In any case they added enormously to the general effect—as of Sealyham crossed with club man.

"And here," announced a disembodied voice, "on forty seconds' private time, a speaker who prefers to remain anonymous. Let's just call him, shall we, a Man with a Message?"

"It's the first time I've ever seen *that*," commented Paul interest-edly. "I believe it costs the earth . . ."

Even Mr. Clark's attention was held. Louisa froze. What Freddy was doing with a Message she couldn't imagine—unless he was going to make an appeal on behalf of Distressed British Admirals? She could think of nothing else; but still, presciently, froze.

F. Pennon cleared his throat with easy deliberation. He might have been appearing on television every night of his life.

"There are times," he opened largely, "when what a chap wants above all is to hear a voice from the past. What I mean ter say is, the sound of a voice that is silent, the touch of a hand that is still."

"That's very true," observed Mr. Clark, showing unexpected emotion.

"It's just going to be another Appeal," sighed Catherine.

"And in a Welfare State—!" murmured Louisa censoriously.

But as his next words showed, Freddy's message was uncapitaled. It was simply and strictly a message—like a telegram.

"Not necessarily from the *far* past," continued Freddy, "say just a couple of weeks ago. Still an' all it may mean much, let alone the Admiral mislaying his full-dress uniform. For though a chap may be right as rain—no doubts as to the future, no intention of skating out of his obligations—there are times when that voice from the past would fall like refreshin' Highland dew. All telephone charges to be reversed," finished Freddy, "because I'm not here really, I'm back at Bournemouth. Good night!"

He faded like the Cheshire Cat. It was absurd to fancy that his eyebrows faded last; but that was the impression.

"What an extraordinary thing!" exclaimed Mr. Clark.

It wasn't in the least extraordinary to Louisa. As soon as she'd had a moment to think she saw commercial television absolutely made for old Freddy. She saw him employing it, over the years to come, quite recklessly: to advertise for a cook, to relieve his mind on the subject of super-tax, or just to complain about the weather. It was probably the most rewarding use of money he'd yet encountered. He was probably rarin' to go again already—especially if that voice from the past didn't immediately respond . . .

Louisa's nerves had been steady enough to carry her through his first effort; but if his next, as it well might, began with a *Dammit Louisa, where are you?* she felt disinclined to trust them. She would almost certainly give herself away; and had a strong impression that Mr. Clark might consider the whole thing out of place.

As soon as she was alone next day Louisa telephoned Bournemouth (reversing charges).

III

"Hi," called Louisa. "This is the voice from the past."

"Did you see me on television? I thought you might," said F. Pennon complacently. "How are you, Louisa?"

"Fine," said Louisa.

"Well, *where* are you? I've been telephoning your flat, I've been telephoning that morgue at Broydon—"

"I'm staying with friends," said Louisa. "How are things at Bournemouth?"

"Oh, we're all fine too," said Freddy cheerfully. "You couldn't have been righter, Louisa, about Enid and the Admiral. Enid's all over him, and the difference it's made to me no one could believe. You don't happen to know what became of his full-dress uniform?"

"No," said Louisa. "He'll have to hire one.—For heavens' sake, Freddy, you didn't go on television just to ask me *that?*"

"Of course not," said Freddy. "It slipped in. What we really want is to get you to the party. It was Colley's idea," added Freddy loyally, "when I couldn't find you on the phone, to send out some sort of a signal. *I* thought of television, though."

There was no doubt, reflected Louisa, that the Admiral and Freddy were as much made for each other as were Freddy and commercial television. What with the Admiral's ideas, and Freddy's money, she foresaw a thoroughly enjoyable future for the pair of them.

"Dear Freddy, I think you're both very sweet," said Louisa fondly. "When is it, the party?"

"Tomorrow. That's what the hurry was about. Tomorrow at six, here. Of course you'll stay overnight—"

Just as though he could see her, Louisa shook her head. She was sorry. The beano at Broydon Court was still fresh in her mind; however vowed to domesticity, the idea of such another—and probably her last—had its appeal. If she could have nipped up to Town and back, to Gladstone Mansions, or Claridge's, the thing might have been feasible; but not an absence of two days, in the middle of her first week at Glenarvon . . .

"I'm sorry, I can't possibly," said Louisa.

"I never knew such a gel for refusing," complained F. Pennon. "First I ask you to marry me, then I ask you to come and live with me and Enid, now you won't even come to a party.—It isn't an *ordinary* party," persuaded F. Pennon.

"I don't suppose any of yours are," said Louisa.

"Actually, in a way, it's more Enid's."

Louisa waited.

"She's invited a lot of nice friends."

"From Poole?"

"That's right. She started out with just a couple, but it's quite remarkable how they've bred.—To tell you the truth, Louisa," said old Freddy, coming clean at last, "it's an *engagement* party."

Louisa understood. Right as rain though he might be—no intention of skating out of his obligations—an engagement party called for reinforcements. She did her best to encourage, if only by telephone.

"You'll have the Admiral," pointed out Louisa.

"*He* just keeps telling me what a lucky chap I am. *He* just wants you to come because he likes you," argued Freddy, "whereas what *I* need is, well, moral support.—Don't think I'm squealing," added Freddy bravely, "I'm not. No one's ever heard a whimper out of me. But it 'ud mean a lot, Louisa, to have you there, just to catch my eye from time to time, perhaps nip out for a spot of brandy—"

But however touched, and she was, Louisa had at last learned to put her own concerns first. Only a month before, so appealed to, she would probably have wrecked all her chances with Mr. Clark to rush to old Freddy's aid. But not now! Now, she wasn't even torn.

"I hate to say it, Freddy, but there's no question. I can't possibly be away a night. Not possibly."

"If that's all—" began Freddy resourcefully.

"And it's no use saying you'll send me back by car—and getting me here at four in the morning."

There was a slight pause. Then—

"Wait," said Freddy. "Hold on."

He was away a couple of minutes. Louisa (the charges reversed) quite agreeably employed the time in composing suitable messages to Enid and the Admiral. She felt sure of the Admiral's getting his; the one to Enid she composed on the off chance.

"Louisa?" called back Freddy.

"Still here," said Louisa.

"Is there a decent-sized lawn where you are?"

"Fair," said Louisa, surprised.

"The Admiral says we could charter a helicopter."

Again Louisa reflected with pleasure, and now admiration, on the happy results of money allied to enterprise.—Not that old Freddy wasn't enterprising enough on his own hook, but undoubtedly the Admiral stimulated him; while for Admiral Colley how delightful to see his good ideas—each as wild as helpful—so immediately and unquestioningly translated into action! "In two shakes, they'll be *buying* themselves a helicopter," thought Louisa . . .

For a moment, she was undeniably tempted on her own account. Not only was the gesture uncommonly flattering; she'd flown only twice in her life before, to Cannes and back, and had adored it. (To whomever under B for Biography equated heaven with caviar to the sound of trumpets Louisa would confidently have recommended trying lunch in a jet.) But now, for once, she thought before she leaped.

Prudently.

Prudently Louisa attempted to visualize the reactions of her new-found, potential family to the sight of a helicopter descending on their back lawn—come to fetch herself, Louisa, to a cocktail party at Bournemouth.

Though with the children, especially Paul and Toby, it might send her stock up, Louisa fancied their father not caring for it at all.

In Mr. Clark's picture of a conscientious, home-loving help-mate—a picture Louisa hoped he was picturing—that helicopter, felt Louisa, was distinctly out of place.

Especially to take her to a cocktail party. (To a *lighthouse* would have been another thing; and had Louisa been a female surgeon. Louisa whipped out an appendix in parenthesis, but not seriously; had her oilskins off almost before she put them on.)

She sighed; but didn't weaken.

"Dear Freddy," said Louisa, "try and get it into your head. I couldn't be fonder of you, but it's no go. Tell the Admiral to phone Moss Bros. about his uniform, lay on enough champagne for the party, and you won't have a care. But get it into your head: the voice *is* silent, also the hand is still. I'm very, very fond of you, Freddy; but it's no go."

With which last words she cut the connection.

IV

Unhappily, this act of prudence and sacrifice looked like being ill-rewarded. It was that same night that Louisa overheard the row between Catherine and Mr. Clark.

Chapter Twenty-Two

I

Louisa always went up to bed first; she punctiliously left the Clarks alone together whenever possible, in case they wanted to discuss her. It was rarely more than a few minutes, however, before Toby, then Paul, then Catherine came up too; and then ensued the cheerful sounds of a family settling down for the night.—There were no unnecessary inhibitions, Louisa was glad to note: not only did Paul march in on Toby soaking too long in the bath, Catherine marched in on Paul (and audibly pulled the plug out). A little Alsatia each night was the first-floor landing, a little riotous enclave within the bounds of a benevolent dictatorship; and Louisa loved to hear its rumor. There was nothing at Glenarvon she enjoyed more than hearing the children come up to bed.

On that Saturday night, she heard something else besides—from down below, in Mr. Clark's study. Paul had left the bath taps running for his sister; Louisa, when Catherine didn't come up, crossed the landing to turn them off; and the study door below was open.

Not this time—as once at Bournemouth—did Louisa deliberately eavesdrop. The ethos of the family was already sacred to her; as Catherine's voice rose, and the voice of Mr. Clark rose in answer, she loyally hurried back to her own room. All the same, she couldn't help catching a phrase or two. "But we don't *want* to have a home made for us!" cried Catherine. "Be quiet; Miss Datchett will hear you," ordered her father . . .

Louisa crept into bed and put her head under the pillow. If there were to be any arguments, before the children finally accepted her, she wisely determined to know as little of them as possible.

And how loyally, and successfully, must Mr. Clark have defended her! Because at breakfast next morning Cathy couldn't have been more amiable.

II

"Marmalade, Miss Datchett?" asked Catherine sweetly. (Louisa shot Mr. Clark a grateful glance.) "Toby, pass Miss Datchett the marmalade!"

"Unless she'd rather have honey?" suggested Paul. "Was it you who got it for us in the comb, Miss Datchett? It's smashing!"

"Mrs. Temple *never* did," said Toby.

Three fresh young faces turned innocently towards her like flowers to the sun. "*They've been talking,*" thought Louisa, with sudden insight. She saw them all talking and talking—probably into the small hours of that morning: Paul wrapped in an eiderdown on the foot of Catherine's bed, Toby squatted on the sheepskin rug and finally agreeing to accept her. How otherwise explain this more than even their usual courtesy?

"Unless it's part of a plan," thought Louisa warily . . .

At least Mr. Clark had no such unworthy suspicions. (That is, Louisa hoped they were unworthy.) He basked in domestic sunshine; his glance, from his children to Louisa, was warm with self-congratulation. Whatever storm had raged the night before, to Mr. Clark the barometer was evidently set fair, glass rising; and if he didn't know his family, who should?

"Who's coming with Father to church?" inquired Mr. Clark pleasantly.

"But all of us, sir!" answered Paul at once.

"That will be very nice indeed," said Mr. Clark. (Louisa fancied his eye to rest with particular pleasure on Catherine.) "And you, Miss Datchett?"

"I'd like to," said Louisa sincerely, "very much. Only Mrs. Temple doesn't come on Sundays, and there's the dinner to cook."

"Mightn't we have something cold?" suggested Mr. Clark.

Evidently the idea was revolutionary.—From the corner of her eye Louisa saw the children exchange a glance of mingled astonishment and gladness. Instantly—

"Or an omelette?" cooperated Catherine.

"Or bangers?" offered Toby.

"In any case, I don't see that we need leave Miss Datchett behind," adjudged their father. "Whatever she provides I'm sure we shall find very acceptable.—All ready, then, at ten-forty-five?"

III

As she entered the Clark pew at St. Michael and All Angels, such was Louisa's happiness that she temporarily forgot every anxiety.

It was a splendid pew, well up in front, and she entered it immediately after Mr. Clark; with Toby and Catherine and Paul filing in behind, she felt just like one of the family. ("Every Sunday!" thought Louisa uncontrollably.) The fact that she hadn't her own prayer book was but a trifling fly in such precious ointment; and in any case there was a spare one on the ledge. Louisa had been brought up chapel, but she soon found her way about, and with genuine reverence and thankfulness joined vigorously in all parts open to the congregation . . .

During the second lesson—what a landmark in her career!—she said "Hush" to Toby. The footstool before him was the big old-fashioned kind, adapted to take a tophat; his fidgeting toe tip prized the lid open, so that it fell back with a gentle thud. "Hush!" said Louisa . . .

It was only during the sermon that her mind wandered. St. Michael and All Angels had an uncommonly broad aisle: all her talks with Enid Anstruther rushing back on her, Louisa absolutely couldn't help filling it with three pairs of bridesmaids. Even in crinolines, there'd be ample room; while for the cloud of white tulle about four foot clearance on either side . . .

What color for the bridesmaids? Pale amber?

"Not that I'd ever round up six," thought Louisa, more practically; in fact Catherine's (if Catherine *would)* was the only name that came immediately to mind. Louisa cast a fleeting glance towards Pammy—towards Pammy and four other Pammies. "But they'd ham it!" thought Louisa—and in their place substituted Enid Anstruther as matron of honor in very pale blue. Undoubtedly Enid would do matron of honor quite beautifully—and why not F. Pennon to give away the bride?

Or the Admiral?—Freddy could provide the wedding breakfast, decided Louisa, there was nothing he'd enjoy more; she herself would make a better effect on the arm of Admiral Colley's full-dress uniform.

"He'll be hiring one anyway, for Enid," thought Louisa. "He may just as well use it twice!"

To strains inaudible, except to herself, of the Wedding March, she stationed Mr. Clark by the front righthand pew—only two up, Louisa noted, from where they actually sat. To those joyful POM, POM, per-umph-um POM strains—

("I'll ask Number Ten," thought Louisa. And why not Mr. McAndrew? At least he'd look well, and he'd stood her a splendid lunch.)

—the small but exquisite cortège advanced: first Louisa in a cloud of white tulle, on the arm of Admiral Colley in full-dress uniform; then Enid in very pale blue and probably a hyacinth toque, followed by Cathy in an amber crinoline. (Which she could afterwards wear to dances, reflected Louisa—with already maternal forethought.) How to work in Paul and Toby? It was a pity they were too old to be pages; but perhaps they'd care to have a bang at ushering . . .

The sermon neared its end. Louisa was in fact just saying "I do" as they all stood up for the final hymn. She had experienced such happiness, she thoroughly regretted not having more than a shilling for the collection, but that was all she could find in her purse. The children, she observed, put in shillings too; their father a folded note.

Paying for the family!

IV

Sunday dinner was almost a picnic. They didn't actually have it out of doors, but because Louisa decided on omelettes ate in the kitchen; the unusualness, the general sketchiness of which arrangement produced a picnicish euphoria. Catherine laid the table, Mr. Clark and the boys sat around watching Louisa crack eggs. And it was just as she began to beat that Paul suddenly answered the question so long present in her mind.

"I see Miss Datchett's is an expert hand," observed Mr. Clark approvingly.

"Miss Datchett, who's going to serve?" asked Catherine.

"Are you putting in ham, Miss Datchett?" asked Toby.

"Look here," said Paul, "why don't we all call her Louisa?"

Louisa naturally glanced first at Mr. Clark, before she beamed.— He accepted the look approvingly; approving her tacit submission to his judgment. His approval broadened to include Paul—and Catherine and Toby, who by their cheerful looks were obviously welcoming the idea.

"If Miss Datchett has no objection—" he began pleasantly.

"Indeed I haven't!" cried Louisa. "I'd love it!"

"—then on high days and holidays, and while you're all behaving yourselves, I think 'Louisa' might be very well admissible—to us all," said Mr. Clark.

V

What could have been more delightful, or more promising, or more thoroughly flattering to Louisa's hopes? Nothing. She still wasn't easy. Her experiences at Bournemouth and Broydon had taught her, all too painfully, to watch out for the stone in the snowball, the gunshot in the partridge, the horseshoe in the mitt.

The children's behavior to her was perfect—it always had been. Nor had she now to fear what they might be saying about her to their father. Their line was too plainly taken, and Mr. Clark the last man alive to countenance double-dealing. What she still needed to know was what they said about her among themselves—in Tomboy's stable, or while overhauling their Vespas, or late at night in Cathy's room . . .

As usual, that Sunday night, Louisa went up first. But almost immediately the pleasant sounds she'd grown accustomed to—the to-and-fro between bed- and bathroom, the subdued family chatter—followed. (No arguments tonight!) It seemed that the children were turning in early too; perhaps leaving Mr. Clark to do a little extra breadwinning.—Louisa cast a thought towards Henry Peel and his criminal neglect of proofs. Compared with Mr. Clark, what a feckless breadwinner was *there!* She wondered his wife ever got a night's sleep.—But this was merely a sidewind, so to speak, blowing lightly across the strong current of her own preoccupations. As soon as she heard Catherine leave the bathroom, Louisa ungratefully dismissed the Peels—to whom she owed her very presence at Glenarvon—completely from mind.

There is always one way of finding out what one wants to know, and that is to ask.

In a few moments of intense activity Louisa leaped out of bed, wiped off face food, applied powder, pulled on her zebra pattern housecoat, sprang between the sheets again, and not without a certain nervousness called through the door.

"Catherine!"

The padding footsteps halted.

"Catherine," called Louisa nervously, "come in a minute, will you?"

Chapter Twenty-Three

———— ❋ ————

I

If Louisa was nervous, Catherine wasn't. (Or didn't appear to be. Where the children were concerned, Louisa found herself thus perpetually hedging.) Catherine, in a blue woolly dressing gown, made straight for the foot of the bed and curled herself thereon as readily as if by nightly habit, while Louisa at the other end unnecessarily plumped pillows.

"Is it anything in particular," inquired Catherine amiably, "or just a cozy chat?"

—For a moment Louisa was as tempted as she'd been by a helicopter. Cozy chats with Catherine were precisely what she longed for; why not have one now? A dozen suitable topics sprang to mind: the health of Tomboy, Catherine's chances at the pony-club gymkhana, Miss Lindrum's extraordinary ill judgment as to breeches— all these beautifully linked to Catherine's passion for horses—while by way of Catherine's own plaits the whole field of hair-dos enticingly opened. ("She ought to be brushing a hundred times each night," thought Louisa. How delightful to dispatch Catherine for a hairbrush *now*, and chat cozily while she brushed!) But such pleasures, to be truly enjoyed, lay on the other side of the hurdle Louisa had deliberately brought herself up to.

"In the first place," said Louisa, "I want you to tell me the truth."

"Well, of course," said Catherine readily. (Louisa hoped she wasn't keeping her fingers crossed; as children give themselves absolution in advance when about to tell a lie.) "What about?"

"I don't know if your father consulted you," continued Louisa bravely, "before I came?"

"No, he didn't. At least, he told us at breakfast—but I don't think one can call that *consulting*," said Catherine, still readily.

"It must have been rather a surprise?"

Catherine reflected.

"Not exactly. I mean, Dad loves giving us surprises. So that though things may be surprising in themselves, they're not exactly *surprising*."

It was a rather neat piece of dialectic, but little help to Louisa. She pressed on.

"Given that you weren't surprised, how do you feel about the results?"

Once again Catherine reflected.

"Well, how long are you staying?"

Louisa's heart sank. She'd asked for the truth, now here it came!

"That depends a good deal on what you tell me. In fact, on what you and Paul and Toby really think about me. If you could think of me as—well, as a *permanency*—" hazarded Louisa.

The sentence was never finished. Catherine instantly seized its every implication. For a moment she simply stared. Then—

"Louisa! *D'you mean to say you'd marry our Dad?*" cried Catherine.

Ravished by delight and surprise as she was—

"Don't say it!" cried Louisa superstitiously.

"But *would* you?"

"If you and the boys—"

"But, darling Louisa, there's nothing we'd like better!" cried Catherine. "We just didn't dare hope! We're all *for* it!—If you've any doubts, just wait while I fetch Toby and Paul!"

II

"Step-Mamma, your health!" said Paul gravely. "We shall still doubt-less address you as Louisa for the moment, but we may as well prac-tice step-mamma too."

There they sat, the family of Louisa's dreams, assembled dressing-gowned about her bed. Catherine was back on its foot, Paul occu-pied the dressing stool, Toby squatted on the rug. All had brought tooth mugs, Paul nipped down for a bottle of lime juice and a soda syphon; in which heady mixture (for so in the circumstances it was) to drink Louisa's health.

"Don't say it!" repeated Louisa anxiously. "For heaven's sake don't jump the gun! He hasn't asked me yet."

"But he will," said Paul confidently. "We've seen it in his eye. It was only you we had any doubts about, dear Louisa. There must be more to our Dad than one suspected."

"*I* believe Louisa likes *us,*" said Catherine gently.

"Well, I've always wanted a family," confessed Louisa. (It wasn't strictly true; she hadn't wanted one until about a week ago. But now that she did, she wanted one so earnestly, the exaggeration was surely forgivable.)

"So do we want a step-mamma," said Paul warmly. "The fact is, dear Louisa, you've turned up in the absolute nick of time."

"In fact, if you *hadn't* turned up," said Catherine dreamily, "I dare say we'd have been found all laid out in sizes beside the gas oven."

"Being all, you see," explained Paul, "practically poised for flight on the edge of the family nest. Only it happens to be smeared with birdlime."

"He means Dad," glossed Toby.

Louisa was so shaken, her fair picture of the Clark family life seemed to dissolve so suddenly before her eyes, all she could think of to say was, "You shouldn't call your father birdlime."

III

"I thought it a rather neat metaphor," apologized Paul. "And it *is*, you know, exactly how he's behaving."

"You forget how much Louisa doesn't know yet," said Catherine practically. "We may have given her quite a shock."

"Yes, you have!" cried Louisa, recovering her forces with a bang. "You ungrateful cubs! Good heavens, with a father who—" She cast about among Mr. Clark's thronging parental virtues for just the most striking example. It was an *embarras de richesses*. However nothing had ever impressed Louisa more than that first sight of Tomboy in his stall. "—Who buys his daughter a *horse*—!" cried Louisa.

Catherine sighed.

"If you only knew," she said gently, "how I *hate* that horse!"

IV

Dismayed and astounded afresh, Louisa instinctively glanced at the boys for confirmation that she'd heard aright. But both nodded gravely.

"It's quite true," said Paul. "She loathes its guts."

"I'm always feeding it, and grooming it, and cleaning up after it," sighed Catherine, "and polishing acres and acres of leather for it, and then when I'm utterly exhausted I have to go out and *ride* it. Even if it snows, I have to come back glowing with healthy exercise, actually my feet are always *frozen*, and start feeding and grooming and polishing—"

"But your father told me," protested Louisa, "you were mad about horses!"

Catherine returned a patient glance.

"He'd read somewhere in a paper that *all* teen-agers were mad about horses. Just because I quite enjoyed hacking once a week didn't mean *I* was mad about them. But that never occurred to him. Because he's never thought of me as an individual. I was just a mad-about-horses teen-ager."

"She never *asked* for a horse," put in Toby loyally. "It just came."

"As a lovely surprise," agreed Catherine, with irony. "The day after I left school, there it was. Outside the front door. Lindy holding it and grinning all over her face.—And no wonder, because whatever Dad paid for it, he was rooked. It's a *horrible* horse. But he went and asked her which was my favorite, and she palmed Tomboy off on him . . ."

"Well, that was when you should have said you didn't want it," said Louisa sharply.

Catherine looked at her again.

"If *you* found a horse outside the front door, and your father bursting with glee because he was giving you such a wonderful surprise, could *you* have said you didn't want it?"

"Perhaps not," admitted Louisa.

"People talk about children being ungrateful," said Catherine somberly. "They don't know what children go through, *not* to be ungrateful. Then Dad led me round to the old out-house—I knew there'd been some sort of alterations going on there, but I thought it was just for improvements—and there was this *lovely* little stable, for me to look after all by myself and ruin my hands."

There was a brief silence. Though Louisa was beginning to see Catherine's point of view, her sympathies were still far more with Mr. Clark. He might have been in error, but wasn't the imaginative generosity of such a gift something quite remarkable?

"Wasn't it still wonderfully *kind* of him," persuaded Louisa, "to give you Tomboy?"

"It was a bribe," said Catherine sternly. "Like the boys' Vespas. To keep me in the nest—because he thought I was mad about horses. What *I* want to be is a nurse—not a stablehand. That's what the row was about, I don't know if you heard, last night."

V

Now they were back to really important matters. Not that the Tomboy-excursus hadn't been useful in its way; as each young Clark realized, it had softened Louisa up.—She was in fact still recognizing an in the circumstances forgivable error: not horsewomanly, the neatness that had so struck her, the first time she saw Catherine, but a nurse's; apt to meet with confidence the most formidable of Sisters' eyes. Not a bowler hat were those neat braids designed for, but a nurse's cap . . .

"It's quite true," repeated Paul, in this fresh context. "It's what she's wanted to do ever since I can remember. She goes to the hospital here every day as an aide. She has to tie Tomboy up with the ambulances."

"Can you think of anything more *respectable*," continued Catherine bitterly, "than nursing? From Dad's attitude, you'd think I wanted to join the chorus of the Folies Bergères. Simply because I'd have to live in a hostel! As for the boys—"

"Jets," said Toby simply.

"Jet engines," corrected Paul. "D'you know, Louisa, we're both of us such bright boys, Rolls would take us on as apprentices in the next batch? They've practically *applied* for us, through our head. What one means to say," added Paul, pointedly echoing his sister, "is that one isn't trying to join the Foreign Legion. One would simply have to go and live in carefully selected digs. Only being under age, we need Dad's signature on the dotted line."

"Matrons want it too," said Catherine sadly. "That was what the row was about."

"Couldn't we forge it?" asked Toby suddenly.

"A fat lot of good that would do," retorted Paul. "He'd come and buy us out, or something equally embarrassing. Besides we now have hope. We have Louisa. As soon as she marries our Dad the whole picture changes, because we shall no more—to quote his favorite sickener—be leaving him all alone."

Louisa felt it high time to speak up on her own account.

"Yes, but what about *me?*" she demanded indignantly. "You don't seem to realize that what *I* want is a family!"

They regarded her with their usual bright intelligence.

"That's what Cathy thought," said Paul. "But surely it isn't too late to start?"

"Look at Sarah wife of Abraham," encouraged Toby.

"Thanks," said Louisa. "What I'm trying to get into your heads is that I want a family *now*. It's not fair, if I marry your father and you all clear out next day."

"Ah, but think how we'd come *back,*" said Paul swiftly. "With you here, Louisa, we'd be back whenever we could—rushing home to our step-mamma."

"Personally, I'd call it ideal," offered Catherine. "Just think, Louisa—part of the time a blushing bride, then *wham!* a mother of three. If that isn't having the best of both worlds, tell me what is.— Dear, dear Louisa, say you will!"

"But I haven't been asked!" cried Louisa.

"Of course he'll ask you. We know he'll ask you. Then as soon as he feels safe and cozy you can talk to him about us—"

"Only she mustn't leave it too long," put in Paul anxiously. "We want our applications in."

"Louisa must handle it as she thinks best. Of course there's no question of her going after just a week—and I dare say our Dad needs a little time."

"Yes, but before June the thirtieth, or we'll have to wait another year."

"Well, that gives her nearly a month. That ought to be loads. Then the gates will open—"

"The nest will fall—"

"No more birdlime!"

Louisa looked from one radiant face to another; at something in her glance the children paused.

"We aren't rushing *you*, are we?" asked Catherine anxiously.

"No," said Louisa. "But aren't you fond of your father at all?"

VI

It was as though she'd thrown a cloth over a bird cage. Louisa deliberately allowed the silence that followed to prolong itself, while the children's attention concentrated.

"He's fond of *you*, you know," said Louisa.

They looked at each other. Tacitly, the word was left with Paul.

"But that's just what we don't," stated Paul thoughtfully. "Quite honestly, *we* think he's just got a thing about families. *We* think that if we weren't his children, he'd probably rather dislike us."

"And no wonder," said Louisa indignantly. "But you are his children, as he's your father. Aren't you fond of him at all?"

Almost unexpectedly, a little catspaw of uneasiness ruffled their calm. As they looked at each other again, Louisa thankfully recognized at least an attempt to be fair.

"When we were little—" began Catherine uncertainly. She broke off, evidently recalling as might a centenarian the days of her youth. "When I was really little, he once made me a Noah's Ark with a gangway."

"When I was about ten, and had mumps, he read Kipling to me," acknowledged Paul.

"He used to be pretty good about fireworks, on Guy Fawkes," recalled Toby.

For a moment, while Louisa held her breath, rockets burst above the roof of a homemade Noah's Ark; a boy sat up in bed listening to the tale of Mowgli . . .

"If you think we don't *mind*, not loving our father," said Catherine abruptly, "you couldn't be more mistaken. It's not just that we worry, quite enormously, over what sort of complexes we may be building up; we'd much *rather* love him. Only when he just clamps down like birdlime on all our absolutely vital projects, it makes him very difficult, to love . . ."

Louisa sat back against her pillows and let a tide of happiness flow over her. How earnestly had she longed to *do* something, for

Catherine and Toby and Paul! Now a gift greater than she'd ever contemplated lay within her power: by setting them free to fly, she could give them back their love for their father.

"All right," said Louisa, as lightly as she could. "I'll do my best. And I promise you not to marry him until he's signed on the dotted lines!"

Catherine kissed her first; then Toby, then Paul.—It was like having a litter of puppies on the bed, thought Louisa; only they weren't puppies, they were a family.

Chapter Twenty-Four

I

Breakfast next morning was even pleasanter than Sunday's. Warm as the sunshine that streamed through the windows, the children's affection streamed out towards Louisa; and now she had no fears of what the fair show might conceal. Moreover they were particularly careful not to embarrass her by any suggestion of complicity; and when Mr. Clark suggested that no doubt Cathy meant to profit by such a fine morning to take Tomboy out early, not one so much as caught her eye.

When Louisa went round collecting laundry, she found they'd all made their beds.

She left Mr. Clark at table; he for once was being unusually slow. "Would you mind," asked Louisa, "if I didn't stay to pour your second cup? I want to get on with the wash."—She had a pretty shrewd idea that this wouldn't offend him, and it didn't; "'Those who wash on Monday,'" quoted Mr. Clark humorously, "'have all the week to dry—'" "On a day like this," cried Louisa vigorously, "It'll by dry by lunchtime!"

She had the kitchen to herself, for Mrs. Temple, frustrated in clearing away breakfast, observed that all things being equal she might as well trot off to her own dhobi. ("In the washing machine," observed Mrs. Temple; adding, "If you're still at that lark in a month's time, I'll eat my old man's hat.") Louisa was perfectly agreeable; she had formed the daring project of attempting to iron a shirt, and greatly preferred to be free of the cynical and experienced Temple eye. She didn't overestimate her powers; the shirts she was used to were the drip-dry variety; Louisa meant to start with one of Toby's, and work up by degrees, through Paul's, before so much as setting iron to tail on one of Mr. Clark's.—It is almost impossible to credit; Louisa's happy fancy actually envisaged *starch;* for stiff or evening shirts. But she was well aware that starch must lie in the future; and for the moment just picked out Toby's worst. Even that she set aside until she'd done the woollens, she wanted to get them out as soon as possible in the good drying wind . . .

"A *month!*" thought Louisa, echoing Mrs. Temple—and plunging half a dozen socks into blood-temperature suds. Why, years could pass before she tired of such delightful employment! It still pleased her that Mrs. Temple had said a month; a month was the latter's general time-unit, the equivalent of indefinitely. Mrs. Temple no less than the children, it seemed, considered her as a fixture! And let but a week or two more lapse, thought Louisa happily, just going quietly on as they were now—*che va piano va sicuro*, softly-softly catchee monkey—and she was pretty confident herself that such would be her happy fate.

Without in the least meaning to go back on her word, she had an idea that it might be wise to postpone her good offices on behalf of the children as long as possible—until Mr. Clark, as they'd said themselves, felt really cozy and safe.

Happily Louisa soaked and squeezed and rinsed out socks. She had a dozen pairs out in the orchard before ten. Not one bird but a whole family were going tweet there. "Suet for Christmas!" Louisa promised them. "Pass the word!"

It hadn't occurred to her, all this time, to wonder what had become of Mr. Clark. Subconsciously, she presumed he'd taken himself off like the children. But just as she'd put in the third batch of woolens to soak, there at the kitchen door, coffee cup in hand, Mr. Clark appeared. In the other hand he held two more coffee cups, neatly piled on a plate.

As the children had made their beds for her, so now their father was clearing the breakfast table. Louisa's heart beat.

—Rapidly she checked over the times when it had so beaten, at least recently, before. When old Freddy, recalled Louisa, suddenly rose from a game of chess; when Jimmy Brown, by candlelight, sat down beside her opposite a bamboo coffee table; neither moment could compare, for true romance, with this; as Mr. Clark bore in the washing-up . . .

"I thought you were gone," said Louisa inadequately.

"So I should be," agreed Mr. Clark. "So I shall be, in a few moments. I just thought I'd bring out these."

"Put them down, will you?" said Louisa. "I'll wash up afterwards."

"What are you so busy at now?" inquired Mr. Clark.

Actually what Louisa had in the suds at that moment were his own longs. What a delightfully intimate circumstance! But instinct warned her to suppress it. She suspected in Mr. Clark a more than maiden modesty about his underwear. And while she hesitated—

"If you imagine I didn't hear, last night," said Mr. Clark, smiling at her, "I did. All the children chattering in your room!"

II

For a moment Louisa was thoroughly disconcerted. Hadn't she just decided to wait, before taking up the children's battle?—but if the opportunity turned out as fair as it promised, it might have to be seized.—Just at the moment, however, she hastily threw Toby's shirt into the suds as well, in order to have something unembarrassing to pull out.

"I must say I liked to hear it," continued Mr. Clark. "Not of course as a regular thing, bedtime is bedtime; but just for once I admit it pleased me very much. It seemed to confirm an opinion."

Louisa's heart started thumping again. *If the opportunity turned out as fair as it promised—*! What if the opportunity was for *her?*—Mr. Clark overcome by sudden recklessness?

She found just enough breath to say she was very glad.

"I wonder if you can guess what I thought it sounded like?"

The suds rose in a sort of enormous meringue as Louisa, now unconsciously, added a pair of Paul's pajamas.

"It sounded like the hum of a happy hive."

Lunatically, Louisa tipped in some half pound of soap flakes. Meringue thickened to porridge.

"About the queen bee."

By this time there were thick, glutinous suds not only all over the draining board, but also all down the front of Louisa's apron. Probably there were suds in her hair. One at least Louisa wiped off her nose. But it was with as much confidence as though she'd just emerged from a beauty parlor that she at last turned to meet Mr. Clark's eyes.

"What were they talking to you about?" asked Mr. Clark.

III

Reaping the fruit of her forethought, Louisa pulled out Toby's shirt. It was so full of soap it felt like a chamois leather; however the mere attempt to wring it afforded her a moment's grace. She needed one: the sudden shift of focus, from her own future back to the children's, was peculiarly unwelcome. But the opportunity to speak for them—Mr. Clark stood waiting inquisitively—wasn't so much offered as absolutely thrust upon her.

"Well, about their ambitions," said Louisa nervously.

"Ah! In the publishing business," nodded Mr. Clark. "Naturally it will be some years before the boys join me; but I'm glad to know they have ambitions about it! I dare say," he added whimsically, "they've some rather revolutionary ideas?"

"Well, yes," said Louisa.

"I fully anticipate so. Paul will probably want me to put out Primers of Russian by the Direct Method—whatever that may be!"

What the hell was Louisa to say next? Her impulse, on purely selfish grounds, was to cozy Mr. Clark on every point; moreover she sincerely found his attitude not only reasonable, but sympathetic. Wasn't there an endearing parental pride implicit in his very jest at Paul the revolutionary? But Louisa had made a promise not to Mr. Clark but to the children; and she kept it.

"I'm afraid it's a bit more revolutionary than that," confessed Louisa. "They want to go and make jets."

IV

The sun still shone outside. The big kitchen, warmed by both sun and Louisa's reckless use of hot water, was still warm as a greenhouse. Yet from some quarter blew a chilly wind. The big mound of soap suds slowly collapsed.

"So that was what they were talking to you about," said Mr. Clark ominously. "I hope you gave them no encouragement?"

"I *tried* not to," apologized Louisa, "only they seemed to have everything so worked out. And if they really *can* go to Rolls's—"

His glance cut her short. It wasn't definitely accusing, but it cut her short.

"That headmaster of theirs has much to answer for," said Mr. Clark coldly. "I don't blame my sons; but I shall see their headmaster today."

"Honestly, I don't believe anyone's been influencing them," persisted Louisa. "They've both got very strong characters—like yours. I believe it's just that they both know exactly what they're interested in; and it's jets."

"Machinery!" snapped Mr. Clark contemptuously. "Didn't I give them their Vespas?"

"And how wonderfully understanding of you!" agreed Louisa eagerly. (If this was her private opinion, unshared by Paul and Toby, she was still firm in it. She didn't speak to mollify. Louisa still refused to regard the boys' Vespas, any more than Catherine's horse, as a bribe.—The thought of Catherine's treachery, yet to be revealed, made her almost quake; she hurried on to get the boys over first.) "In fact, what really worries them," said Louisa—skipping several intermediate stages—"is that they'd have to go and live in digs."

"I'm glad to hear it," said Mr. Clark bitterly. "That the idea of leaving the family roof arouses at least some little worry. To me it's simply unnatural." He paused, and with an unexpected gesture dropped his hand—as he might have dropped it on Toby's head—on Toby's shirt. "Isn't their natural place here with their father?" asked Mr. Clark sadly.

Louisa hesitated. She found both plea and gesture deeply touching; yet by some trick of memory what struck her most was Mr. Clark's reference to himself in the third person. It was a locution she recalled of old—*If you'd only show your aunt a little gratitude*, or, *Your aunt is only doing her best for you*—and Louisa recalled also how extraordinarily irritating she'd found it. She did her best to put the memory aside.

"They'd be home quite often," pleaded Louisa. "They're looking forward to that already. All of them!"

"All of them?" repeated Mr. Clark incredulously. "*All* of them? Do you mean to say that Cathy too has some such preposterous notion—of leaving home?"

Whether because she'd just remembered Aunt May, or whether from sheer nervous strain, Louisa suddenly lost her head.

"But she's told you about it herself!" cried Louisa impatiently. "Just as the boys have told you about Rolls's! For heaven's sake, you can't pretend you don't know *anything!*"

The hand on Toby's shirt dropped.

"I am not aware of 'pretending' in any sense," said Mr. Clark coldly. "All three of my children have, I agree, from time to time talked a great deal of rubbish to me; naturally I paid no attention."

"That wasn't very respectful," said Louisa sadly.

Fortunately he misunderstood her. His look softened.

"I'm glad you agree with me there. I did, as I thought, end the whole foolish business—at least as concerned Cathy—so recently as on Saturday night; I'm only sorry she brought it up again to pester *you* with." He smiled. "I see she *got round* you!" accused Mr. Clark. (Accused and forgave as it were in the same breath.) "My daughter Cathy is a very beguiling young miss. No doubt a nurses' hostel seems very glamorous to her; no doubt she sees herself as a modern Florence Nightingale. But if you were as accustomed to handling a family as I am," said Mr. Clark, now quite mildly, "you'd realize that there are times when to seem harsh is to be most truly kind."

Louisa, she couldn't help it, thought of birdlime.

"I dare say the boys *got round* you too," added Mr. Clark forgivingly. "Young fools! Some day, naturally, they will leave the—"

"Nest?" supplied Louisa.

He looked pleased.

"I like to know that you think of it as that too.—When my sons are old enough to marry, and if they find nice suitable girls—*not* the sort who'd be content with mechanics!—I shall naturally expect them to leave. I shan't even suggest splitting up this house—though it could well be managed—into self-contained flats. But *until* that day arrives, the place of all three is obviously here at home with their father."

He looked confidently at Louisa for agreement. He was reckoning, and rightly, on her natural desire to take his side. He knew just as well as Louisa, did Mr. Clark, what was in the wind! But he reckoned without Aunt May.

"I do wish," exclaimed Louisa uncontrollably, "you wouldn't keep calling yourself their father!"

A last soap bubble rose and burst, as Mr. Clark's brow grew dark.

"Since I *am* their father—" he began, ominously again.

"Yes, of course, but haven't you ever noticed how irritating it is," begged Louisa, "to the young? I mean, look at Hamlet; 'Let not thy *mother* lose her prayers, Hamlet!'—one can't wonder that he almost throttled her. I'm only trying to help," said Louisa.

"You make it hard for me to believe," stated Mr. Clark. He paused, regarding her, all too obviously, with fresh eyes. "In fact, what I'm beginning to believe, though with what disappointment I can hardly express, is that you would positively abet my children in their foolishness."

It was at this point that Louisa, ever a realist, recognized herself in the position of one who may as well be hanged for a sheep as a lamb.

"Yes, I do," said Louisa brusquely, "because it isn't foolishness. I've never in my life met three such thoroughly sensible young people making such thoroughly sensible plans. I only wish you'd given birth to Hugo Pym—or any of the Pammies! Then you *would* have something to complain about!—But there's another thing as well," said Louisa, pausing in turn; "something that as an outsider I dare say I've no right to talk about at all. Only I must, because it's so important..."

Mr. Clark waited—no more.

"They all *want*—Catherine and Toby and Paul—to be able to love you again."

He didn't flinch; he froze.

"It's only your holding them back," continued Louisa recklessly, "from everything they want to do—Paul and Toby from going to Rolls's, Catherine from taking her training as a nurse—that's made them *stop* loving you. They remember Guy Fawkes Night and—and everything. Can't you see what a serious thing it is," pressed Louisa, "to stop the flow of love?"

She made no more impression than the bird of legend brushing its wing across a granite pillar.

"A disappointment all the more bitter," said Mr. Clark, going on from where he'd left off, "in that I had built, I admit, certain hopes. I had hoped that this week you've spent amongst us might have been but the first of many. I will be frank: I had hoped to see a united and happy family benefiting by your affection for many a year to come."

"So had I," said Louisa sadly.

"Instead of which it seems that your presence has been positively disruptive."

"I suppose it *was* because I was here they felt they could get cracking," admitted Louisa. "Because they felt you wouldn't be left all alone . . ."

Cool as a hardened villain—in the circumstances—Mr. Clark lifted his eyebrows.

"They could hardly imagine your remaining after they were gone? That would scarcely I think be suitable. However, after all you have told me—and, more importantly, after all they have seen fit to tell *you*—the inmost secrets of our family life bandied with a complete stranger!—I begin to feel their absence almost preferable. *Let* my children leave me!" exclaimed Mr. Clark, with sudden vigor. "It is possible I may be less lonely than they expect! With no childish likes and dislikes to consider—"

For some reason the image of a Saxon head and ruddy cheeks flashed into Louisa's mind. Could it be a *reflected* image?

"—I may even find the permanent companionship of a wife," said Mr. Clark cruelly.

Then he did something Louisa was never to forgive. He sat down at the kitchen table, and took out his pen and checkbook, and wrote her out a check.

"I imagine five guineas will be sufficient?" said Mr. Clark. "For a week?"

"As I've had my keep as well, yes," said Louisa.

He held his pen poised; as though he'd expected more gratitude for his liberality.

"You have also done a certain amount of laundry work?"

"Five guineas covers that too," said Louisa. "Just sign on the dotted line, will you? Because when you get back tonight, I shan't be here."

V

She felt without seeing the children again either. She couldn't bear to. She just wrote a note for Catherine. *"Darling, I'm sorry I can't help, tell the boys,"* scrawled Louisa. *"Try Lindy. And anyway try to love all the same . . ."* She paused, and with mingled wryness and yearning signed *"Your affectionate failed step-mamma, or Louisa."*

There was no love in her own heart, however, as she propped the note on Cathy's dressing table, in that flowery bedroom of a young girl's dreams; rather Louisa herself now saw its roses spoiled by birdlime . . .

In fact, lacerated as she was, Louisa bore away from Glenarvon far more substantial profit than five guineas. At last, she'd met a man she positively disliked. She was no longer *indiscriminately* fond of men. Moreover it may have been remarked that both her attention and her emotions, during that past week, had centered far more on the children than on their father. The male no longer, exclusively, filled her horizon.

In fact, it seemed as though she had come to a point where she could just take men or leave them.

Not without a pang, recalling each event of the two or three weeks preceding, she resolved to leave them.

—Not without a pang, but at least, after Mr. Clark, with the calm of final disillusion.

PART FOUR

Chapter Twenty-Five

I

"I must say you get around," observed the milkman. "How was the grub this trip?"

With some surprise, Louisa realized that at Glenarvon she'd hardly noticed the food at all. Only one meal stayed in her memory: a picnic Sunday lunch . . .

"I suppose I ate," said Louisa.

"But nothing tasty?" sympathized the milkman.

"Just plain family fare," said Louisa.

"Well, why not treat yourself to a spot of cream?" suggested the milkman.

"Look," said Louisa, "I may be what suffragettes chained themselves to railings for, I may be the *femme sole* with all her rights—"

"I remember you telling me," said the milkman.

"—but all I've got out of it is that I can't afford cream. So lay off the high-pressure salesmanship."

"I'm not on commission," said the milkman, hurt. "That go for yoghurt too?"

She hesitated.

"Keep it on till the dairy cuts up rough," said Louisa. "At any rate I've got a profession."

II

She still had a profession. It was a defeat, in a way, to subside upon it; Louisa was still intellectually convinced, on behalf of all *femmes soles*, as to the desirability of either rich or steady husbands—now with a family if possible thrown in. But each of her own three attempts in this field having failed, at least she had a profession to fall back on.

"Let's face it," thought Louisa. "I'm where I started. From now on, it's the dogs . . ."

Which made it all the more a pity that she'd forgotten, that last morning at Broydon, to load her camera. The shot Louisa now visualized was an absolute world-beater. She saw Ivor and Ivan on the cover of *Life*. She saw herself getting a gold medal for it. She saw everything, in fact, but the actual print, which didn't exist.

"Yes, and why doesn't it exist?" thought Louisa grimly. "Because my mind, that's why, wasn't on the job."

It had been on Jimmy Brown; or, in other words, upon matrimony: just as at Glenarvon she hadn't thought to take a shot of Tomboy—the very subject for Pony Club Christmas cards!—because her mind had been on Mr. Clark. Louisa perceived that if she was to make anything of her profession at all, she'd better stick to it.

Mentally she burned her matrimonial boats; and being never one to do things by halves, immediately after a thin breakfast telephoned Hugo Pym.

III

"My dear Louisa!" cried Hugo warmly. "I've been trying to get hold of you for days!—How did he like it?"

It took Louisa a moment to think back—past Mr. Clark, past Jimmy Brown, to F. Pennon.

"It's all off," said Louisa baldly.

There was an incredulous pause.

"If you're talking about the *show*, darling—" began Hugo Pym.

"No," said Louisa. "I'm talking—"

"Because if you are, naturally it is. We're a rep. company."

Louisa took a deep breath.

"Listen," she said. "I'm talking, believe it or not, about myself. I'm not going to get married after all. So if you've spread the news around, you might just unspread it."

Again there was a pause. Louisa had known explanations would be difficult, and they were.

"My dear girl," returned Hugo firmly, "I simply don't believe you. It's too ridiculous."

"Not ridiculous. Sad."

"I meant, fantastic," Hugo corrected himself. "Good heavens, Louisa, only a couple of weeks ago there I saw you with my own eyes absolutely *wallowing* in devotion! Absolutely biting my head off at the least *breath*—! Are you sure," suggested Hugo hopefully, "it isn't just a lovers' tiff?"

"Quite sure," said Louisa.

"I mean, it would be a pity if I couldn't put on my Aristophanes just because you've had a slight run-in with your intended."

"Dear Hugo, I feel for you," said Louisa. "I'm still not going to marry—"

She hesitated. It was an added distress that she had to hesitate between more than one name. Had she ever told Hugo F. Pennon's? She couldn't remember . . .

"—anyone at all," finished Louisa.

IV

Deliberately she burnt her boats. Her visit to Soho was at an hour deliberately chosen to encounter Mr. Ross.

"Keeping up on the job till the last?" joked Rossy.

"It's all off," said Louisa.

In the very tones of Hugo Pym—

"What d'you mean, it's all off?" demanded Mr. Ross.

"I'm not going to get married. I've changed my mind."

At least Rossy had no ax to grind. His concern was disinterested. It was nonetheless extremely irritating to Louisa's current mood.

"I remember you phoning me," said Mr. Ross anxiously. "But if it's just a matter of settlements—"

At least, after her conversation with Hugo, Louisa knew at once whom they were talking about; and without a break skated over Jimmy Brown and Mr. Clark to do F. Pennon justice.

"The settlements would have been all right. They'd have been fine. I just couldn't stand," explained Louisa, "the life."

Rossy's concern simply deepened.

"If there's a door still open, I'd like you to talk to my sister. She had doubts herself—though I must say not many. Why don't I get you together?"

"I wouldn't waste her time," said Louisa, "though thank you all the same, Rossy dear. I'm back on the old stand: Datchett Photographer of Dogs."

V

Datchett Photographer of Dogs still had her profession; but it was at low ebb.

A peculiar mood of cheese-paring seemed to have settled over the entire dog world. No client old or new, during the days that followed, wrote or telephoned to ask Louisa's services. Already grudging each penny, Louisa wrote or telephoned herself—without results. Even Supreme Champions were making do with last year's photographs; even the famous York establishment let her down. ("Dear Miss Datchett, fine as the last lot were, we don't seem to need anything fresh just now. Salaams and all the best.") The Bow-wows to Baby check was the last to come in.

What did come in were last month's bills. The dairy's was the worst, but even the lesser ones added up alarmingly. Louisa began to wake at four in the morning, adding them.

It was a new thing for her to wake at all. All her life, hitherto, she'd put her head on her pillow and passed out for the next eight hours. She'd even thought it an inconvenience, that if she didn't get to bed till three, she didn't wake up till eleven. Now she woke regularly.

Her chief liquid assets were the two bottles of brandy pressed on her by F. Pennon when she left Bournemouth. Carried round to a famous wine merchant in St. James's Street, so astonishing, and authentic, their labels, they almost doubled Louisa's capital; even so, it was under thirty pounds.

When the thought of hocking her camera entered her mind, Louisa realized that the time was past for any false pride.

After all, hadn't she always photographed *en plein air?*

VI

"Look, Rossy," said Louisa, "outside Burlington House, do they ever have dogs with them?"

Mr. Ross considered her with what had become a habitual expression of affectionate disapproval. ("Dammit, if *I* can get over three husbands, why can't he get over one?" thought Louisa impatiently.)

"Not that I recall," said Mr. Ross. "It's the quarantine."

"But just now and again?" pressed Louisa. "They can't *all* be foreign visitors! Don't tell me you've never seen a peke in Piccadilly! What I mean is, would the boys mind if I strung along?"

"I'm not sure I quite see what you're getting at," said Mr. Ross uneasily.

"Well, *you* say, 'Take your picture, lady—'"

"'Madam,'" corrected Rossy. "Sometimes adding," he admitted, "'in that lovely hat.'"

"Well, *I'd* say, 'Take your dog?'"

Mr. Ross hesitated. He had a genuine affection for Louisa; also strong business instincts. As the two emotions—the sentimental and the professional—struggled in his breast, he looked less and less happy.

"It wouldn't do," he stated at last.

"Why not?"

"You've told me yourself about getting 'em to stand on tables—sometimes with a bone nailed to it. You couldn't set up a table with a bone nailed to it in Piccadilly. The police wouldn't let you."

"I don't *have* to have a table. I could squat down."

"I don't believe the cops would care for that either. You'd hold up the traffic," said Mr. Ross firmly, "and get us all a bad name."

Louisa paused in turn. Rossy's cooperation was vital to her. She made a final effort.

"Look, Rossy," said Louisa again, "this may be something really big for me. It may be a whole new career. I swear not to poach! Unless there *is* a dog, I'll just be admiring the view. Just tell the boys to give me a chance—and you can remind 'em there'll be no whip-round, now, for a wedding present."

It wasn't her words that swayed him. The boys enjoyed giving wedding presents. They liked to feel the generous sentimental glow. What swayed Rossy was the expression on Louisa's face.

"Okay," sighed Rossy. "I'll tell 'em. Though you'd still do better, in my opinion, to have a word with Sis."

Chapter Twenty-Six

I

High-hearted nonetheless stood Louisa next morning outside Burlington House. Rossy's word, however reluctantly given, had gone
round. Josh and Manny grinned at her companionably, from the
opposite side of the street Benny sketched a double-handed boxer's
salute. And if it took a certain courage, on Louisa's part, so to decline
to the pavement, she'd always been, if nothing else, courageous . . .

She was there in readiness soon after ten. (Coffee-colored linen
suit, beechnut boutonnière brushed free from mites, an appearance
altogether as un-dashing as she could make it. She felt the beechnuts
a particularly reassuring touch—for country cousins.) Until eleven,
however, not so much as a schipperke crossed her field of vision. Mr.
Ross bagged a brace of Texans, Josh, an Australian; Benny opposite, a turbaned Sikh. Loyally Louisa hung back, fingering the camera about her neck only as might any tourist; and as at last a dog
appeared, loyally the boys hung back in turn; leaving her a clear
field.

Surprisingly, it was a Sealyham.

The dogs proper to Piccadilly are poodles and Pekingese. Sight-
ing a Sealyham, Louisa for one wild moment (she was a little over-
strung) felt as though F. Pennon in person had come to her aid.

The resemblance was indeed uncommon: thick, springy, brindled hair, bushy eyebrows, even F. Pennon's keen and skeptical old eye, were so accurately reproduced in canine miniature, the collar and lead looked to Louisa like a collar and tie.—How thoughtful of old Freddy to wear them! There had been a slight, entirely amicable discussion on the point; any pooch actually *carried*—any peke, or poodle, tucked under arm—was to count along with its owner as out of Louisa's field. ("They hold 'em up against their faces," explained Josh. "And often a good thing too.") But with the Sealyham, or F. Pennon, trotting on a lead, Louisa hardly advanced.

"Take your dog, madam?" invited Louisa.

Her prospects, anthropoid and quadruped, at least halted. Surprisingly again, the anthropoid wasn't the regulation tweed-clad, county-type Sealyham owner, but a fluttering blonde. ("Dammit, it *is* F. Pennon!" thought Louisa wildly.) In Mrs. Anstruther's exact voice—

"Ducky, someone wants to take your picture!" fluted the anthropoid to her quadruped. "Shall us say yes?"

Louisa was already down on one knee. Behind her she felt Rossy and Josh emanating waves of encouragement—all disapproving thoughts forgotten, urging her on to make good. The pavement was comparatively unencumbered, the sun was in the right place, and the moment practically historic as Louisa—the first canine photographer in Piccadilly—dropped to one knee and set her shutter at 1/300th.

Unfortunately, the quadruped said *no*.

With an absolute reflection of Freddy's most ill-tempered glance—called to the telephone, so to speak, in the middle of a cigar—Ducky jerked free his lead and attacked a Western Union messenger. "Stop him!" shouted Mr. Ross. "Catch the b—r!" shouted Josh. "My poor frightened lamb!" wailed the blonde. Ducky raced on, snapped at two more Sikhs in passing, and nipped a South African delegate to an economic conference.—The latter came out best; as Ducky plunged into the traffic, with all the élan of his ancestral impis he plunged after; and at least brought back news of where the culprit had gone to ground—down the Ladies beside Green Park.

Meanwhile the pavement round Louisa had become quite crowded. If opinions diverged—all the foreigners agreeing with each other that all dogs were dangerous, all the British agreeing that it was a shame to frighten them—Louisa was equally censured all round. As a policeman approached, she felt the eyes of even Josh and Rossy fixed on her in justified rebuke . . .

"Now then, what's all this?" inquired the policeman.

("See what I mean?" sighed Mr. Ross.)

"He was frightened by the horrid camera!" wailed Ducky's owner.

"Now he's probably biting Ladies right and left," said the delegate, rather jovially. "You'll have to send for a policewoman . . ."

Fortunately Ducky chose this moment to reappear. No one could have guessed from his demeanor that he'd just been whacked on the behind by a cleaner's broom; he ambled back through the traffic with all the dreamy, dignified assurance of an absent-minded professor. The sight of the policeman, however, appeared to give him pause; with what Louisa couldn't help feeling an absolutely cynical switch to pathos, he began to shake all over. "What a shame!" cried one and all—with the exception of a few foreigners—as Ducky crept back to his mistress's protection. "He was *frightened!*"

At least the policeman moved off. He wasn't looking for trouble. His eye just registered the presence, at the scene of the riot, of Louisa and Josh and Manny and Mr. Ross.

"See what I mean?" repeated Mr. Ross. "Dogs won't cooperate. We're on tricky enough ground as it is, and if one of the public got *bit*—"

"Okay," said Louisa sadly. "You needn't go on."

"It's not we don't want you, it's just that we can't afford the risk."

"Okay," sighed Louisa; and made the best amends she could by going straight home.

Chapter Twenty-Seven

I

If at this point Louisa plumbed her professional nadir, there is always this about a nadir, that any subsequent motion must inevitably be upwards.

Unless, of course, the pendulum has stopped.

Louisa's view was that it had. Perhaps this was because she wasn't eating enough. The debacle in Piccadilly had thoroughly dismayed her; during the succeeding week, in a panic attempt to conserve her capital, she not only didn't pay any bills, she ate less and less. Remorse kept her from sharing even a cuppa with Mr. Ross; if Hugo Pym had a spare sausage (which was unlikely), she wouldn't have shared that either, at the price of being urged to make up a nonexistent quarrel with a nonexistent intended. Louisa was down to a steady diet of bread and margarine, she was very nearly pinching Number Ten's yoghurt, before the pendulum swung up again.

It hadn't stopped after all. It had but paused to gather momentum.

II

"There was a letter for you," said the milkman. "I brought it up."

"Does it look like a bill?" asked Louisa nervously.

"No, stuck down," said the milkman. "Very nice quality envelope."

"What's the postmark?" asked Louisa—still wary.

"Chesham Oaks," said the milkman. "Best part of Bucks."

It was as a sort of propitiary libation that Louisa took, along with the envelope, a spot of cream.

III

She looked at the signature first: Sybil Fox. The name meant nothing to her, but below was typed the encouraging word *Secretary*. Also the paper itself was crested.

Dear Miss Datchett (read Louisa)

Lady Mary Tablet asks me to inquire whether you would be free to come down next Thursday the 11th, at three-thirty, to photograph her corgis? There is a good train from Baker Street at 2:36, and a bus from the station yard will drop you at Chesham Hall. (There is no need to bring any lighting apparatus, as the photographs will be taken out of doors.) I may add that Lady Mary was very much struck by some pictures of poodles you had in the Tatler—she thinks they belonged to some film actress, but cannot remember the name—and would rather like the same sort of thing. Will you kindly let me know if this date suits you, also your fee? Lady Mary suggests three guineas, to include the finished prints.

Yours truly,
Sybil Fox
Secretary

IV

Datchett Photographer of Dogs kept her head.

The fee suggested, for half a working day, including prints, was outrageously low; and something told her it was all she could shake down. On the other hand, there is no world more snobbish than the dog world; the corgis of a Lady Mary Tablet would have their own built-in publicity.

A more disturbing point was what Lady Mary intended by the same sort of thing. The film actress was undoubtedly that Italian star to whom Louisa owed her trip to Cannes; could Lady Mary possibly be contemplating a Rescue by Corgis from Ornamental Water? If so, it would probably take not half a day but half a week, with a few movie technicians thrown in.—Louisa made a hasty check, and gratefully recalled the famous Rescue by Poodles fake as appearing only in the local French press. What then had Lady Mary seen in the *Tatler*? Louisa searched about, but couldn't find the issue; she must have left it at Broydon Court. After some thought, however, she remembered a previous shot taken in Green Park, of Coco and Cocotte affectionate to their mistress's celebrated underpinnings. Louisa had suspected at the time that it was those ankles, rather than those pooches, the *Tatler* paid for; and was not discouraged. If Lady Mary herself had any ankles at all, if she wasn't on absolute hockey sticks, something could be managed . . .

Fortunately corgis are very low-slung.

Louisa kept her head, but with increasing difficulty. It was her chance at last. A really good job done on Lady Mary's corgis, and ankles, could put Datchett Photographer of Dogs into the very top class.

—And how had it come to her, that chance? Through keeping her mind on her work. Inconceivable, in Green Park—before she'd heard from F. Pennon, before remembering Jimmy Brown, before encountering Mr. Clark—that she should have forgotten to load her camera! ("If I'd kept my mind on my work at Broydon," thought Louisa, "I'd have syndicates bidding now, for that shot of Ivor and Ivan.") It was astonishing, now, to remember how easily she'd let the rot set in: she'd just felt jaded one morning, had a talk with the milkman about Ibsen—was that really all, had no more than that been sufficient to arouse her so disastrous impulse towards matrimony? It seemed so; not otherwise, now, could Louisa account for her subsequent aberrations . . .

"I was a fool, but I've learnt my lesson," thought Louisa. "I'm not the marrying sort. But what I am is a damned good photographer of dogs, and here's my chance, it's all I ask, and I'm going to take it."

She answered Miss Fox, Secretary, by return of post. (To telephone, or telegraph, might look over-eager.) The three days that intervened before the eleventh she spent mostly in bed, conserving energy; also she dipped so far into her capital as to add to her diet of bread and margarine sardines and kippers.

V

Taking every possible pain with her appearance, on the crucial day, Louisa oddly enough found herself dressing for Chesham Hall as for the pavement outside Burlington House. (Discreet coffee-colored linen, spray of beechnuts on shoulder.) This time however, she added a hat, a practically county hat, a green felt porkpie once worn by Bobby at Cannes. Louisa stuffed as much of her hair under it as she could; her rowdy locks were always a weak point, when it came to inspiring professional confidence, and she was taking no chances.

She was taking no chances. She was resolved to keep her mind strictly on the job, also not to waste an ounce of energy until she reached Chesham Hall.

Before boarding her train she looked for a compartment without a man in it—men in trains constituted a particular hazard. (All too often, getting out at their destinations, they told Louisa how much better they felt for talking to her; leaving Louisa flat as a pancake. Sometimes she even had to get out herself; once, and three stations early, to accompany a nervous juvenile to his audition at a local rep.; which was how she'd first met Hugo Pym.) At that hour, half past two in the afternoon, and headed out of London, the train was by no means full: on the other hand, this allowed the native passion for privacy full play; to each smoker its solitary occupant—the worst possible hazard—and past each Louisa's experienced eye hurried her on. As she reached the last, doors were being slammed all down the train; Louisa nonetheless, perceiving again a solitary male within, hesitated. The young man looked cheerful enough, indeed uncommonly so; but appearances could deceive, and Louisa was taking no chances. Sticking her head through the door—

"Are you in any sort of trouble?" asked Louisa forthrightly.

As well he might, the young man looked surprised. But only for a moment. He was evidently a true child of his age.

"Is it for the telly?" he countered interestedly.

"No, just a private poll," said Louisa.

"Then put me in the opposite column," said the young man—disappointed but still cheerful.

Louisa entered and relaxed. The train drew out. With a whole side of the carriage to herself, she had plenty of room for her long legs. She stretched them comfortably out, and deliberately slackened every muscle; allowing herself to be swung with the train's motion limp as a rag doll. If now and then there was a jolt, it didn't worry Louisa; it merely kept her from dozing completely off. "An hour of this is just what I need," thought Louisa. "It must be as good as Zen . . ."

She didn't exactly kick off her shoes, but she loosened her heels; the train did the rest. At eye level opposite an impression of Burnham Beeches pleased without exciting; rather soothed . . .

"Aren't you going to take it down?" inquired the young man.

"Take what down?" asked Louisa thoughtlessly.

"Why I'm in the other column."

Louisa continued to contemplate Burnham Beeches. Once again, she'd bought it; but this time she didn't mean to pay. As the young man waited expectantly—

"I don't need to take it down, I've a trained memory. But fire away," said Louisa—deliberately closing her ears.

VI

It was still impossible that something shouldn't percolate. The train had decided to run with uncommon smoothness, the young man leaned enthusiastically towards her. However unwillingly, Louisa picked up certain vital statistics: name something like Hally How, age twenty-something, National Service somewhere overseas, present occupation some sort of clerk. Dim, decent Hally How! Behind dropped eyelids Louisa's thoughts wandered to the Meares' dachshunds: so easy to photograph, decent little clerks of the dog world . . .

"After *which*," said Hally How earnestly, "we were finally able to get married."

. . . whereas borzois, in their skiing trousers, had always the air of being off to winter sports . . .

"I don't know if you're married yourself?" pressed Hally How.

Louisa shook her head. It would be nice for him if he thought she was memorizing, but really she didn't care.

"You ought to try it," said Hally How earnestly. "I can't tell you how—how smashing it is. Not just, if you'll pardon the expression, how jolly in bed, but what self-confidence it gives a chap. Fr'instance, you must have wondered why at this time of day, when I work in London, I'm headed out of London."

"It doesn't matter," murmured Louisa.

"I'll tell you. It's Marlene's birthday. 'I've a good mind to take the day off,' I told her, 'in celebration. Why don't I phone and say influenza?' She wouldn't have it. Her mum was in the ATS—searchlights, a very picked bunch, I've heard tell—and brought Marlene up according. 'Go along to the office, ask for the afternoon,' said Marlene, 'tell 'em why you want it, and I'll have a smashing tea laid on for when you get back.' Never doubting, d'you see, that I'd pull it off. Which is the whole secret," said Hally How. "Mind you put it in."

"Sure," murmured Louisa.

"I set it up to the boss without a frill. 'I would very much like the half-day off,' I said, 'on account of its being my wife's birthday. In fact, I intended to take the whole day off,' I said, 'only Marlene wouldn't stand for me having flu.' And d'you know what he replied?"

"No," said Louisa.

"'Your wife's made more of a man of you than the Army,' he said. 'Take her out shopping and buy her a new hat.' As I intend," said Hally How, "up to three quid. If any of this is immaterial—?'"

Louisa shook her head; or rather the train shook it for her.

"I'm glad, because I've often wondered how much is missed, when taking polls. (Rock cakes, now, I do see might be set aside. Marlene makes smashing rock cakes.) But as we're getting to my station, I'll just re-cap: what puts any chap in the okay column, nine times out of ten, is happy matrimony; and for women, of course, even more so."

VII

Louisa swung her feet up on the seat and stretched frankly recumbent for another thirty minutes of Zen.

Not that she needed it. She felt indeed like a successful candidate after a particularly grueling examination. Such a build-up for matrimony, but a month before, would have thoroughly distracted her from the job in hand. But not now. Even the numinous word rock cake aroused but a vague feeling of affection for Molly and Teddy Meare . . .

Louisa had settled for a profession. Beyond the stately portal of Chesham Hall beckoned solid fame, solid fortune. It was without either regrets or misgivings that Datchett Photographer of Dogs got out at the right station and mounted the waiting bus.

Chapter Twenty-Eight

I

It was a stately portal all right. Louisa gazed appreciatively at carved stonework scrolling up to an escutcheon above, at a great oak door ajar upon squares of black and white marble, with beside it a brass bell-pull, beautifully polished. "Staff!" thought Louisa, as she pulled it; and confidently awaited the arrival of a butler.

In the few moments' interval that followed she noted, more practically, the excellent condition of all the paint. Chesham Hall, a rarity among stately homes, was as well kept up as Mr. Clark's Glenarvon; moreover was not merely being kept up, was being improved—for Louisa sighted, on the south flank, what looked like an old winter garden under such scaffolding as suggested additions. Mentally congratulating the aristocratic owners upon either a transatlantic marriage or a successful bout with the income tax, Louisa congratulated herself too; it seemed out of the question that Lady M.'s check—such things had been known to happen—would bounce.

A butler answered. He was so perfect a specimen, from his graying hair to shoes polished like the bell-pull, Louisa momentarily suspected he'd been hired from the local rep. But his reserved, inquiring glance, as he in turn surveyed Louisa, was surely the result of more than clever direction; reserved and inquiring as it was, it explicitly placed her—somewhere between a collector for charity and an ex-service salesman. Without rancor, but firmly, she enlightened him.

"I," said Louisa, "am Datchett Photographer of Dogs. I have an appointment with Lady Mary Tablet for three-thirty. And let that," she added mentally, "teach you a lesson, my man!"

Undoubtedly he looked more respectful.

"An appointment did you say, madam?"

"To photograph Lady Mary's corgis."

"I will inform her ladyship you have arrived," said the butler—exiting within.

He still didn't invite Louisa to follow, but if she were to wait anywhere on so fine an afternoon she rather preferred to be outside. Indeed the prospect before her, as she strolled a little way past the tall windows, and sat down on a stone bench, was of great beauty. On either side the drive—about five minutes' walk long, even for Louisa—stretched a miniature parkland of lush grass and handsome trees. Clumps of oak or beech, rising like islands in a green sea, made each its stately point; each in turn led the eye on to the next; and over all lay the temperate sunlight proper to an English nobleman's country seat.

"This," thought Louisa, "is the sort of place I shall come to often . . ."

Why not? Her foot once within a first stately portal, how many other stately portals might not open to her? And remain open? No one knew better than Louisa the conservatism, as a class, of stately-portal-owners: until a favorite photographer of either their dogs or their children actually died or went gaga, to that same photographer they stuck with a loyalty Louisa now perceived as admirable. In her own field the doyen already touched seventy; Louisa sincerely hoped he'd get the O.B.E. before packing up, but when he did pack up, why shouldn't she herself step into his shoes? ("Not that they'd ever give me the O.B.E.," thought Louisa—leaping the next twenty-five years. "I'm not the right type." It was a pity; the suffragettes would have been proud of her.) But even without any explicit honor in view, what rewarding week ends might not lie ahead, photographing ducal pooches behind stately portals!

"All I'll need," thought Louisa, "is one really good dinner dress"; and determined to watch the *Times* personal column for the next Model Disposing of Balenciaga Wardrobe . . .

The sun lapsed a degree while she contemplated grouse served by footmen. For the first time in her life it struck her as fortunate that she had a taste for game. It struck Louisa, and rightly, that the nobility no less than F. Pennon might like to see a woman eat. She saw herself as a more than acceptable, as a positively popular week-end guest—pressed by dukes to stay over Monday.

"And I can do it," thought Louisa—mentally up-ending a couple of boar hounds to support a coat-of-arms. She couldn't help wishing corgis more heraldic; but there was the glamour aspect as well (which had obviously appealed to Lady Mary); Louisa trusted that many a duchess, observing how Datchett Photographer of Dogs had glamorized Lady Mary with just a couple of corgis, would hasten to be superiorly glamorized with borzoi or peke. "It's my chance and I'm going to take it," repeated Louisa to herself. "I'm going to bleed and die and get the best shot since Gelert . . ."

More time had passed then she realized, in these happy plans. It was nearly four o'clock before an elderly woman with an inherited face came loping towards her from the house.

II

She was so obviously Lady M., Louisa instantly glanced at the shins below the short tweed skirt. Though on the hockey-hardened, beagling model, there was a quite noticeable diminution towards the ankle.

"Miss Datchett? You poor dear!" exclaimed Lady Mary remorsefully. "I've kept you waiting *hours!* Johnson couldn't find me. I'm so ashamed I could *die!*"

"That's all right," said Louisa. "The light's fine. You do want them—your corgis—taken out of doors?"

Lady Mary clutched her untidy gray head.

"But that's just what's so *awful!* I don't know how to *tell* you! They aren't *here!* They're in Scotland. They went up yesterday with the boys. I'm so madly sorry, but my secretary must have made a real *bloomer*. So I'm afraid there's nothing for it," finished Lady Mary brightly, "but to call the whole thing off."

It was an irrelevance that Louisa at this moment observed upon Lady Mary's cardigan a spray of beechnuts matching her own. Could it be Number Ten who was going to get into the top class?—She pulled herself together.

"I'm madly sorry too," said Louisa formally. "The fact remains that I'll have wasted half a day. Let alone my fares—"

"But of course you'll come again," consoled Lady Mary, "when they're *back*. My dear Miss Datchett, you mustn't be cross with me! Be cross with poor Fox if you like—as I must say I often am myself— but you and 7 are just companions in distress!"

Possibly because there is a solidarity amongst professional women, Louisa remained unconvinced. Herself and Miss Fox, felt Louisa, were what suffragettes had chained themselves to railings for—not herself and Lady Mary.

"I'm not cross with anyone," said Louisa. "I'd just like my three guineas."

Lady Mary started back as might a thoroughbred hunter before a knacker's cart.

"But my dear good creature," she protested, "isn't that perfectly— I'm sure you'll see it is, when you've had a moment to think—*absurd?* I mean, three guineas just for nothing at all—!"

Louisa looked at the scaffolding on the south wing. How much was *that* going to cost?

"For a wasted half day," she corrected stubbornly.

"Ah, but what would you have been doing with it?" countered Lady Mary. "You'd have been having your hair done, or at a movie.

I know what happens, with a spare afternoon in Town! Instead of which here you are in the fresh air, enjoying a nice little outing—"

"I didn't want an outing," said Louisa. "And my fee is three guineas."

Lady Mary looked injured but resigned.

"If you really *insist*—though I must say this isn't the way one's *usually* treated—I'll tell my secretary to send you a check."

"If she's as inefficient as you make out, I'd rather have cash," said Louisa.

Lady Mary brightened again.

"But my dear Miss Datchett, I *haven't* any cash! I never carry sixpence! I'm just at my secretary's *mercy!* I do truly, don't imagine I don't, appreciate your position—but only Fox knows where to find my checkbook."

"Okay," said Louisa. "Where is she?"

"As a matter of fact, *she* left yesterday too," said Lady Mary, "for a holiday in Athens. (Something poor *I* could never afford!) So until she comes back I'm afraid we're really at a *standstill*. But I shan't forget! And now I'm going to send Johnson out to you," said Lady Mary kindly, "with a nice—"

She paused; the kindliness twinkled to democratic bonhomie.

"—with a nice *cuppa!*" finished Lady M.

Louisa didn't wait for it. Instead, with what she hoped was sufficient dignity, she walked out.

Straight-backed, with sufficient dignity, she reached the drive's end; and there outside the great gates, on the grassy bank behind the bus stop, for the first time in her adult life, sat down and cried.

III

When she'd wept in a Broydon attic, she'd been a child; and her tears all too natural—for loving if casual parents, for no more balloons brought back from a *palais de danse*. What she wept for now was

the collapse of a career. After ten years' work, after establishing herself (or so she'd fondly believed) as Datchett Photographer of Dogs,
she hadn't been able to squeeze three quid out of Lady M. She was
so little established, anyone with a title could do her down.—Here
Louisa was possibly in error. With a steak inside her, instead of sardines, the issue might have been different. But the upshot, whatever
its cause; was as disastrous to her confidence and to her self-esteem
as to her pocket. Outside the gates of Chesham Hall, on the grassy
bank behind the bus stop, Louisa sat with unchecked tears running
down her face.

Only the wind, from time to time, dried them. No fellow traveler
appeared, to rouse her pride, or even a spark of vanity: in addition to
all else, she'd just missed a bus.

—No wolf appeared either. The road was unfrequented; but Louisa sensed a deeper reason. Any number of men might have come
by, without one stopping to make a pass at her. What attracted them
of old (at a bus stop, outside a telephone booth, in any public place)
was their recognition of her special gift for aid and succor. (Wolf out
of work, recalled Louisa, wolf misunderstood by wife, wolf needing musical instrument getting out of hock.) Now that she plainly
needed aid and succor herself, they'd hurry by. Louisa didn't blame
them, she wasn't resentful; there it just was . . .

She turned her back on the road, and wept anew.

Chapter Twenty-Nine

I

In all folklore, the tear has its own and special place.

Witches, for example, cannot weep; nor mermaids; or if they do, they lose their magic nature. Only a tear, in the legend of Little Gerda and the Ice Queen, had power to shatter the frozen palace-prison. Some principal constituent, in that dropping of the eye, modern science has even discovered therapeutic against the evil of the Crab. Thus Louisa, weeping, invoked stronger forces than she suspected.

Sheer animal instinct for warmth had driven her into a last patch of sunlight; when the car stopped, and a man got out, she had her face half-buried in the hedge.—Her hat lay beside her, pulled off long since, or perhaps pushed off, by stiff hawthorn twigs; the declining sun turned her foxy head to gold.

"You look as though you're wearing a halo," observed Andrew McAndrew. "Though I must say it's no' a thought that would have occurred to me at Broydon."

II

So far as Louisa was concerned, this was the end. Of all men breathing, the last she'd have chosen to find her so disconsolate was Mr. McAndrew.

She looked at him and hated him. Everything about the man—his calm and solidity, even his good car, his good clothes—pointed all too painfully her own vagabond dishevelment; the recollection of how she'd slammed him down at Broydon Court (and at Stack's in the Strand) made the impossibility of doing so now—from a sitting position by the roadside, face and hands wet with tears—her very hat like a beggar's cap beside her!—all the more humiliating. As a first move in the direction of dignity, she rose stiffly to her feet.

"If it's the bus you want, you're previous," remarked Mr. McAndrew. "There's none due for an hour."

"I've been here an hour," retorted Louisa.—To her extreme annoyance, reaching down for her hat she felt her knees shake: she had sat too long without stirring, while the heat of the day declined to evening chill. The support of a large warm hand under her elbow, however, merely annoyed her more; she flinched back as from a viper, and took a grip of the bus sign instead.

"They pass every three. It's a very poor service," said Mr. McAndrew. "Why not let me drive you where you're going?"

"Because there happen to be two things I enjoy particularly," said Louisa—holding her eyes wide open to let the wind do its best. "One is fresh air, and the other is a nice bus ride."

"Don't be foolish," said Mr. McAndrew. "We'll stop on the way for a drink."

"Do I look as though I needed a drink?" snapped Louisa—rather unwisely.

"To be truthful, aye," said Mr. McAndrew. "You're shivering with cold.—Not that it doesn't seem to be a habit with you," he added censoriously. "I've not forgotten all that champagne yet."

"When you were so childish about your whiskey," retorted Louisa.

"Be your opinion what it may, you're still shivering," said Mr. McAndrew. "Will you get into the car, or do I lift you?"

He was undoubtedly capable of it. (Also the only man Louisa knew who was. Mr. McAndrew weighed about fourteen stone, in good trim. He played Rugby football, Louisa almost guessed it, for the London Scottish.) It still wasn't the threat of such a last indignity that swayed her. There was no bus for another hour. (However odious in other respects, Louisa felt Mr. McAndrew reliable about timetables.) And when she did get a bus, or if she walked, to the station, she had no idea when the next train was. Why cut off one's nose to spite one's face? Louisa got into the car.

III

Within a matter of minutes, she nearly got out again.

It had been easy enough, after but the briefest period of conjecture, to connect Mr. McAndrew's appearance outside Chesham Hall with the scaffolding over the Hall winter garden; didn't he specialize in stately homes? So far, so good; Louisa's curiosity was satisfied—for she must have been a little curious—without the need to encourage Mr. McAndrew (instead of slamming him down) by showing it. But as she considered the circumstances more fully, a really horrible suspicion stirred.

"Did you by any chance pinch that *Tatler* I had at Broydon Court?" asked Louisa abruptly.

Mr. McAndrew grinned.

"There was a pair of very fine ankles pictured in it—along with the couple of wee dogs."

Louisa wasn't deceived. That would-be salacious grin masked, she was almost sure, the even more repulsive aspect of a Good Samaritan.

"Did you by any chance show it to Lady Mary Tablet?"

"I might have done."

"Did you by any chance suggest *me* to photograph her beastly corgis?"

"Not at all. That was entirely her own notion," affirmed Mr. McAndrew.

Louisa wasn't deceived. On top of all else, he had managed to *patronize* her.—His mere proximity now revolting, she glanced at the car door, half-minded to pull it open and hurl herself out. They weren't doing much over thirty—or if she did break her neck, what matter? Wouldn't a broken neck solve her every problem? So felt Louisa, at the moment, most sincerely; nor was the thought of Mr. McAndrew involved in all the nuisance of an inquest at all displeasing. She only hoped he'd get his license endorsed . . . While she hesitated, however (indeed while she still had him in the witness box), the latter so far misread her look as to reach across and wind the window up, then back for a light overcoat which he pulled about her shoulders. The resultant warmth was so grateful, Louisa at least temporarily abandoned thoughts of suicide. Moreover, she'd remembered a come-back.

"It may still interest you to know," retaliated Louisa nastily, "that your Lady Mary Tablet has just gypped me out of three guineas."

She continued to feel humiliated nonetheless. Probably no car of its size ever bore a greater burden of resentment, and humiliation, and general ill-feeling.

IV

When they stopped, not long afterwards, it was at a very small village inn. The benches against the walls were so narrow and hard, if Louisa suddenly recalled the Meares, it was only to hope that when they left her at Dorking station—

How long ago? Only a month? To Louisa it felt like a lifetime.

—they'd been able to sip their one small sherry apiece in brighter surroundings. Louisa couldn't think of any other reason for thinking of the Meares; though perhaps the landlady's expert glance (in this case how mistaken!) showed a slight diminution of umbrage as before a properly respectable couple. ("It's his size," thought Louisa vaguely, watching Mr. McAndrew insert himself between narrow bench and narrow table.) She looked about again; for all gaiety of décor there was a stuffed pike, under glass, behind the bar, and on one wall an old broadsheet commemorating an eighteenth-century murder. The leaves of a pair of rubber plants shone with a sickly, mortuary phosphorescence—probably floor-polish; which hadn't been applied to the floor. In all, it was one of the most depressing hangouts Louisa had ever struck; and thus at least matched her mood.

"Not that the Meares would notice," mused Louisa aloud.

They were the first words she had spoken for some time. Mr. McAndrew looked at her.

"I'm glad the cat hasn't got your tongue altogether," he remarked. "Who might the Meares be?"

Impossible to go back to Kerseymere Kennels, to Teddy and Molly Meare standing hand-in-hand on a railway platform! Taking a short cut—

"Well, they were married," explained Louisa.

"Most folk are," said Mr. McAndrew. "I don't see what way that specializes them."

"Yes, but she didn't know Teddy was a vet."

Mr. McAndrew glanced at Louisa's tumbler. She'd had only one small whiskey, as yet unfinished.

"No doubt I'll plumb your mind in due time," he reflected. "I'm still glad to hear you've a few decent acquaintances. A vet's is a very respectable profession."

"Of course I've never seen them since," said Louisa discouragingly.

But somehow, just as they'd have wished to do, the Meares broke the ice. Moreover, Louisa was now at that stage of fatigue when it is easier to talk than not.

"They were really why I came to Broydon at all," she added, "to meet Jimmy again . . ."

"I understood the name was Freddy," objected Mr. McAndrew.

"No, Freddy was the one before," explained Louisa.

"The one before what?" inquired Mr. McAndrew patiently.

"The one I tried first, when I first thought of getting married at all."

"You surprise me," said Mr. McAndrew. "I'd never have credited you with such a sensible notion. From the way you carried yourself at Broydon, one would have thought photographing wee hounds—by which I intend canines in general," said Mr. McAndrew pointedly—"the whole aim of female existence. I never remember a woman," recalled Mr. McAndrew, "annoying me more."

Why the thought occurred to her Louisa had no idea. It occurred nonetheless.

"Was it you," asked Louisa suddenly, "who kissed me when the lights went out?"

V

Now it was Mr. McAndrew's turn to flinch.—He looked a little aside; then up at the stuffed pike.

"Aye," admitted Mr. McAndrew. "Though more out of opportunism than anything else."

"Was it you who turned the lights out?" demanded Louisa, pressing her advantage.

"Certainly not," said Mr. McAndrew, recovering a little. "At a guess, it was some silly young lad wishing to make a pass at a silly young lass. As I've told you, on my part it was sheer opportunism."

"*I* didn't even know who it was," said Louisa. "*I* thought it was Mr. Wray."

"Maybe he could have made a jump, at that," agreed Mr. McAndrew.

"At least you're not jealous," said Louisa coldly.

"Of that wee fellow? How should I be?" said Mr. McAndrew. "It was only I you bothered to slam down. I repeat, I felt if anything rather an aversion for you."

"You still came and took me out to lunch."

"I've a maybe foolish dislike of eating alone," explained Mr. McAndrew. "Go on with what you were telling me. You had a notion to get married."

VI

Sadly Louisa thought back over the past weeks: recapitulating, and reviewing, and regretting.

"Well, I suppose it *began* with talking to the milkman about Ibsen."

"I don't know whether to give you another whiskey or not," said Mr. McAndrew.

"Freddy would," said Louisa. "—Actually I don't want one, but I've never, you must have noticed it, met any man freer with drinks. Freddy's is a quite wonderfully generous nature," said Louisa.— "What I would like is something to eat."

"It surprises me you didn't marry him yourself," observed Mr. McAndrew, returning from the bar with a meat pie, "if such was your aim, and you've so fine an opinion of him."

"It surprises me too," acknowledged Louisa, "now. But perhaps it wasn't just Enid—"

"The widow?"

"Or butterfly on buddleia."

"I hope you're not running a temperature," said Mr. McAndrew. "Do you feel any warmer?"

"Warm as toast," Louisa assured him.—It took her a moment to discover why; then she realized that she was wearing his overcoat. At some point she must have thrust her arms into the sleeves. As a garment it was far too big, but the ample tweed folds were wonderfully cozy, over a linen suit . . .

"It's to be trusted you've a good thick dressing gown," said Mr. McAndrew worriedly.

"Two," lied Louisa.

"You'd better take that back with you," said Mr. McAndrew—obviously a hard man to deceive. "If it wasn't a butterfly on a buddleia—for heaven's sake!—put you off the old rip, tell me what did."

"Well, perhaps I felt even then—subconsciously, you know—that he was past starting a family."

"In my opinion, it's an aspect that might have struck you outright," commented Mr. McAndrew.

"At least I'm not as old as Sarah wife of Abraham!" retorted Louisa, stung—also slightly confusing the point. "I didn't know I wanted a family, then, myself. It was only after Mr. Clark—"

"I'm glad to find you read your Bible," said Mr. McAndrew. "But just for the record, what's become of this Jimmy?"

Louisa sighed.

"*He* turned out to have something quite different in mind altogether."

"Ah!"

"Bamboo," corrected Louisa.

Mr. McAndrew went back to the bar and fetched a couple more meat pies.

"At least old Freddy taught me money isn't everything," mused Louisa. "Won't you have one yourself? They're very good. All I learnt from Jimmy was to steer clear of bamboo.—Which I suppose was useful too in its way; now that I look back, I can see I spent far too much time in the pansy beds among the bamboo bushes . . . Isn't that pie all right?"

"It beats me how you can tackle a second," said Mr. McAndrew frankly.

"Well, I'm hungry," said Louisa. "I generally am," she added thoughtlessly.

"O my dear lass!"

Louisa looked at him in surprise. He instantly fixed the stuffed pike again.

"We'll find some more decent place on the road," he promised. "Get on now to Mr. Clark."

Louisa sighed anew.

"One thing *he* taught me I hope I'll never be ungrateful enough to forget. I'd never, really, disliked a man before, I was so fond of them; after Mr. Clark I don't see how I can ever be such a sucker for them again. I only wish," sighed Louisa, "he hadn't had such a nice family ..."

A silence fell, as she remembered Paul and Catherine and Toby; a tear fell, salting not unacceptably the meat pie.

"Is yon the last?" prompted Mr. McAndrew.

Louisa nodded.

"I've given it up," she explained. "I suppose you could say I've made a pretty fair fool of myself. But I only wanted to get married!"

"Well, there's nothing wrong with that," said Mr. McAndrew kindly. "Still, what a daft way, by your own account, you set about it! Don't you know that a woman wanting to marry should let herself be *courted?*"

VII

"For instance, if you'd thoughts of marrying *me*," continued Mr. McAndrew, after a further pause, and now transferring his gaze to the broadsheet about the murder, "you should begin by letting me take you out a bit. To Sunday concerts at the Albert Hall, for example. So we'd get to know each other.—D'you happen to be free this coming Sunday?"

"Well, yes, I am," said Louisa.

"Then there's Kew Gardens, if the weather doesn't break. Wet or fine, there's the British Museum."

"Or Westminster Abbey," suggested Louisa, more and more interested.

"London's filled with suitable spots," said Mr. McAndrew. "The point I'm making is, that's how you should let yourself be courted."

The more Louisa considered it, the more the notion appealed to her. Wasn't it indeed something she realized herself—*che va piano va sicuro?* And how delightful (recalling the other half of her device) to be oneself in the position of monkey softly-softly padded after by Mr. McAndrew! But there was a serious drawback.

"How long would it take?" she asked anxiously.

"Say a year to eighteen months."

"Then I'm sorry, but I can't wait," said Louisa.—"I don't mean I can't *wait*," she added hastily, "I mean that any job, anywhere, if I can find one, just now I'd have to jump at. Even in Australia as an Assisted Immigrant. At Broydon," confessed Louisa, "I was just putting on the successful woman act.—*You* thought I was successful, didn't you?" she asked wistfully.

"Indeed I did," said Mr. McAndrew. "O my dear lass!"

The thread of her thought momentarily broken—

"You called me that before," said Louisa uncertainly.

"Let it pass," said Mr. McAndrew. "Though you might try my own given name of Andrew."

"Didn't your mother call you *Andy?*"

"She did not.—Nor am I seeking a mother," stated Andrew McAndrew. "In my view, the man's part is to provide and cherish, not be taken care of like a bairn.—D'you mean you're in any real financial difficulty?"

Louisa put it as plainly as she could.

"Well, if I don't pay some rent pretty soon, and if I do I don't see how I'm to eat, I'll probably be sleeping on a park bench."

"Are you telling me you owe for *rent?*" demanded Mr. McAndrew incredulously.

"Aye," said Louisa. "And you should see the dairy bill."

It wasn't the stuffed pike he now regarded, nor the broadsheet about a murder, but Louisa's chrysanthemum head.—Rather droop-ing, like a chrysanthemum under rain. Louisa didn't consciously droop, she was just very tired; but at the same time the thought washed over her, in a warm relaxing tide, that before a man so pre-pared to provide and cherish it didn't matter whether she drooped or not. In fact, she slightly revived.

"You're putting me in a very awkward position," complained Mr. McAndrew.

"It was your idea," pointed out Louisa.

"Might you not hold on for just a couple of months?"

"Well, I dare say I could borrow from old Freddy," offered Louisa.

"Don't speak merely to irritate me," said Mr. McAndrew. "Can't you see that what I'm being driven up to is a Special License?"

Louisa sat back in his overcoat and let him worry it out. At last, she was being taken charge of—and how gladly! Only because it wasn't in her nature to be unhelpful—

"O my dear lad!" breathed Louisa tenderly. "O my dear lad!"

About the Author

Margery Sharp (1905–1991) is renowned for her sparkling wit and insight into human nature, which are liberally displayed in her critically acclaimed social comedies of class and manners. Born in Yorkshire, England, she wrote pieces for *Punch* magazine after attending college and art school. In 1930, she published her first novel, *Rhododendron Pie*, and in 1938, she married Maj. Geoffrey Castle. Sharp wrote twenty-six novels, three of which, *Britannia Mews*, *Cluny Brown*, and *The Nutmeg Tree*, were made into feature films, and fourteen children's books, including *The Rescuers*, which was adapted into two Disney animated films.

MARGERY SHARP

FROM OPEN ROAD MEDIA

OPEN ROAD

INTEGRATED MEDIA

OPEN ROAD

INTEGRATED MEDIA

Find a full list of our authors and
titles at www.openroadmedia.com

FOLLOW US
@OpenRoadMedia